# If the Shoe Fits

### Sandra D. Bricker

**MOODY PUBLISHERS**

CHICAGO

© 2013 by
SANDRA D. BRICKER

Published in association with the literary agency of WordServe Literary Group.

Edited by Cheryl Dunlop Molin
Interior design: Ragont Design
Cover design: DogEared Design, LLC
Cover images: iStock 15363933, 4431227, 3379029

Library of Congress Cataloging-in-Publication Data

Bricker, Sandra D.
If the shoe fits / Sandra D. Bricker.
     pages cm
Summary: "Julianne used to believe in fairy tales; she's been watching for Prince Charming to come charging in on his white steed ever since the day her mother read her Cinderella for the first time. But she's never come close to finding the perfect man--instead she's always tripping over her childhood best friend, Will. And who finds her Prince Charming on a 10-speed bicycle on the other side of the cul de sac? She and Will are attorneys now, and they've joined up in private practice in a beautiful Cincinnati office building that overlooks the Ohio River. And then one day Julianne is on her way to court, and runs right smack dab into Prince Charming. But when she looks again, all she finds is a metaphoric sign she is certain came straight from heaven: The Prince's toolbox has fallen off the back of his truck, and a work boot along with it. What better way for God to grab the attention of a Cinderella-in-training than to show her a glass slipper...errrr, work boot?...waiting to be reunited with its owner? So she sets out to track down the mysterious Prince Charming. He's the most gorgeous guy she's ever seen...and a caring animal rescuer, too. Surely he must be the soul mate God has prepared her for. But, Julianne's prince is starting to look less and less charming all the time"-- Provided by publisher.
     ISBN 978-0-8024-0628-6 (pbk.)
     1. Women lawyers--Fiction. 2. Cincinnati (Ohio)--Fiction. I. Title.
     PS3602.R53I3 2013
     813'.6--dc23

                                        2012044784

We hope you enjoy this book from River North Fiction by Moody Publishers. Our goal is to provide high-quality, thought provoking books and products that connect truth to your real needs and challenges. For more information on other books and products written and produced from a biblical perspective, go to www.moodypublishers.com or write to:

River North Fiction
Imprint of Moody Publishers
820 N. LaSalle Boulevard
Chicago, IL 60610

1 3 5 7 9 10 8 6 4 2

*Printed in the United States of America*

*Once upon a time, in an enchanting village*
*called Cincinnati, a beautiful fair-haired princess*
*went in search of her prince. She searched high*
*and low for the one who'd been set aside just for her.*
*And right about the time that temptation*
*persuaded her to abandon all hope of finding him . . .*

# 1

"**Hang on!**" **Julianne** shouted at the cell phone already in flight and hurtling toward the empty passenger seat of her white PT Cruiser. "Ooooh, hang on, Will!"

She pumped the brakes frantically, clutching the steering wheel so that her fingers ached, and virtually ignoring the stream of diet Coke running from the overturned paper cup in her lap. Speeding toward the rear bumper of the sport utility in front of her, she squeezed her eyes shut in anticipation of the impact.

When her car jerked to a violent stop, Julianne cautiously opened one eye and then the other.

"Jules? What's going on? Jules? Are you all right?"

Julianne looked down to find the cell phone teetering in the half-filled bowl of water on the floor of the car. A bug-eyed goldfish swam around it in wide, frantic circles.

"I'm sorry, sweetie," she said and cringed, gently lifting the phone from the water and shaking it drip-dry. "I'll bet that was scary for you, huh?"

"Jules? . . . Talk to me."

"Oh," she said with a start, crinkling her nose as she held the damp instrument to her ear. "Will. Sorry. Some guy up ahead of me slammed on his brakes and nearly caused a three-car pileup, with me as the caboose!"

"Did anyone get hit?"

"No. It seems like we all narrowly escaped the impa—"

Before she could complete the thought, squealing tires traversed into grinding steel and shattering glass, falling to silence after one final *thud!* from somewhere behind her.

The monotonous clank of her windshield wipers drew Julianne from her state of shock. She pushed the button to lower her car window and poked her head out into the rain.

"What's going on?" Will's muffled voice called out to her.

Julianne watched the sight before her in gaping silence.

He had to be more than six feet tall, and his shaggy, blondish hair fell past the collar of the long black coat that seemed to float behind him as he stalked toward her, straight down the double yellow line in the center of the road. A day's worth of stubble shadowed his suntanned face, along with an intense form of resolve. The soles of his boots pressed puddles in the road into tiny geysers at each determined step, and he glided through without notice. But the best part: the way he gazed down at the enormous bulge of pale yellow fur in his arms as the large dog tilted its loving, grateful gaze upward.

Before she could fully register the pair as anything more than a momentary vision, they disappeared into the pickup truck in front of the SUV ahead of her.

"No," she found herself squealing right out loud. "No! He's . . . *leaving.*"

"Who?"

"Will, he's driving away! How do I stop him!"

"Stop who? Was it a hit-and-run? Can you see a plate?"

"N-no," Julianne stammered, straining out the window for a better look at the driver of the cherry-red Chevy truck.

"It looks like a dog was hit. And God sent an angel to the rescue."

"What are you babbling about, girl? . . . Jules, *did you hit your head?*"

The pickup sped away around the corner, and the four-wheel drive ahead of her followed suit, swerving angrily before screeching through the intersection.

"Hey! Something fell off the angel's truck," she said, distracted. "I'm going to pick it up."

"Pick up . . . *What?*"

Julianne thoughtlessly pitched her cell phone to the seat beside her and flicked on the hazard lights. She heard Will scolding her in the distance as she let herself out of the car into the rain and hurriedly approached the obstruction in the road ahead.

There before her—as oddly out of place as, say, a woman standing in the middle of a busy intersection in the pouring rain— sat a red toolbox with one leather work boot propped innocently against it like a billboard advertisement.

Julianne cocked her head and gaped at it for a moment before the blast of car horns propelled her into action. The muscles in her arm flexed painfully all the way up to her neck as she struggled to lift the box, and she grabbed the boot by the laces and ran, dropping them both into the backseat of her car once she reached it. She'd barely closed the door behind her as she thrust the gearshift into drive, and she squealed away just in time to miss the impact of oncoming traffic by a stone's throw.

"What are you doing now? Jules?"

"His toolbox fell off his truck," she said as she pressed the speaker button on her iPhone.

"Whose truck?"

"And a boot. So I stopped and picked them up out of the road."

"A boot? Jules, what are you talking about?"

"I grew up with two older brothers," she continued as she took the turn onto Ninth. "This kind of toolbox is really expensive. He had the truck bed stacked with all kinds of lumber, and the box fell out when he stopped to save the dog."

"What dog?"

"The dog that was in the road, Will. Pay attention, would you, please?"

His groan of exasperation was mostly lost on Julianne.

"I'm going to have to find him," she thought aloud. "I wish I'd have gotten his plate number."

The idea of finding the dog-saving angel in the red Chevy

9

pickup set her pulse to pounding an octave above the steady beat of windshield wipers that matched her heartbeat.

"Maybe I could call the newspaper and place an ad," she said as she veered onto the shoulder of the road to avoid the traffic blocking her from turning into the city lot. "Tools like these don't come cheap. Oh, and the way they were sitting there in the road, the work boot propped up against the box, it was like . . . a sign. God was telling me something, I just know it. He drove away—"

"Who? God?"

"—but I'm supposed to find him."

"Find him?"

"Yes, find him," she declared. "I'm not going to stop searching until—"

"And, by George," he interrupted with dramatic flair, "you'll take that boot to every workshop in the kingdom if you have to! Every man shall try it on until, at last, you find your prince."

Julianne didn't reply. She just grinned and shrugged slightly. It was the germ of a plan, after all.

"Will, I'm due in court. I've got to run."

"I'll see you back at the office when you're through."

Once she found a parking spot, Julianne slipped her phone into her bag as she ran. As she skidded around the corner and through the double glass doors into the courthouse, water sloshed from the fishbowl to the rubber mat lining the floor.

"Oh, phooey!" she cried as she scampered up the stairs to the second floor, shielding the open top of the bowl with her hand in an effort to keep the stunned fish inside it while squeezing her briefcase beneath one free arm.

"Ms. Bartlett," Judge Hillman greeted her the moment she burst through the door to the courtroom. "We were just speculating as to whether you were going to join us this afternoon."

"Oh, Your Honor, I am so sorry. The weather is horrible out there, and the traffic trying to get off Ninth Street is impossible. I apologize for—"

"Ms. Bartlett, is that a fish?" he interrupted.

"Oh, yes, sir. Yes, it is."

"What, pray tell, is it doing in my courtroom?"

"Th-this is Jonah, Your Honor. He's my pet goldfish, sir. And I had him in my car, planning to take him over to our new office before I was due in court. But because of the weather and the traffic, and this really amazing man . . . a vision, really . . ."

"And the tie-up on Ninth?"

"Yes, sir, because of that, I didn't have time to stop by the office first, and I couldn't just leave him in the car."

"No, you couldn't do that. Why again?"

Julianne set the fishbowl and her briefcase on the table before her, slipping out of her diet Coke–splotched raincoat as she continued. "Begging Your Honor's pardon, I thought I could set him right here on the corner of the table."

"Bailiff? Is there a No Pets rule for my courtroom?" Judge Hillman asked Bridget, and the stocky woman grazed Julianne with a serious eye.

"Yes, Your Honor. But I don't think we've ever found the need to exercise it until now."

"Ms. Bartlett," Hillman said seriously with an arch to his rather bushy gray eyebrow, "you may leave, um . . . "

"Jonah. Like the guy inside the whale?"

"Yes. Leave it right there on the table for today. But be advised that there will be no further allowances for pets of any kind in my courtroom. Is that understood?"

"Y-yes, Your Honor. Thank you so much."

Julianne ran her hands through her damp hair and pressed the front of her navy suit.

"Are we ready to proceed then, Ms. Bartlett?"

"Yes, sir. I'm ready." Casting a casual glance toward opposing counsel, she added, "If Mr. Flannigan is ready, that is."

"Oh, I've been ready for quite some time, Your Honor," Flannigan replied.

"All right then. Let's play courtroom, shall we?" he asked them. "I'll be the judge. Is your client present, Ms. Bartlett?"

"Uh, no, sir, he's not."

Flannigan groaned, and Hillman released a sigh from behind the bench.

"Did your client understand that part of the arrangement of being out on bail includes showing up in court?"

"Yes, sir," Julianne answered politely. "But there are extenuating circumstances surrounding this case."

"Your Honor!" Flannigan exclaimed, and he went silent when the judge raised his hand.

"Your client was caught on videotape in Leffler's Jewelry Store stealing a two-carat diamond, Ms. Bartlett."

"Yes, sir."

"A diamond which he swallowed, but which never passed through his intestinal tract, is that correct?"

"Yes, sir."

"And Mr. Bertinni does not contest his guilt in this matter?"

"No, Your Honor. In fact, he is hoping to make full restitution to Leffler's, which is why he's not present in the courtroom today and why we're hoping for a continuance on this matter."

"Can you explain that to me, Ms. Bartlett?"

"Well, sir, Antonio Bertinni is currently a patient at Good Samaritan Hospital."

"The aforementioned diamond?" Hillman asked.

"Yes, sir. It's passing through his system as we speak."

"Continuance granted," the judge declared without expression. "We'll hear the details of this case on the twenty-third at 9:30 a.m."

One firm rap of the gavel punctuated the judgment.

"You are the luckiest broad on earth," Flannigan cracked as he passed her and walked out the door.

Julianne inwardly acknowledged his statement and lifted the fishbowl to carefully inspect its occupant.

"He called me a broad, Jonah. Are you going to let him talk to me like that?"

When the fish did a quick circle around the inside of the glass bowl, she blew him a kiss and hurriedly gathered her things.

●　—　●　—　●

Julianne couldn't get the vision out of her head. He'd looked like something straight out of the movies, his long black coat flowing behind him as he walked purposefully toward her, the misty haze of rain clouding him into a dreamlike apparition, yet still allowing enough clarity to make out the shadow of stubble along the line of his jaw. And the way that dog looked up at him! Appreciation, admiration, and blessed relief.

"Must love animals as much as I do." That was the third point on her ten-point mental checklist for her very own Prince Charming!

The only thing that had been missing from their first almost-meeting was slow-motion movie effects, and maybe a soft dissolve as his truck peeled out of the intersection.

"He was like nothing you've ever seen before, in person."

"Well, congratulations," her best friend and business partner said sourly. "Now can you give me a hand with this?"

Julianne glanced down at the floor where Will peered up at her from beneath the desk, his dark hair rumpled and his brown eyes narrowed as he glared at her. But a spontaneous burst of laughter coughed out of Julianne in retort.

"Go ahead. Laugh it up, Jules," Will said with a frown. "But my computer's already hooked up. I could easily leave you without one."

"No, no, don't do that," she replied, gazing first at the end of a computer cable dangling from Will's extended hand, then at the look of sheer exasperation on his perfect, square-jawed face.

"What do you want me to do with it?" Julianne asked him, taking the cable cautiously into her hand.

"Don't tempt me with questions like that, Jules," he said, miming the wrapping of the cable around her neck.

Julianne mouthed an unamused, "Ha ha ha," and she gently smacked Will's leg with the cable.

"Run it around the length of the desk, and hand it to me through the opening in the back."

Julianne did as she was told and, several minutes later, Will emerged from underneath the desk with a victorious grin.

"What are your plans tonight?" he asked her. "A dinner, silent auction, fund-raising effort for dogs, cats, starving armadillos?"

"Very funny. I am completely free tonight. The plight of starving armadillos will have my full attention *tomorrow*."

"Of course they will," Will answered with a chuckle.

"And the dogs were last week when you graciously dusted off your tuxedo and accompanied me."

Will grimaced. "Whatever. You are now up and running, my friend. Once more connected to the planet via the Worldwide Web." He took Julianne's outstretched hand and groaned as she tugged him from the floor. "It looks like we're official. The Law Offices of Hanes & Bartlett, open for business."

A surge of excitement shot through Julianne. She'd been waiting for this moment since the day she and Will had graduated from law school just five years prior. Today was a banner day, and it deserved some serious celebration.

* — * — *

Will trailed behind as his father and Julianne headed for the kitchen. Being there in his family home again, so much familiarity between his dad and his best friend, Will half expected his mom to bound through the back door, a sack of groceries in her arms and a beaming neon smile on her pretty, suntanned face.

"You get the ice cream, and I'll get the root beer!" Julianne exclaimed.

Will's father nodded. "Anywhere else in the world, a celebration like this might involve popping champagne corks and glasses of wine raised overhead," he declared. "But here . . . root beer floats are the stuff that toasts are made of."

"Don't forget we've ordered Chinese," Julianne reminded him with a grin. "The celebratory meal of champions."

"Where's Amanda?" the elderly man asked as he dipped a scoop of vanilla ice cream into a tall glass.

"Mom's just back from her sculpting class. She's changing into a clean blouse and said she'd be over in two shakes of a lamb's tail."

Will grinned, knowing that was a direct quote. Julianne's mom always said things like that.

"Shall I make her a float, too?"

"Please."

Quick flashes of past root-beer-float celebrations blinked through Will's memory. He and Julianne had become quick best friends when her family moved in next door, both of them ten years old at the time, her with her pigtails and gangly long legs, and him with his scruffy hair and debilitating shyness.

"Remember our first floats?" Julianne asked as if she could hear his thoughts.

"In the backyard," Will replied. "We barbecued chicken on the grill, and your mom brought that horrid potato salad she makes with the green olives in it."

"Shh," Julianne said playfully. "She'll be here any minute."

"That was the day the doctors told my mom she'd beaten her cancer."

"Round one, anyhow," his dad chimed in, and the mist of emotion in his eyes inspired Will to touch his father, Davis, on the shoulder.

"I miss her, too."

"Adele was awesome," Julianne added as she took Davis's hand into hers. "So beautiful, and so kindhearted."

"Yes, she was," the older man agreed with a nod before glancing up at Will. "Your mother would be very proud of you, Son; proud of you both."

15

"She would have been the first one to the root beer!" Julianne exclaimed, and Will nodded.

"Who might have ever seen this day coming?" his dad asked, returning his attention to crafting four perfect floats. "Those two kids racing their bikes around the cul-de-sac—lawyers now! And starting their own practice."

"Am I too late for the toast?"

Will offered his hand to Julianne's mother, helping her up the last step and through the back door. "Just in time," he told her with a smile.

"We ordered some beef with broccoli just for you, Mandy," his father announced, pouring cold root beer into four tall glasses.

"Oh, thank you. That's my favorite."

Julianne poked straws into each glass as she distributed them. "Okay! Let's toast!"

"Here's to our two kids," Amanda piped up.

"To Hanes & Bartlett," Will added, and they all clinked their glasses together.

Will and Julianne exchanged meaningful smiles. Their world would certainly take on a new life of its own now that they would be working together every day. They already spoke their own language, a dialect consisting of half-finished sentences and meaningful nods. Even a simple grunt-like murmur had meaning in this wonderland that was the friendship of Will and Julianne.

But they were more than friends, a fact that Will knew more assuredly than he liked to admit. They were best friends. Even more than best friends, if one cared to count the fact that his half of the twosome had somehow managed to fall in love along the way.

"Did anyone feed Isaiah?" Julianne asked as the very fat Hanes family cat sauntered into the kitchen. Isaiah had been around since the dawn of time; Will wondered how the old thing still managed to stay on his paws.

Will's dad nodded. "Turkey and giblets tonight."

"His fave," she replied.

Uplifting praise music wafting in from the living room drew Will's attention as Julianne began to sing along. The sour clank of her tone tickled at the center of Will's heart. She couldn't hold a tune if it were packed up for her in a handy little box, but he sure did love to hear her try.

"Hey!" he blurted, as much for his own sake as to stop her from singing. "Another toast! To Pop's clean bill of health from the doctor today."

"Davis, that's awesome!" Julianne declared.

"Yeah, the medication seems to be working well. You sure can't cure Parkinson's, but I'll settle for holding it at bay for a little while."

"Well, here's to dreams coming true all over the place!" she added, and she clinked her glass against his dad's before grinning at Will with a mustache thick with foam. "Today is the start of something big. I can feel it."

He suddenly sensed the dawn of a case of root beer indigestion coming on.

"Mom!" she exclaimed. "I saw the man of my dreams today, just walking down the center line of the road, headed straight for me."

"Ohhh," Amanda growled as Will downed half of the root beer from his float and suppressed the belch that tried to follow.

"On the very day that we open our offices," she went on.

"Julianne, really."

"I'm not joking, Mom. It was a sign . . . especially since I was just thinking about those things that horrible Lacey James said about me at the pediatric AIDS fund-raiser the other night. You heard her, Will!" Julianne looked at Will with narrowed eyes before darting her attention back to her mother. "She had half the table full of my peers making fun of me for never being able to keep a guy around for long. They said the only long-term relationship I'd ever had in my life was with Will, and that there's something wrong with me. But then this . . . *vision!* . . . stepped onto the horizon. I'm telling you, Mom, he's the kind of guy who would really show them. He'd show them all!"

Amanda cocked her head and looked at Will for a long moment. Her hazel eyes, almond-shaped just like her daughter's, told him she knew about his secret feelings. And she appeared to apologize for Julianne's insensitivity.

He wanted to release her from the regret, tell her that they'd never made any promises to each other; both of them had dated other people over the years, after all. They weren't an actual couple or anything. . . .

Julianne's creamy round face looked so expectant, her pale blue eyes brimming with such hope that he almost wanted to believe it for her—which struck him immediately as nothing short of absurd. Will expelled a chortle that surprised even him.

"Will?" she asked softly, and the disappointment cutting through her eyes with catlike precision sliced him right to the quick. "Are you laughing at me?"

Fortunately, the doorbell rescued him.

"Dinner," he announced, thumbing through his wallet for a tip as he headed for the door. She was sure to ask him again before the final crack of the almond cookies, but for the moment he was safe.

# 2

**Will's dad's diagnosis** of Parkinson's had been a pretty big motivator to do what he couldn't have imagined doing just six months prior. But moving back into his family home to provide care hadn't actually been so bad, after all. The move gave him a chance to spend time with his dad while his health was still relatively good, and the place was loaded with great childhood memories; not to mention three times the space of the cozy little house in Forest Park that he'd reluctantly sold. Lots of room to move around in . . . and he loved that massive stone fireplace on the largest wall of the living room.

Early September was far too early for a fire, at least in Cincinnati, but Will and Julianne were never ones to stand on ceremony. And so the crackle from the hearth provided a soft rhythm against the whisper of the air conditioner.

"You're joking," Amanda remarked as she carried a tray of coffee mugs and set them on the oval table in front of the sofa. "A fire? It's seventy-four degrees outside. You two are loony tunes."

"Ah, let them be," Davis said on a chuckle. "They're dreamers."

"Winter will be here soon enough," Amanda replied, shaking her head as she poured a dollop of creamer into one of the cups. "I wonder how attractive the cold weather will seem when there's snow to be shoveled."

"I don't have to shovel," Julianne chimed in. "The super at my condo takes care of that."

Amanda handed Davis the mug and he thanked her. "And I've got a new roommate," he cracked, nodding toward Will. "He'll take care of the snow on my walk. Play your cards right, Mandy, and maybe I can hook you up."

"Do you hear this?" Will asked Julianne, and she giggled. "I move home to take care of the old man, and he's got me out shoveling the sidewalks of every pretty woman in the neighborhood."

"Hush, boy."

Will grinned at Amanda. "I hope you realize my father is working you."

"Oh, yes. He's a charmer all right."

The casual, familiar banter acted as a reminder of days long since gone. The lyrical music of Amanda's laughter, in particular, warmed Will's heart. Her husband left just weeks after Will and Julianne had graduated from law school, leaving Amanda alone in the house next door, looking very much like a deer caught in the headlights of an oncoming semitruck. A full year had passed before her mom even started to recover from the blow of unexpected divorce, and Will felt certain that his parents had been instrumental in nursing that healing along. They'd invited her over for dinners, dessert and coffee, evenings of board games and snacks; they'd even taken her along to church more than a few times. When Adele's cancer returned with a vengeance, Amanda had assisted Davis with her care. After more than two decades with just a small plot of grass and a rose garden between them, the households seemed more like one family than two.

"You need to head home," Will told Julianne as he gathered the coffee mugs.

His voice seemed to shatter her deep thought, and Julianne popped her head up in response, and dropped it again with a sigh.

"What time is it?" she asked him.

"Past eight. And you're in court first thing."

She seemed surprised that he remembered, and she grinned at him. "Thank you, Uncle Will."

"Don't forget, the new secretary starts tomorrow," he commented as he passed her. "She arrives at noon, and I'm deposing

20

in Springdale at eleven, so you've got to be there to show her the ropes."

"Oh, I forgot."

"How could you forget? I put it on a sticky note and pasted it to your computer screen."

Julianne chuckled as she headed for the door. "I do appreciate a good sticky note."

"I know!" he teased.

Once Julianne and Amanda made their way out the door, Davis groaned and shoved upward and to his feet.

"Long day," he said with a yawn. "I'm headed to my room to watch *CSI* before bed."

"Don't forget to take your pills."

"Yeah, yeah." Davis tossed up his hand in a sloppy wave and shuffled down the hallway.

Will plopped down to the sofa as the final embers of the fire struggled against their demise. Suddenly, that bed in his childhood room seemed as vast as Ohio itself to Will, and he settled back into the sofa cushions instead.

Her PT Cruiser was probably headed down Winton Road by then, he speculated as he closed his eyes. The night's full silvery moon shining through the window, giving life to the streaks of multiple hues highlighting Julianne's beautiful hair . . . and her sweet crystal-blue eyes narrowed so that the fringe of golden lashes caressed the top of her perfect, porcelain cheek.

Ah, Lord. When is she going to get it? But not my will . . .

Will's eyes popped open wide and he stared at the ceiling for a long moment while he wrestled his thoughts down to silence. Then with one punch to the sofa cushion beneath him, he flung himself over onto his side and pulled the cotton throw from the back of the sofa.

Quickly filling his mind with thoughts of tomorrow's deposition, he snapped shut his eyes and let go of the sigh that had been building in his chest.

Davis snorted out a chuckle that roused Will from his sleep.

One arm hung haphazardly over the side of the sofa and lolled limply toward the floor, and one of his legs, stiff from the slight bend at the knee, rested atop the coffee table.

He stirred slightly in response to the scent of the Colombian coffee his father had brewed. Leaning over him, he waved a mug close enough to Will's nose to bring him around, like caffeinated smelling salts.

Poking Will's shoulder with his sock-covered foot, his father sang, "Rise and shine, oh son of mine. You fell asleep on the sofa again?"

He opened his eyes reluctantly, squinting up at him as he groaned. "What time is it?"

"Seven," he replied, raising his foot again for one more poke. "Now move over so I can sit down."

"Coffee," Will muttered, his eyes closed again.

"Mm-hm. Strong and black, just the way you like it."

He peeled his eyes open only far enough to see the mug. He took hold of it with both hands and drew a sip from the cup. Isaiah, his father's enormous cat, launched an assault on his foot when it moved beneath the blanket, and Will groaned as he nudged the feline to the floor.

"Morning," he finally greeted his father.

"Morning," he grunted back with a grin that Will returned.

He loved mornings like these with his father. He thought of all the time he'd have missed if he hadn't sold his house and moved back in with his dad.

*Such a good son*, everyone said when they heard. *What a selfless thing to do!*

Will never admitted out loud to anyone—not even Julianne—that he gained as much as he gave from the move. Especially after his breakup with Holly, Will's dad had become a bit of a security blanket. Familiar and comforting, compassionate and ever-present, his father had provided an emotional safety net that Will really needed. The best he could hope for was that he returned the favor by making his dad's life less lonely, and maybe even more interesting, while they figured out the health challenges together.

"So what's going on with you and Julianne, Son?"

A needle screeched suddenly across the record album of his thoughts.

"What do you mean?"

"Why don't you just tell her how you feel?"

Will froze, the mug of coffee suspended in the air before him for several thumping seconds.

"I'm gonna be late," he finally replied. "I need to jump in the shower."

"You're just like your mother," Davis called out after him. "Running out on a conversation if it gets too tense. Well, I'll tell you what I always told her: I'll be here tomorrow, too. I got nowhere else to be."

●  —  ●  —  ●

Julianne looked up from her desk in response to the soft whoosh signifying that the reception door had opened.

"I'll be right with you," she called out, completing the note on the pad of sticky notes before her.

"It's just me, Miss Bartlett . . . Phoebe?"

"Oh, good!" she said as she peeled off the note and stuck it to the frame of her computer monitor with a dozen others in multiple pastel colors. "Come on in."

Phoebe stepped timidly into the office and greeted her with a warm smile. "I came a little early in case there was anything you needed from me," she said. "Paperwork to fill out. Coffee to be made."

"That's fine," Julianne acknowledged. "You're off to a great start. I'm so happy Pastor Dean recommended you!"

In her work as a public defender, Julianne had shared a secretary with six other attorneys in the office for the first years of her career. She'd been dreaming of her very own assistant for all that time, and Phoebe would fit the framework of that dream just fine.

"There are insurance forms on your desk," Julianne said as she rounded her own and led Phoebe out to the reception area. "You'll want to fill those out first, and fax them over to our agent. The number is on the sticky, here, on the monitor. And then Will has set up your email at your computer. Your password to get in is *Reception*. Will likes to make things easy."

"Okay," the girl said and nodded, pushing her wavy brown hair away from her face to reveal lovely golden-brown eyes that Julianne hadn't really noticed on their first meeting.

"I've made up a list of your general duties," she continued. "Sort of like a job description. And I've emailed that to you, so you can pick it up when you're through with the insurance forms. Your official title is executive assistant. After you've had a chance to look everything over, why don't you come into my office and we'll have a chat."

"All right."

"The restroom is down the hall that way, and the coffee is in the conference room. There's diet Coke and ginger ale in the fridge. If you like something else, just go ahead and order it."

The ringing phone interrupted Julianne's thought process, and Phoebe grinned excitedly before she picked it up for the first time.

"Law offices of Hanes and Bartlett," she said in a businesslike tone. "How may I help you?"

Julianne raised both thumbs and grinned.

"Yes, sir, let me check on that for you," Phoebe replied. She put the caller on hold and turned to Julianne. "Did you call about placing a classified ad?"

"Oh, yes!" Julianne cried, and she hurried to retrieve the torn piece of paper from the corner of her desk and delivered it into Phoebe's hand. "I want this to run in tomorrow's paper. Will you take care of that for me? Oh, and . . . could you put it on Craigslist too?"

"Certainly, Miss Bartlett."

"And Phoebe?" she added. "When no one else is in the office, we're just Will and Julianne, okay? You can save the titles for when we're in the company of clients."

"Thank you," she said, clumsily adding, "Julianne."

"You're welcome, Phoebe."

As their new executive assistant set about placing the ad that was going to bring Prince Charming home to her, Julianne sauntered casually into her office and closed the door. Once behind it, she suppressed the excited squeal, settling instead for a quick little happy dance around the corner of her desk.

"I'm a real attorney now, Father God!" she whispered in the form of a song as she danced toward her chair. "I got an of-fice . . . and a de-esk . . . and a Phoe-a-ee-ee-bee!"

She attempted an ultimately unsatisfying high five in the direction of Jonah's fishbowl before settling into the enormous leather chair behind the carved oak desk. Looking around her office once more with glee, she sighed and returned to the unfinished task before her.

Less than half an hour later, commotion from the other side of her office door snagged her attention.

"I'm sorry," Julianne heard Phoebe call out in a loud tone of voice. "Can I tell Miss Bartlett who would like to see her? If she has the time, I'm certain she would—"

Before poor Phoebe could finish the thought, Julianne's office door burst open and Lacey James floated through it on a cloud of Chanel and peroxide.

Oh, great.

"Well, lookie *hee-ah*," she sang in her thickest Southern Belle. "I guess it's ta-rue. Almost anybody can rent themselves an office and call themself an attorney these days."

*Kind of like how anyone can take on a Southern drawl and call themselves a Southerner, huh? . . . Sorry, Lord. That slipped.*

She'd been razzing Lacey about concocting her heritage ever since they'd first met a few years ago at the Bar Association gala, and Lacey retaliated by attacking Julianne's forever-single status at every possible opportunity. These zingers had become the nature of their relationship; without them, Julianne realized there would be no relationship at all.

"I'm so sorry, Miss Bartlett," Phoebe offered genuinely. "I tried to—"

"It's fine," she replied.

"C-can I get you anything then?"

"Nothing, thank you. Miss James won't be staying."

Phoebe retreated, wisely leaving the door standing open wide to enable the intruder's quick departure.

"To what do I owe your swooping in?" Julianne asked Lacey.

"Careful now," Lacey warned her with the outstretched tip of one of her sharp red nails pointing right at her. "You're going to hurt my feelings."

Julianne resisted the urge to question the existence of feelings in Lacey, and she said a quick prayer for self-control.

"Well, I imagine you're on a reconnaissance mission," Julianne stated. "Checking out the new digs?"

"Yes, and to congratulate you and William."

*Ah. William*, Julianne repeated internally. *Now we get to the point.*

"And where *is* William this afternoon?"

"William had a deposition to conduct," she supplied with a knowing smile. "But I'll be sure and tell him you stopped by."

Lacey masked the disappointment quickly with a smile that seemed to crack her face right in two. "You don't mind if I just take a quick little look-see around, do you now?"

"Don't believe me?" Julianne replied, but Lacey was off on her private tour of the offices before she could complete the thought.

"Oh, don't be silly," she said upon return. "I just wanted to see

26

the new place, *Julie*. It's just lovely. It really is. Could use a woman's touch though, couldn't it?"

Pausing a moment to clench the words between her teeth with crocodile persistence, Julianne decided to let the insinuation pass.

"A plant or two, or some flowers?" she went on. "Oh, but I'm sure the new secretary can help with that."

"If that's all I can do for you," she said so courteously that it nearly choked her, "I'll let Phoebe see you out. We're doing a little something here we like to call *practicing law*."

"Isn't that just like you, Julie. Sturdy and rock-solid. Always knee-deep in the grunt work."

*Dear Lord, give me strength.*

"I'll leave you to it then."

Julianne followed her out to the reception area with the thought of asking Phoebe to prevent similar situations at all cost in the future, but her heart nearly leapt into her throat as she glanced through the beveled glass panel to the side of the office doors. She'd recognize that shadow anywhere! It was Will, heading up the hall toward the office.

"Wait!" she called suddenly, taking Lacey firmly by the elbow and whirling her around until she nearly smacked right into her. "You didn't see my view!"

Will flung open the reception door and started inside at just that moment, and Julianne frantically mimed a slashing motion to him as she practically dragged Lacey back toward the door to her office.

"You have to check this out!" she cried, waving one arm toward the window, cautiously using the other to direct Will toward his office, and quickly! "You can see all the way across the river, into Kentucky."

"Yes. It's nice," she managed, and Julianne sensed the irritation in her tone.

Suddenly, Lacey softened. "Oh, you poor dear. I understand. This is really all you have in your life, isn't it? Well, yes. Yes," she said as she glanced out the window with a patronizing nod. "It's just lovely. I'm glad you shared it with me, Julie."

*Next time, Will's on his own.*

"But I really do have to be on my way. You'll give my best to William, won't you?"

"You know it."

Once Lacey left the office, Will rounded the corner from behind his door and leaned on the frame.

"She drives me batty, Will!"

"And she knows it. Don't let her get to you. Besides, if you didn't have someone like Lacey in your life, how would you—"

"Learn to love the unlovable," she joined him, in unison.

"Right."

Phoebe stifled a giggle, and Will shot her a quick wave.

"Welcome to our law office, Phoebe." He reached across the desk to shake her hand. "Good to meet you."

"Thank you."

"Never again, Phoebe!" Julianne called before heading into her office. "Do you understand?"

"Yes, ma'am, I understand. Never again."

●　—　●　—　●

"I wish you'd have contacted me before you made the big leap," Judd said, and Will shrugged at the phone.

"Well, if you returned a guy's calls every now and then, that wouldn't be an issue, would it?"

Judd's laugh rumbled through the speakerphone. "Look, I know it might be too late for you to give it any consideration, Will, but we'd love to have you down here. Just think it over."

"It's not even a matter of just opening the law office here with Julianne," he told his old friend. "I've got my dad to think about. He's been diagnosed with Parkinson's. In fact, I've sold my place and moved in with him to help with his care. I can't uproot him, and I certainly can't leave him."

"You know, we've got a center here in Lexington that specializes in clinical trials and advancements in neurological diseases like Parkinson's, bro. It would be a great place for him. Just think about it."

Will agreed to think it over, but only to appease his old friend from law school. He had no real intention of making a move two hours south, especially at this point. He and Julianne were hardly out of the gate yet with the practice, and his father had lived in that house on Winlake Drive for twenty years.

The better part of the afternoon had been spent making notes for Greg Rush, the guy from Will's former practice who would handle the arbitration hearing scheduled later in the week. He closed the file and leaned back in the chair for a good stretch.

The sun left the marks of a rainy day across a sky splotched in rose and faint purple outside the window of his new office. There were no words to express the relief of freeing himself from exclusive attachments to commercial transactions, business loopholes, and federal regulations. With the last of his loose ends all tied up, he could now handle anything that came his way, and he could hardly wait to see what that would be. He hoped for a good criminal defense, or even a hairy accident settlement in which to sink his teeth. Anything other than the exclusive and dry Sahara of corporate law.

He squinted at the clock on the wall to make sure he hadn't misread it.

*Can it really be after six?*

Phoebe had already gone for the day. He heard Julianne turning pages in the conference room and noticed the yellowish beam of light glowing from her general direction.

Will crossed the lobby and stood in the doorway observing her for a few moments. Chewing on a lock of honey blonde hair, Julianne sat hunched over one of several law books spread out on the table before her. She tapped the fingers of her right hand as she read, and Will watched them as they drummed against the varnished oak tabletop. Her fingers were long, with short, manicured nails lightly frosted with pale pink polish. The thin circle of silver she always wore on her right thumb glistened as it caught a reflection of light. He'd bought it for her a couple of years back when the group from church went to Mexico to help rebuild an orphanage, he recalled.

They hadn't been allowed much R & R time while there, but how beautiful she had looked that singular afternoon when the group had gone to the beach. She'd been wearing a modest bathing suit, and the deep purple of the suit had blended with the silky floral sarong she wore tied in a knot just above one hip. He remembered thinking, as the setting orange sun reflected off her sun-kissed hair, that she was the most radiant beauty he'd ever seen.

Of course, he also remembered that she'd burst into a fit of laughter at just the moment when he'd been about to tell her so.

"What in the world are you thinking about?" she'd teased him as she nibbled on the wedge of lemon balancing on the rim of her glass of iced tea. "You look like you're just about to declare your undying love or something."

"Too many taquitos," he'd commented quickly. And it had become a private joke between them after that.

Julianne didn't look up as he crossed the conference room to the miniature fridge tucked into the corner of the counter and yanked out a small bottle of ginger ale. She finally noticed him at the hiss of the opened bottle.

"What's this?" she asked as he filled two paper cups and walked toward her.

"A toast," he replied. "To the end of our first day in our new offices."

Julianne smiled as she accepted one of the cups, and she tapped it against the side of the one still in his hand.

"There's nobody I'd rather partner with." She smiled up at him and took a sip.

*But only in law,* he thought. *Partnered in practice, but not in life. That's never even crossed your mind, has it, Julianne?*

Will fell deep into his own thoughts, and he jumped as she waved her hand playfully in front of his face.

"He—*lloooooo*?"

He blinked several times, hard. "I'm sorry. What?"

"Where were you just then?"

"Forever-Everland, I guess."

"Hey, that's my hometown, not yours."

Will managed a smile, but it didn't quite make it up to his eyes. "I heard that."

Will's heart began to race.

"Pardon?" he asked her.

"Your thoughts. I can hear them."

He could feel the thunderous pounding as it pushed against his chest.

"Oh, really?" he asked casually.

"Yep. I can hear your thoughts, Will Hanes!"

# 3

**Will's mind clouded** over with visions from a regrettable movie he'd seen as a teen. Some poor guy's stomach had burst suddenly open, and the monster within exploded out for everyone to see.

"You don't believe me?" Julianne asked him, stepping back and looking him squarely in the eye. "You think I would lie?"

"No," he finally replied, and his own voice sounded as frozen as a couple pounds of chicken legs tucked into the back of the freezer at home.

"Want me to prove it?"

All Will could manage was a slight shrug and an awkward smile.

"All right then," she said confidently, and she crossed her arms as she glared at him. "You're thinking how lucky you are to have a best friend like me."

When the corner of her mouth twitched in amusement, Will snickered, more out of relief than amusement.

"And you're thinking that this ginger ale is good, but not as good as a fruit punch and a plate of citrus shrimp from Vandella's will be."

The inward sigh of emancipation would have thundered overhead and rattled the windows had he released it.

"Jules the Magnificent," he said with a nod. "You really are remarkable. Like the prophets of old."

"Pastor Dean is treating the volunteers to a night out, remember? Let's walk over, and I'll be your date!"

"I'll get my jacket."

Several tables were pushed together, the only two seats available at opposite ends. Vandella's had become a favorite for church fellowship. Tabletops vividly painted with renditions of various landmarks exclusive to the Cincinnati area displayed truly appetizing food on brightly colored platters. It was situated conveniently right near Fountain Square at the center of town. As everyone exchanged greetings, Will walked Julianne over to the far side and held out the empty chair next to Maureen Alden, the pastor's wife. Once Julianne settled down into it, he made his way to the other end and sat between the pastor and Jimmy Rudd.

"You two look like you've been together all your lives," Maureen said to Julianne as she offered a basket of warm tortilla chips.

"We almost have," Julianne giggled, popping one into her mouth. "Will was my first crush back in grade school."

"Have you ever dated?" Maureen asked curiously.

"For about a minute in high school," she replied. "But we were always best friends. Nothing more."

"What a shame," Maureen commented softly, and Julianne wondered for a moment what she meant. There was no shame in what she and Will had settled into. Their friendship was one of the most valuable relationships of her life.

"Hey, everyone!" Jimmy Rudd announced from the other end of the table. "Will and Julianne have opened their law office."

"Yep. We're all moved in to the brand-new digs," Will told them, and he cast a quick smile at Julianne.

"Well then," Maureen said sincerely, raising her glass of raspberry tea. "Here's to a long and lucrative partnership." Leaning toward Julianne, she whispered, "If only in the practice of law."

The evening was great fun, just as they all were when this group of men and women got together. Julianne adored her pastor, and she enjoyed watching his interactions with others. Pastor Dean Alden, one of those very unusual combinations of true wisdom and absolute humor, always seemed to exude love and understanding, no matter what the challenge or situation.

She especially enjoyed the exchanges between the pastor and his wife. Their mutual love and respect almost crackled in the air around them, and it trickled down to even the tiniest parts of the church.

"Julianne?" Beth Rudd said as she walked up behind her at the bathroom sink after dinner wrapped up.

Julianne tugged a paper towel from the dispenser and dried her hands with it as Beth said, "I was talking to Maureen. And, well . . . you really aren't attracted to him in the least?"

"Who?"

"Will!"

"Attracted to Will?" she clarified. "That would almost be like incest, Beth! Will is my best friend. You don't cross over lines like that one."

"For goodness' sake, why not?" she asked through the reflection in the mirror, fussing over her helmet of ebony hair. "I'd have given just about anything if Jimmy and I were friends from the start. It took us years, and no small amount of turmoil, to find that part of our marriage."

Julianne's amused chuckle was cut short when the bathroom door slipped open and Linda Barnes poked her head inside. "Are you riding with us?" she asked Beth.

"I'll be just another minute," Beth replied with a nod. Turning to Julianne, she said, "The reason I'm asking is . . . I don't want to step on any toes. You know what I mean?"

"Not entirely," Julianne admitted with a smile, and she tapped the used towel down into the bin. "What are you getting at?"

"I was thinking of setting up Will and my younger sister, Alison. You remember, you met her at the Christmas pageant?"

Julianne thought back and shrugged. "I'm sorry. That was such a crazy night. I had twenty-seven crazy junior choir kids to look after."

"Oh, well, Alison has just broken up with her boyfriend of three years, and I know Will and Holly split last year. Anyway, she's just not meeting any nice Christian men, and I was thinking . . . if you wouldn't mind . . ."

"Oh! Well, of course not!" she replied, stunned. "It's not like that with Will. Really. I mean, fine. Go ahead."

"Really?"

"Sure," she said with a shrug. "Yes. I mean, if Will wants to."

"Oh, I think the two of them will be perfect for each other!"

Julianne hated to admit to the little scratch of irritation she felt right in the hollow of her chest at the thought of Will being set up with someone. She wondered why, but recalled how long it had taken to get a handle on his devotion to Holly. Whatever the source of the irritation, it settled in as if it might plan on staying awhile.

That Vandella's had developed a following among the legal community over the years went a little sour for Julianne as she exited the ladies' room just in time to find Lacey James standing with Will near the front door.

"Ready to head out?" she asked Will as she reached them.

"Oh, William, you don't have to leave just yet, do you?" Lacey asked him as if Julianne hadn't entered their airspace.

"I do. I'm in court first thing."

"Oh, how disappointing."

"You take care, Lacey," Will said kindly, and he turned to Julianne. "Ready?"

"More than."

She had to run to catch up to him at the crosswalk.

"What's up with you? Did she get to you?"

"Who?" he asked as the light signaled them to cross.

"Lacey!"

"Lacey? No," he said, shaking his head. "She's all right. She gets to you way more than she gets to me."

"Oh. Well, could you slow down? I can't keep up with you!"

He glanced down at her four-inch heels and grimaced. "Well, they're not much for walking, are they?"

She clicked her tongue. "Then don't make me run, Will."

He paused and looked at her seriously before his face melted down to a smile that cut straight to her heart. "Sorry."

"You know what? Let's head down to The Wall," she suggested. "Can we?"

Will didn't respond with anything more than a shrug, but he changed course, up the street toward the river.

One of her favorite places in the area, Julianne came to The Serpentine Wall as often as she possibly could. A huge construction of what looked like perfect concrete stairs leading straight down into the Ohio River, she and Will had been going there together for years. Whether for a quick lunch, or a jam-packed Fourth of July celebration for fireworks over the river, it was one of their most beloved spots. They'd been seated right there on the third stair from the top, in fact, when they planned the opening of the law partnership.

A party seemed to be going on at one of several riverboats moored at The Wall, and lively Dixie music wafted gently up toward them from the river below.

"You're not yourself tonight," Julianne commented once they'd settled into their regular spot. "Please tell me you're not having second thoughts about going into business with me, Will. I want you to know—"

"No," he interrupted. "You know better than that."

"Well, I thought I did. But you're behaving so strangely. Like someone kidnapped your dog."

"I don't have a dog."

"Maybe that's the problem. You want me to get you a dog, Will?"

"You're all the family pet I need," he quipped.

"Smarty pants."

After a moment, Julianne looked into Will's glazed eyes. She saw something unusual there, something she didn't think she'd ever seen before.

"Talk to me. What is it?"

"Ah, nothing. Too many taquitos," he remarked with a lop-sided smile.

"Come on, Will. Don't joke. If there's something on your mind—"

"You know what's on my mind?" he interjected. "I'm exhausted. Let me enjoy a few minutes with my best girl, and then we'll head out and I'll get some sleep."

With both hands on her shoulders, Will guided her around until she faced the river. The water glistened like glass under a perfect, full silver moon, the kind of moon a girl made wishes on. The kind of moon that caught those wishes like stardust and held on to them until the time was right.

"I wish I could sleep until noon tomorrow," she said on a sigh.

"Me, too."

●　—　●　—　●

"Hey, you were a killer in there today," Benton Rhames declared as he hurried to board the elevator behind Will, slipping in just before the doors slid shut.

"You had your chance to settle before you dragged your client into litigation, Bent. I gave you every opportunity."

"Blah, blah," he replied as the steel doors yawned open. "I'll see you on appeal."

"New day, same decision, my friend," Will told him.

"No mercy. I'll remember."

On the walk over to the office, those words spun around inside Will's mind several times.

*How could it be*, he asked the Lord, *that You could have created me to be such a formidable opponent in the courtroom and yet such a lame excuse for a hunter on the field of romance?*

"Talk to me," Jules had said to him the night before down on

The Wall, but he hadn't even spent a moment trying to summon the words. Because those words were buried deep, covered over with layers upon layers of excuses and justifications and, truth be told, fear.

He'd known her since they were kids, but it had taken him until freshman year of high school to work up the courage to ask her to LaRosa's for pizza.

She'd looked like an angel that night. Her honey blonde hair hung halfway to her waist back then, and she'd curled it up into wavy spirals of spun silk and golden threads of light. She'd been waiting outside her house when he'd walked across the lawn to pick her up, and the lamp on the porch backlit her as if she were posed for a portrait. She looked to Will like one perfect white candle standing on the steps of a cathedral, and he remembered losing the air from his lungs when he saw her there. He supposed he'd fallen in love with her long before that moment, although he didn't get around to admitting it to himself for a good many years. He'd never been quick on the draw when it came to love.

Will let a chuckle escape from his throat as he crossed the lobby and pressed the button to summon the elevator to go up to their new offices on the seventh floor. Julianne had remained the pristine portrait of perfection hanging on the wall of his life, the bar against which all other women were measured.

You couldn't just yank a painting off the wall and take it for a spin, after all. Once he went that direction with Julianne, there would have been no turning back. Gambling with a friendship as important as theirs wasn't an option, and so the dice were simply packaged away, the wheels of chance forever silenced. Friendship with Julianne: a sure thing. Love? A risk with too high a cost, if they lost. Holly had been the one and only woman who ever came close; but that ended in disaster, too.

Will punched the panel before him once more, and this time the elevator doors glided shut.

"Seven's a good number in the Bible, isn't it, Will?" Julianne had exclaimed when she'd originally found the office for rent on the seventh floor. "It's a sign, Will! It has to be."

Julianne saw signs from God around every corner of the world, Will thought with a smile. Every song on the radio was a message just for her, every rainbow a handwritten note to her from Him, posted on the sky like one of those sticky notes framing the screen of her computer.

If he were to read the map of their relationship in the Language of Julianne, Will believed he might certainly come away convicted of their ultimate destiny, the great State of Meant-to-Be, in the County of the Land of Soul Mates. All the signs were there, if one were the type to look for them.

And Julianne had always been the type.

So why had it never crossed her mind? She had prayed about everything from going to law school to teaching the kids at church how to sing when she clearly could not hold a tune herself. So why hadn't He ministered to her or even whispered into her ear about Will?

*Or perhaps You have, Lord.*

Will's heart thumped at the possibility as he recalled how drastically she had changed after those few dates they had in high school. Cold sweat beaded on his forehead and both palms. But . . . what if he weren't the only one feeling it? What if, all these years later, Julianne had actually, on occasion . . .

*Don't be ridiculous! She's still searching.*

And just for an instant, the idea burned at his insides like a bad case of indigestion. Maybe she just needed to be shown the general direction in order for her to ponder the actual journey. He wouldn't have to let on the intensity of his feelings, just the possibility of their focus.

"Why don't we go out on a date," he might suggest to her casually. "No pressure, or expectations. Just a date, to see if there's something here."

The appeal of the idea was alarmingly refreshing, like an ad he'd once seen for a chocolate and peppermint candy where the partaker was blown backward off the side of a cliff.

Will wondered for a moment if he'd begun to mentally unwind. He hadn't entirely decided yet when he opened the office door, greeted by a frantic Julianne excitedly hopping from one foot to the other, squealing incoherently.

"I'm . . . so glad . . . you're . . . back!" she cried.

"What's going on?" he asked, looking at Phoebe over Julianne's shoulder.

"He called!" Julianne sang. "He called!"

"Who?"

"Paul Weaver," Phoebe stated, and Julianne backed up like a rush of wind had driven her.

"That's his name. Paul Weaver."

Will didn't know what to say. He just looked at her expectantly, nodding tentatively, awaiting the rest of the story that might fasten it all together.

"Paul Weaver," she repeated insistently. "The angel."

*The angel.*

"With the dog?"

*The dog.*

"The work boot? And the toolbox?"

*The—Oh . . . no.*

"He saw the ad!" she cried. "And he's coming here at six o'clock today!"

"Six o'clock," Will repeated, and he glanced at his watch.

*In two hours.*

"Two hours," she squealed. "Come on!"

She tugged Will's sleeve and started for the door.

"Where?" he asked, confused.

*That's right. We'll just leave Phoebe to meet him. She can return his toolbox, fall madly in love, and ride off with him into the sunset. And—*

"I need new shoes!" she cried. "I can't meet him in these shoes!"

And with that, Julianne snatched Will's briefcase from his hand and flung it at the sofa across from Phoebe's desk.

"We'll be back in an hour," she declared, and she yanked Will behind her as she headed toward the office door.

"Oh, no, I won't, Jules," he said while pulling his arm from her grip. "You're on your own. I draw the line at shoe shopping."

*And in the radiant glow of yellowish light*
*from the candelabras in the foyer,*
*the knight bowed at the waist.*
*"Pleased to make your acquaintance, fair maiden."*
*Her heartbeat thumped in her ears,*
*and her breath caught in her throat as she forced out the words.*
*"The pleasure is mine, my Prince."*

# 4

"**I'm here about** my tools."

"Yes," Julianne managed to croak. Her hand popped up and she pressed two fingers gently against the hollow of her throat. "I . . . uh . . . I have brothers so I know how expensive a toolbox like that can be. I'm so glad you saw the ad."

"Well, I appreciate it," Paul Weaver told her, and when her gaze met his, Julianne felt the blood rush to her cheeks at the sight of those blue eyes of his. "I guess I should give you a reward or reimburse you for the ad or something like that. What do you think is fair?"

She shook her thoughts away from his impressive chiseled jaw and the perfect curl of the wayward lock of sandy hair that brushed his forehead.

*A date or two, perhaps a diamond eventually . . .*

"No!" she exclaimed. "No, no. That's not necessary. No."

"Are you sure?"

"I'm sure," she said, motioning to the chair angled toward the corner of her desk. "Have a seat, will you?"

"Oh, I can't stay. I just—"

"Please. Just for a minute."

He shrugged and folded into the chair. "I guess if you're a lawyer, you don't really need a reward from me, do you?" With a nod toward her computer monitor, he added, "That's an interesting filing system you have there."

Julianne narrowed her eyes for a moment before glancing at the layers of sticky notes that had piled up on top of one another around the frame of her screen. Her lips curled into a broad smile. "Oh. Yeah, I like to make notes of reminder."

"It looks like you need a shovel to dig through them. I don't think that would help me remember any one thing."

She grimaced before diverting the conversation. "Anyway, about your toolbox. I just did what anyone else would do in that situation. Tell me, how did it turn out for the dog you rescued that day?"

"I don't know."

"You don't know?"

"Well, I mean, I dropped him off at the emergency vet clinic over on Taylor Mill, but what happened to him from there, I don't know."

"Oh."

Julianne tried to imagine how he could have gone to the trouble of rescuing the dog and getting him to a clinic, but never followed up to—

"I was headed out of town on a job that afternoon," he said, and she sighed.

"Oh, of course! That's why you don't know. You were called away, and you *couldn't*—"

"Well, I really do have to go," he told her. "If I could just get my toolbox?"

"Oh. Right." Julianne stood up, and Paul followed suit. As she rounded the desk and stood in front of him, she realized for the first time that he towered a good six or eight inches above her 5'6" frame. "You're very . . . *tall*," she observed, looking up into his steel-blue eyes.

"Six-four," he said with a nod. "My tools?"

"Oh. They're in the supply closet. I'll just . . ." When she headed toward the door of her office and he didn't follow, Julianne rolled her hand at him. "Come with me."

Paul trailed her out into reception where Phoebe straightened to full attention and Will stood curiously in the doorway to the conference room.

46

"Everyone," she said, tugging open the door to the supply closet. "I'd like you to meet Paul Weaver. He's the angel of mercy I told you all about the other day. Paul, this is my business partner, Will Hanes. And our executive assistant, Phoebe Trent."

It took no longer than seven seconds for Julianne to retrieve the boot, but when she reemerged, Paul stood there fidgeting like a lone lobster in the tank at King Wok.

"Ah, you found my boot, too!" he exclaimed, seemingly relieved to be thrust out of the spotlight. He took it from Julianne and tucked it under his muscular arm. "That's great. I didn't think there was any shot of getting this back."

"Well," she groaned as she lugged the toolbox out of the closet and clanked it down at his feet, "I couldn't leave it lying there in the street."

Paul picked up the forty-pound monstrosity as if it was the plastic Tonka version she'd gotten both of her nephews at Christmas, and he gave her a nod as he headed for the door. "Nice to meet you all," he said. "And thanks again."

"Well . . . uh . . . Wait!" she managed, and Paul turned back and pressed the full weight of his spectacular eyes down on her meager 120-pound frame. "I . . . I'll . . . walk you to the elevator . . . is . . . what I'll do."

Julianne snatched the work boot away from him and clutched it with both arms.

"You don't have to," he said, gazing at his lost-again boot.

"I want to. Let's go."

Will shook his head at her, and she tossed him an animated cringe before following Paul through the door.

"So, Paul," she said as they waited for the elevator car to arrive, "you're in construction of some kind."

"Yeah. A carpenter. I'm working on a Victorian restoration over in Wyoming."

"I love that part of town," she said as she arched her leg and dug the peep-toe of her new color-blocked Marc Fisher platform

Tumble pumps into the carpet, wondering if he noticed them. "All those beautiful tree-lined streets, with the cute little gas lamp streetlights."

"Yeah," he said with a shrug. "I guess. A little uppity for my tastes."

"Where do you live?"

"I have a loft in Clifton."

"Oh, near the university."

The elevator door slid open and Paul stalked inside and pushed a button on the metal panel. "See ya."

"You know, Paul," she said, and she handed the boot back to him as she stepped into the way of the closing door and leaned back against it to hold it open. "I'd love to come around and see what you're doing on the Wyoming house."

"There's no visitors allowed on the site."

"Oh. Well, maybe we could have lunch sometime. You do get a break for lunch, don't you?"

His blank expression punctuated the humiliation setting in on Julianne.

"We usually have food brought in," he replied. "And we just toss it back and get back to work, you know."

"Oh." Julianne didn't like the idea of surrendering, but she also didn't like riding in circles around a cul-de-sac and getting nowhere. "Okay. Well, have a nice day, Paul."

"Yeah, you too."

*And they both lived separately ever after.*

Julianne stepped back and watched the metal doors close on her fairy tale. But at the very last instant, Paul's large hand reached through and yanked them open again.

"Hey," he said. "You wanna get a bite or something Friday night?"

*Like pulling teeth.*

"Yes!" she replied, a broad smile beaming. "I'd like that."

"I'll give you a call."

When she popped back through the office door, she gave a dramatic and triumphant bow.

"You got a date?" Phoebe exclaimed.

"I got a date."

Will stared at her in disbelief for several beats before he shook his head and rolled around the edge of the doorway, slamming the door behind him.

"Jealous!" she called after him. Tweaking out a little grin at Phoebe, she added, "He's jealous."

"*I'm* jealous," Phoebe said with a chuckle. "That was kind of strangely masterful."

Julianne shrugged. "Yeah, it was, kinda."

She headed for her office, but Phoebe stopped her. "Oh. Wait," she said, tapping her desktop with the clicking end of a pen. "Someone named George Flannigan called. He said to tell you the package you've been waiting for has been delivered over at Good Sam, and he's headed over to pick it up."

Julianne stared at her for a moment while she mulled that over. "Not without me he's not!"

Grabbing her purse and rain slicker from the Shaker coat hooks on the wall inside her office, Julianne sprinted through reception and out the door.

●　—　●　—　●

"Seriously, George?" she called out to him as she slipped out of her jacket and closed the distance between them. "What do you think you're doing?"

"I'm taking ownership of my client's property, that's what I'm doing," Flannigan replied as he stuffed his paperwork and identification into his pocket. Without looking up, he scratched his name across the bottom of the clipboard held by a bald guy in a lab coat.

"Can I just see that?" she asked as she reached them, and she snagged the plastic bag out of the attendant's hand before Flannigan could stop her.

She held the small bag up to the light as she examined the diamond. "Nice and brilliant." Smiling at the attendant she added, "Thanks for polishing it up for us. That couldn't have been a very pleasant job, but I guess you guys see just about everything around here, don't you?"

"Uh-huh." Without further exchange, he stuffed the clipboard under his arm and headed off down the corridor.

Flannigan made another grab for the bag, but Julianne yanked it away.

"You and I both know that there is paperwork to be completed, George. There's a nice judge involved. You know the one, over in the big nine-story building downtown, the one with the lovely columns in front."

"We'll appear before Judge Hillman when—"

"When he can see us," she interrupted. "Which is right now. I called Bridget from the car and she says we can take this directly to his chambers—" she dangled the plastic bag in front of him, pulling it away before he could snatch it from her "—as proof that my client has made full restitution. Then Judge Hillman will hear my argument for dropping all charges against him, and you can return this beautiful diamond into the hands of Mr. Leffler. Everybody wins."

Julianne turned on her Marc Fisher heels and stalked down the hall.

"Coming, George?" she called over her shoulder, knowing full well that he matched her stride for stride. "We don't want to keep Judge Hillman waiting."

Judge Bradford Hillman had been on the bench in Hamilton County since long before he lost most of his hair. Will sometimes said Hillman grew a moustache to make up for it, but Julianne thought he looked rather dashing. Not every man in his early sixties could get away with a moustache. Just Hillman.

And Tom Selleck, of course.

Julianne racked her brain as she tried to think of another one, but Hillman joined them in his chambers before any more moustaches sprang to mind.

"Miss Bartlett," he said as he dropped into the large leather chair behind his desk. "How is your fish doing? Jonah-like-the-whale?"

"Swimmingly, Your Honor. Thank you for asking."

"And Mr. Flannigan. I hear birthing congratulations are in order."

"Yes, sir," Julianne replied, and she produced the plastic bag from her pocket and dropped it on the desk. When Flannigan reached for it, she sent the bag sliding across the desktop. It landed against Hillman's hand like a base runner coming into home plate. "Mr. Bertinni has expressed deep remorse, Your Honor. In light of restitution of the diamond he borrowed from Leffler Jewelers—"

"Borrowed?" Flannigan objected.

"—we'd like to see the charges against him—"

"Not a chance, Julianne."

"—dismissed."

"I think that's for me to decide, isn't it?" Hillman asked, and he took a serious look at his judicial robes before nodding. "Yes. I'm the judge here. And Mr. Flannigan is right, Miss Bartlett. There's not a snowball's chance in a sauna."

"Then perhaps we can agree to probation and six months of community service?" she suggested. "Since this is his first offense, I think it's a more than adequate—"

"There's nothing adequate about it, Judge," Flannigan interrupted. "She knows very well that jail time is—"

"Oh, come on, George!"

"Enough." That was all it took for both of them to zip it. "Mr. Flannigan, restitution has been made, an act I would venture to say did not come easily or without great discomfort for the defendant. Can we at least agree on that?"

"Yes, Judge."

"And Ms. Bartlett, do you have anything to add to the usual first-offense-heart-of-gold yada-yada defense?"

The corner of her mouth twitched as she tried to keep the grin under wraps. "No, Your Honor. I'd say that about covers it."

"Good then. Mr. Flannigan, you can see my bailiff in thirty minutes for the paperwork to return the diamond to its rightful owner. And Ms. Bartlett, I want to see Mr. Bertinni *in person* in my courtroom next week for sentencing. Bridget will schedule it for you. In the meantime, bail will stand. My gavel is at the bench, so this will have to do," he said, and he pounded his fist on the desktop. "Now get out, both of you."

"Thank you, Your Honor."

Julianne and Flannigan parted company the moment the judge's door latched behind them.

"Dr. Phil," she muttered as she waited for the elevator, then she slapped her hand against her raincoat. "Dr. Phil has a *great* moustache!"

In fact, Judge Hillman looked a little *like* the television psychologist.

"I beg your pardon?" the woman standing next to her asked as the doors slipped open.

"Oh," Julianne replied with a snicker. "I was just counting men with good moustaches."

The woman followed her onboard and pressed the call button to the lobby while Julianne checked email on her iPhone. A reminder from Will about dinner with the parents. Two messages from Rand Winters, her old cubicle neighbor at the public defender's office. An invitation from Suzanne to rejoin the game of Words with Friends they'd begun three days prior.

"Why?" the woman asked her, and Julianne broke free from her phone.

"Why, what?"

"Why were you counting men with moustaches?"

Julianne sighed. "Because . . . they're there?"

The woman gave her a halfhearted nod as the elevator doors opened.

The sun had finally broken through the clouds, coloring a happy blush on the afternoon. Julianne lowered the tan convertible top on the PT Cruiser and dug her sunglasses out of the side pocket of her hobo bag. She stopped to convert Suzanne's "draws" into "drawstring" on Words with Friends before poking the key into the ignition and rolling out of the parking lot.

"Hey, Phoebe," she sang as she barreled through the office door. "What'd I miss?"

Phoebe looked up from her computer screen and smiled. "Someone named Randall Winters stopped by looking for you, and—"

"Ohh. You can divert that connection however you see fit." She'd put the public defender's office behind her now, and she wasn't really interested in hearing all the scuttlebutt going around in her absence.

"Well, that might be a little hard to do," Phoebe said, and she leaned forward and whispered. "He's in Will's office."

"Oh." Julianne cringed, staring at the closed door between them. "Why?"

"I'm not sure. When you weren't here, he asked to see Will."

She nibbled on the corner of her lip for a long moment as she considered whether to go in or not. "How long have they been in there?" she finally asked.

"About half an hour."

She groaned, folding her body into it as she contorted her face. "That guy just really *bugs me.*"

Phoebe chuckled. "Want to hide in your office? I can tell you when the coast is clear."

"Yes!" she exclaimed immediately. On second thought, she deflated. "No." And with that, she tapped lightly on Will's door before pushing it open slightly.

"Jules, good. I'm glad you're here," Will greeted her. "Can you come in a minute?"

She tossed a helpless glance over her shoulder at Phoebe before mustering her most charming smile. "Rand. Phoebe mentioned you were here. How are you?"

Rand squirmed out of the chair and pulled a face at Will before replying, "Not . . . good."

"No?" Julianne stepped inside the office and latched the door behind her as Will stood up behind his desk. "I heard you and Debbie split. I'm really sorry."

"Yeah," he muttered as he twisted a string hanging from the cuff of his sport jacket. "Divorcing."

"Well, Phoebe can pull together a list of attorneys who—"

"Rand isn't here about his divorce," Will interrupted, his eyes unusually round as he stared a hole right into her. "Why don't we all sit down."

Rand sank into the chair, and Julianne folded into the one beside him. "So what's going on?" she asked him, and she turned toward Will and arched an eyebrow.

"Rand is facing a rather delicate situation," Will explained.

"And I need it to go away," he blurted. "I can't have this coming back at me on the job, you know? I'm making a bid for the open Assistant D.A. post next month, and I can't have this hanging over me. It's not like I did it on purpose." He narrowed his eyes at Will as he continued. "It's not like I'm some sort of monster."

Julianne swallowed the retort born out of five years' experience working alongside Rand Winters.

"Rand. What did you do?"

His gaze darted back to Will again.

"What did he do?" she asked Will.

"I shot someone."

# 5

"You what?" Julianne exclaimed. "You shot someone? Who?"

"Not so much some *one*," Will clarified, "as some *thing*."

"You shot . . . *some thing*? What was it?"

When Rand hesitated, Will finally answered for him. "A pig."

"A pig."

Rand groaned. "Yes."

"You shot a pig?"

"Yes."

"And you're afraid someone will find out."

"Yes. I need this to go away."

Julianne grimaced. "So you said. Who's going to care that you shot a pig? Aside from the owner of the pig, I suppose."

"Well, that's the thing."

"The owner is the thing."

"Yes."

Julianne sighed, looking to Will for more help.

"Rand shot Dean and Maureen's granddaughter's pig," he told her.

"Pastor Dean has a great-grandpig?" Turning in her chair, she asked Rand, "Why did you shoot Emily's pig?"

"I didn't know it was her pig. I heard a ruckus outside the back door, and I thought it was one of the neighborhood dogs getting into the trash cans again."

"And you intended to shoot the neighborhood *dog*, Rand!"

"No, of course not. But when I opened the door and saw that

thing. . . . Well, it came charging at me like a wild boar or something. . . ."

"How big is this pig?" Julianne asked Will, and he only shook his head and pulled a face. "Is it one of those giant hogs or something?"

"I remember Pastor Dean talking about it. His son got it for Emily at Christmas last year. It's one of those pot-bellied pigs."

"How big can a year-old pot-bellied pig be?"

"Excuse me." Rand interrupted their exchange, and he rose to his feet, waving one hand between them. "Can we focus? Does it really matter how big it is? I think we're running off the road and into the ditch here. The fact is . . . *I shot it.*"

"It does matter how big it is," Julianne corrected him, circling Will's desk and opening his laptop. "If it's a cute little ten-pound domesticated pet, that's going to be a whole other kettle of pigs than if you had two hundred pounds of bacon charging at you."

Will moved out of the way, and Julianne lowered into his chair without looking up from the laptop.

"What are you doing?" Rand asked nervously.

"I'm searching for Emily's Facebook page. She may have pictures."

When she finally found it, her heart dropped a little at Emily's profile picture: A cute little wide-eyed pink piglet.

"Oh no," she said. "This thing couldn't be any cuter if it was lounging in a laundry basket like that snuggly bear on television. How could you shoot this little guy, Rand?"

He leaned across the desk and turned the laptop to look at the screen. "This isn't the pig I shot, Julianne! It's not. No way."

Julianne took control of the screen again and clicked on the photo section. Fortunately, eleven-year-old Emily had documented the entire first year of her pig's life. Adorable little ten-pound Wilbur, with the cute pink snout and round peach-fuzz body, had morphed into an eighty-seven-pound one-year-old stunner who apparently enjoyed a good carrot cake. Julianne groaned at the picture of the pig donning a pointed birthday hat as he made short history of one decorated like an actual carrot!

"This pig was part of the family," Julianne commented as she clicked through more photos of Wilbur and the Alden clan. "That's going to complicate matters considerably."

"L-look," Rand stammered. "You two know this pastor, right? Maybe you can get him to help us make this go away, huh?"

"Well, has anyone contacted you? Is there a threat that this will go public in some way?"

Once again, Rand glanced at Will before he replied. "That little girl is going to be the end of my career!"

"What don't I know?" she asked him.

Will turned over a pink flyer and slid it across the desk.

A close-up photograph of Rand's contorted and shocked face angled against another picture, this one far more sobering—the bloody corpse of Emily's treasured pig-friend—both photos sandwiched between two lines of giant block letters.

RANDALL WINTERS

MURDERER

"Oh. Well, that's effective, isn't it?"

● — ● — ●

"Davis, you should come to my Movin' & Groovin' class with me next time," Amanda said as she dropped a scoop of macaroni and cheese on Will's plate. "It's nothing strenuous. It's a little like a bunch of doddering old fools doing the hokey-pokey."

The moment Julianne's eyes met his, Will shared a grin with her.

"Babette picks the music. Today it was *Achy Breaky Heart*."

"At my age, Mandy," Will's dad cracked, "everything I got is achy-breaky."

"Well, maybe it would ache and break a little less if you'd get your blood pumping every now and again."

"Stop it, Mom," Julianne warned, waving her fork at her mother. "Davis is still in his prime."

Amanda's face blushed as she told them, "I wasn't saying he's old, really. I . . . was—"

"Yeah," Davis said softly as he leaned toward Julianne, "I'm in the youth of my old age."

She chuckled as her mother continued "—just thinking a little exercise might be a good thing."

Will pushed several asparagus spears from the serving dish before passing it to Amanda. He loved these dinners. Will and his dad provided the kitchen table, and Amanda brought the food from her kitchen next door. And all their talk about nothing in particular; that was his favorite part of all.

"Tell you what, Mandy. You come fishing with me, and I'll go movin' with you." Davis snuck a grin at Will. "Or is it groovin'?"

"You know I'm not going fishing. If Julianne's brothers were in town, they could tell you why."

Julianne giggled. "Mom's afraid of worms."

"I am not afraid of worms!" she corrected. "I just don't like them crawling into my shirt."

Julianne wiggled her eyebrows at Will, eliciting laughter.

"Austin was playing with the worms," she told Davis. "And one of them got away from him and crawled right down the front of Mom's dress. Dad and Travis thought it was funny, so they tossed a couple more of them at her."

"It was not funny," Amanda said with a sniff.

"She hasn't been fishing since."

"And I am not about to start again now."

"Well, you know Pop's not movin' or groovin' anytime soon either," Will quipped.

"Who wants more macaroni?" Amanda rerouted the conversation.

"I'll have some," Will said, raising his hand like a schoolboy and wiggling his fingers.

"None for me," Julianne piped up. "In fact, I have to go in a minute."

Will straightened, holding a forkful of asparagus in the air in front of him. "Where are you headed?"

"I'm meeting Suzanne."

"You should have invited her for dinner," Amanda said. "She hasn't come around in ages. What are your plans?"

"Shopping," she replied casually. "I need a new outfit."

"Oooh. Something special coming up?"

"Very. Remember that guy I told you about? The one who saved the dog?"

"The owner of the toolbox."

Will felt his father's eyes burning a dent into the side of his face, but he held his gaze firmly on Julianne.

"Yes, I found him and returned his toolbox and work boot," she explained casually. "And we have a date on Friday night."

Amanda's eyes darted immediately toward Will as she sang, "Oh, that's nice. I suppose."

Great. Now both sides of his face were melting under careful scrutiny. Will shot his father one quick cut-it-out glance before he returned his attention to the thick slice of ham on his plate.

"Julianne. What do you know about the man?" Amanda asked her with a scowl.

"Paul is his name and he is a carpenter—part of the crew restoring one of the old Victorians over in Wyoming. And he risked his life to save that dog when—"

"Risked his life?" Will questioned without looking up from his plate. "That's kind of an overstatement, Jules."

"What do you mean? He got out in the middle of a downpour, walked right out into traffic—"

"Yes, but did he risk life and limb?"

"All right, kids," Davis declared, "that's enough arguing now, or you'll both go to bed without dessert."

Amanda chuckled as Julianne brightened. "Ooh, is there dessert?"

"Strawberry shortcake. Shall I make a dish for you before you head out?"

Julianne nodded and smiled at her mother, the perfect dimples on either side of her face flashing as she did. "Yes, please."

Amanda got up and headed for the refrigerator. "Does this carpenter meet any of the points on that list of yours?"

Julianne glanced over her shoulder toward her mother. "My list?"

"Oh, I don't know," she replied in an attempt at sounding casual. "I just remember something about a list of qualities you wanted in a relationship. For instance, wasn't there something about how he had to be a Christian believer? Is this boy a believer, honey?"

"Well, it's a little too soon to know that yet, Mom. It's only our first date."

"Okay then," she conceded. "Chocolate sprinkles?"

"Of course."

At first jingle, Will snatched up his phone from the table in front of him. A text from Lacey James beckoned.

*I guess you've heard the news?*

Will typed a quick reply. *What news?*

*Noms r out for Bar Assoc Person of the Year.*

His breath caught in his throat as he read it. Julianne had been hoping for a nomination three years in a row, and Will knew she deserved it for all of the pro bono work and volunteer time she'd devoted to several local charities. He'd submitted her for consideration all three years, but she never quite made the final cut. Perhaps this year would be different. He'd nailed that nomination essay.

*Jules?* he typed.

His throat tightened slightly at Lacey's reply. *Yes. But someone else 2.* Will considered the possibilities as a second text popped up. *ME!*

"Put that thing down and finish your supper," his father reprimanded. Amanda nodded and agreed while Julianne picked up her iPhone.

"Will!" she exclaimed, popping right out of her chair. "The nominations!"

"I was just about to tell you."

"What nominations?" Amanda inquired.

"The Bar Association's Person of the Year awards," Julianne began.

"And your daughter," Will continued for her, "is a finalist."

"Oh, honey, that's wonderful."

"Ohh," Julianne said, deflating into her chair again as she studied the screen on her phone. "And Lacey James."

"Who's Lacey James?"

"I've told you about her, Mom. She's that horrible woman with her radar set on Will."

"There's a woman with her radar set on you, Son?" Davis asked. "What's she like?"

"Oh, Davis, she's awful. Will would never!"

*Lunch tomorrow to celebrate?*

Will examined Lacey's text for a moment and thought it over, weighing it against Julianne's certainty that he *would never*.

"Mom, I'm going to skip out on the shortcake. I can't wait to tell Suzanne we have to shop for *two outfits*! Ooh, Will, maybe Paul will escort me to the awards gala. Wouldn't that be amazing?"

He glared at her for a moment before defiantly typing a reply, *Tan Thai on Court St? 1 p.m.?*

*See you then!*

Will watched Julianne glide out the front door for her shopping excursion with Suzanne, and he made his excuses to Amanda for passing on dessert.

"You headed out too, boy?" Davis asked him.

"I thought I'd head over to Alec's and go for a ride. Clear my head."

After changing clothes and filling a large resealable plastic bag with chopped apples and carrots, Will jogged out to his car and dialed Alec before shifting into Reverse. They'd been chums since grade school, and from then until now, their relationship had been braced by a mutual love of horses. Alec's family owned about fifty acres of trails and rolling hills out off McKelvey Road. When each of the three Ross kids reached the age of venturing out on their own, each one got a home of their own built right there on the family property. Alec's place, built for him at the ripe old age of nineteen, reminded Will of an overgrown treehouse, just halfway between the main family house and the stables.

Alec had given Will carte blanche on the horses, but in all the years they'd been friends, he had never worked up the nerve to just turn up and grab a saddle. He always called first, and Alec said the same thing every time he did: "Bro, I told you. Just come on over anytime." On this particular day, Alec had worked a late day and expressed some regret that he couldn't go riding with Will.

Truth be told, Will didn't want any company aside from Christie, the blond Palomino quarter horse he'd been riding for years. He could hardly wait to saddle her up and pick up some speed before the sun started to set for the day. Twenty minutes after he and Alec hung up, Will climbed into the saddle, patted Christie's mane, and the two of them galloped up the dirt trail and over the first hill.

Will knew the Ross property almost as well as he knew the nuances and slopes of Julianne's face. He gave his head a hearty shake to remove her from his line of sight. The only female Will wanted to think about just then was Christie. He still had an hour or so before the sun dropped beneath the hills, and he determined to make the most of every minute.

"Hah!" he exclaimed, tapping Christie's sides with the heels of his boots and flapping the reins gently. "Let's go, girl. Show me what you got!"

He sensed the horse's excitement as she immediately took off into a full gallop. Alec often said he thought Christie waited longingly for Will's visits because there was a four-beat gait harnessed inside her that no one else accessed. She'd been saving it up for him, and Will let out a bellow of a laugh as they climbed the last hill on the property.

"Whoa. Whoa, girl."

With a slight tug on the reins, Will guided Christie to a stop and he dropped over the side of her, both feet thumping to the ground.

"You're a great horse, Christie," he told her, running both hands along the sides of her shiny golden muzzle, scratching into her thick white mane. He gazed into her amber eyes and nodded his head. "That was a great ride, my friend." Christie snorted and lifted her head with a jerk. "I know. You liked it too, right?"

Will produced a small bag, and the rustle of the plastic drew the horse's full attention until he offered her a chunk of apple on his flattened palm. She lapped it up greedily.

When she'd finished all of the treats he'd brought along, Will led her by the reins toward an overgrown patch of soft green grass. He wrapped the reins loosely around one of the lowest branches of a mature elm before plunking down beneath it and leaning against the whitened trunk.

He stared out across the vista of green, tracing the property line fence until it disappeared behind a dense grove of trees. In the distance, beneath a darkening pink and blue sky, cars had just begun turning on headlights. Will knew he would have to head back soon. But not just yet.

He closed his eyes and tilted his head back against the tree.

"Father, I need Your help right now. I need to look at her and just see my friend, instead of seeing that *Property Of* sign I stuck to the back of her jacket when she wasn't looking. Help me let her go and face reality, to get my eyes off Julianne and back onto You. Lord, help me to move on. I'm ready to move on."

Christie snorted, and when Will opened his eyes and looked up at her, she stared right at him, and it seemed for a minute as though the horse *laughed*.

"What?" he asked her, and one corner of his mouth twitched slightly. "There's nothing funny here. What are you laughing at, huh?"

Will's cell chimed, and he pulled it from his pocket. Beth Rudd, Jimmy's wife. He wondered why she might be calling.

"Beth. How are you?"

"I'm good, Will. How about yourself?"

"Pretty great. I'm out for a ride, actually. A buddy of mine from school lets me take one of his horses out every now and then."

"Oh, that sounds perfect!" she squealed.

"You like to ride?" he asked her.

"Me? No. Absolutely not." Will's mouth quirked with a smile. "But my baby sister does. You remember Alison? You met her at the Christmas pageant."

"Sure. The schoolteacher."

"Yes! I'm so glad you remember because she's why I'm calling you, Will."

"Does she need a lawyer?"

"In a manner of speaking, I think she might."

# 6

"**William, I am so** happy you agreed to have lunch with me," Lacey sang as she sliced her already-cut salad into small bite-sized strips. "I'm just over the moon about being nominated for Person of the Year. Can you imagine?"

Well, in fact, he could imagine. Julianne was ecstatic after hoping to make the cut for three years running.

"So what did they cite as your outstanding accomplishments?" he asked before taking a bite of his orange chicken.

"Oh, that's the best part," she crooned. "They didn't just name my pro bono work for the women's shelter, but they also included the fact that I was elected to the governing board."

"Were you?" he asked. "I don't think I knew that. It's great, Lace."

"Thank you. I'm very proud of the work we do over there, William."

Will chuckled inwardly. No one had ever called him William outside of a couple of teachers in middle school, but Lacey had latched on to his full name since the day they'd met.

"How about Julie? What did they pick for her?"

"Ah, she's involved in every nonprofit in the Queen City," he said with a smile. "They named a few of them."

"Oh." Her ladylike expression slipped away for a moment, and Lacey curled up her face in reaction until she caught herself. "I suppose you'll be escorting her to the gala?"

Will considered how to answer. "I don't know, really."

"Well, it's not like she has many other options," she speculated.

"I mean, the poor girl doesn't exactly keep them around for more than a date or two, does she? And for something like this—a formal evening and all—"

"She's been seeing someone new, actually." He didn't know why he felt so compelled to jump to her defense, but Lacey's catty remarks about Julianne's inability to snag a good man had started to become rather legendary. And Will didn't like it.

"Really." He watched as Lacey's wheels turned, but what came next caught him by complete surprise. "Then would you be willing to escort *me* to the gala, William?"

He took another bite of orange chicken as a short reprieve before answering.

"Can I get back to you on that?"

●— ● —●

Dean and Maureen Alden's quaint two-story home sat on a small parcel of land punctuated by a slight grade in the front.

*Not even enough of a slant for kids on sleds to pick up any real speed,* Julianne thought as they pulled up out front. *But even if they could, the closeness of the street at the bottom of the descent would make sledding impractical.*

"You're measuring sledability again, aren't you?" Will asked as he pushed the doorbell.

How did he always do that?

"I give it a 2-rating," she replied. "Too close to the street."

Will shook his head and grinned as the front door opened, nudging the brushed nickel knocker to rap lightly.

"Hey, you two!" Pastor Dean greeted them. "Come on in."

Maureen served glasses of iced tea on a bamboo serving tray as they all sat around the glossy dining room table. She straightened the floral centerpiece and set down a plate of butter cookies.

*Will's favorites.*

He reached for a cookie and thanked her as he plopped it into his mouth.

"So I'm hoping I know why you wanted to see me," Pastor Dean said with a sly grin. "Why don't you tell me if I'm right."

Julianne and Will exchanged perplexed attempts at smiles.

"It's about Emily," Will told him, and Dean belted out a laugh.

"Oh! Well, I wasn't even close."

Maureen emerged from the kitchen. "Our granddaughter, Emily? Can I sit down with you then?"

"Please," Will said, waving her into the room.

Once his wife had settled beside him, Dean sighed. "Why don't you tell me what's on your mind."

"I guess you know that Rand Winters—"

Maureen wrinkled her nose and groaned loudly at the mention of his name.

"—accidentally shot Emily's pet pig last week."

"Accidental!" Maureen exclaimed. "That's not the version Emily and her father told when she sat right here at this table in hysterics." Dean pressed his wife's hand with his own, and she touched her lips with two fingers. "I'm sorry. Go on."

"I used to work with Rand," Julianne told them, "when I was at the public defender's office. I know better than anyone what a challenging man he can be. But Rand isn't the kind of person who would do something like this on purpose. He is so sorry for what happened. He feels just terrible." When her conscience poked at her, she clarified. "You know. As terrible as he can *feel*, he . . . feels it."

One look from Will told her she wasn't helping at all, and Julianne leaned back against the chair and sighed.

"Rand is concerned," Will picked up from there, "that this accident is gaining momentum that can adversely affect his reputation."

"You mean that people will find out he shot a young girl's pet?" Dean asked.

"Well, frankly," Will replied, "yes."

"And what are you looking for from us?" he asked, glancing from Will to Julianne.

"Well, I was hoping we could start with finding some way to put a lid on the smear campaign."

"What smear campaign?"

Julianne pulled the pink flyer out of her bag and unfolded it, straightening the creases against the edge of the oak table. She handed Will the paper, and he laid it out in front of them. Maureen's eyes grew wide and glossy, and the corner of Dean's mouth quivered.

"Did Em make this?" he asked.

"She's put up dozens of them in their neighborhood," Julianne expounded. "She's left them on parked cars, even handed them to people coming out of Kroger."

After a long moment of silence, Dean sighed. "She's a very passionate girl. And that pot-bellied pig of hers was . . ."

"Part of the family," Julianne said with him in unison.

"Yes," Dean confirmed.

"We know," she told him. "But we're hoping you can help us come up with something that will make this right enough that Emily will stop the . . . umm . . . counterattack."

Maureen's expression told Julianne that they weren't going to get any constructive assistance from her. In fact, she might have gotten an idea from Emily's flyer, might have started wondering how to make one of her own.

"I think an apology might have gone a long way," she said, her face tilted slightly upward. "Frank says the man never even said he was sorry."

"So do you think if he goes over to the house and makes a heartfelt plea for Emily's forgiveness . . . do you think that will put this to rest?" Will asked her.

"I think that would be up to Emily."

"But it certainly couldn't hurt," Pastor Dean added.

● — ● — ●

Will and Julianne decided to walk the few blocks from the office to Taqueria Mercado, and Julianne slipped her arm through Will's as they trekked up Walnut and crossed Seventh.

"Are you ready for your big date tomorrow?" Will asked, and her heart fluttered like the wings of a dozen butterflies trapped in her chest.

"So ready. Although the reality of it started to close in on me around three o'clock this morning."

"What reality is that? The one where you've accepted a date with a perfect stranger based on a toolbox and a work boot sitting in the road? Or the one where you notice that the chasm between your *Once Upon a Time* and your *Happily Ever After* is murky and gray?"

"Yes," she stated. Tossing her hair over her shoulder, she let out a burst of tension by way of a snort and a laugh.

"I have a date of my own tomorrow night. Maybe we should make it a double."

Julianne's fluttering heart went eerily still. She stopped in her tracks, yanking Will by the arm as she did.

"What's wrong?" he asked. "Foot cramp again? I don't know why you insist on wearing those heels, Jules. They can't be good for—"

"No," she replied, shaking her head. "You have a date?"

He grinned at her and tipped his head to the side as he admitted, "Yeah. I have a date. Boggles the mind, doesn't it?"

"Do tell."

"Alison Reece. Beth Rudd's sister."

Her conversation with Beth in the ladies' room at Vandella's skittered across Julianne's memory.

*"I was thinking of setting up Will and my younger sister, Alison. You remember, you met her at the Christmas pageant?"*

She'd asked Julianne if she minded. What else could Julianne have said? She had no claim on Will, then or now, or ever. It did cross her mind now though whether it might be too late to file an appeal.

"The schoolteacher," she muttered. Tightening the loop of

their arms, she squeezed and forced a smile. "That's so great."

Pulling him along, she continued the stroll up Walnut.

"Really?" he said. "You think it's great?"

"Of course," she replied without looking away from the crosswalk ahead of them. "Don't you?"

"Well, let's face it. I haven't had a date in a pretty long time. And it's not like I know much of anything about this girl. We might be pathetically ill-suited to one another."

She mustered up the encouragement she knew Will sought. "Or you might be soul mates. You never know until you spend a couple of hours getting to know each other."

"Soul mates," Will muttered, shaking his head. "Is that what you think the ditch digger is? Your soul mate?"

"He is not a ditch digger," she said, smacking his arm. "He's a carpenter. Like Jesus."

"Really?" he challenged. "You really want to go there and compare him *to Jesus*, Jules?"

"Yeah." She tilted her head upward and apologized. "Sorry, Lord." Her eyes darting back to Will, she added, "I just meant—"

"I know what you meant."

"And by the way," she continued. "He could be my soul mate." When Will didn't reply, she repeated, "He could be."

Will's silence closed the gap between the corner of Eighth Street and the front entrance of Taqueria Mercado. "Here we are."

She spotted Rand Winters at a small table. "Over there."

Will placed his hand on the small of her back and guided her toward him. "Rand," he said as they reached the table, "thanks for coming."

"I ordered a round," Rand told them, "and a little something to nosh on."

"A round of what?" Julianne asked him.

"Yes, Julianne," he mocked, "I remembered that you don't drink alcoholic beverages. They're bringing a pitcher of virgin sangria for the two of you. A beer and a shot for me. Now tell me what you found out about this pig nightmare."

*Oh, he is just so unlikable!* she thought, taking a deep and bracing breath before answering.

The waiter set a platter of quesadillas next to the chips and salsa already there. He carefully unloaded drinks from the tray and asked, "Anything else right now?"

"No," Will replied. "Thanks very much."

Rand grabbed the shot glass and raised it in a toast. "To good news, if you don't mind," and he downed the tequila in two gulps.

"We talked to Pastor Dean, the girl's grandfather," Julianne began.

"Did you get anywhere?"

"That all depends on your perception, I guess," Will told him as Rand sucked on a wedge of lime. "How do you feel about apologizing to an eleven-year-old?"

"*Apologizing.*" Rand spoke the word as if it had been dipped in spoiled milk before crossing his lips.

"Yes, Rand. Apologize," Julianne said. "It's the act of saying you're sorry for picking up a gun, cocking it, and sending her little pig instantly to its grave."

"That pig was not *little.*"

"It might be your only hope of settling things with her," Will added.

Rand took several swigs from his beer and smacked the glass on the table. "So if I hold my hat in my hands and say I'm sorry, the little terror will stop with the flyers?"

"We can't guarantee that. But it's a good start."

He stuffed a quesadilla wedge into his mouth and spoke while he chewed it. "I'll do whatever it takes." He stood up, downing the rest of his beer. "I'll go across the lawn in the morning and give it a shot."

"Try to express some kindness," Julianne suggested. On second thought, she added, "You do have some of that, don't you?"

Rand contorted his face into a balled fist.

"I just mean . . . don't railroad her. Kids are very perceptive."

He plunked the glass to the table with a shrug. "Whatever. I'll call you when it's done, and we'll see where we are."

Julianne's eyes met Will's and locked there as Rand left the restaurant.

"He's a piece of work," Will declared.

"Credit where credit's due," she replied. "He's a piece and a half, at the very least."

"He is that."

"He's just so hard to . . . like!"

"But if the Rands of the world didn't cross our paths," he began, and Julianne grinned.

"How would we learn to love the unlovable!" she finished for him.

"Dinner while we're here?" he asked her.

"Oh, yeah," she answered with a chuckle.

Once they'd both ordered and the meals had been served, Julianne leaned back against the chair, both hands wrapped around her chilled glass, and grinned at Will.

"So tell me more about your date with Alison. Where are you taking her?"

"Riding, up at Alec's place."

"She rides?"

"Since she was a kid. She actually used to compete."

"Compete. *Really.*"

Julianne started to wonder if the fruit in the sangria hadn't agreed with her, and she pressed her hand to the top of her burning stomach.

"You okay?" Will asked.

"Too many taquitos," she teased. With an added chuckle, she admitted, "I actually think it's the sangria. It's very fruity."

"Order an iced tea."

"I think I will." She shook her head and gulped. "So . . . horseback riding. Then what? Out to dinner?"

"Sunset picnic on the ridge, I think."

"Nice," she said, nodding.

"What about you? Where's the ditch di—" He stopped himself. "The carpenter. Where's he taking you?"

"He didn't say. We're meeting first . . . at The Blind Lemon."

"In Mt. Adams?"

"Yes. And I guess we'll decide from there."

"You're *meeting* him? Why isn't he picking you up?"

"He's working in Clifton for the day, so it just seemed easier for me to meet him."

Will shook his head. "No horse-drawn carriage. A shame."

"The horses and glass carriage come later, smarty pants," she informed him. "Right before the *Happily Ever After.*"

"Ah." Will grinned as he stabbed a couple of rogue onions and green pepper strips from his plate and poked them into his mouth. "Thanks for the lesson."

"William? Is that you?"

Julianne looked up and spotted Lacey and her thousand-dollar dazzling-white smile heading straight for them.

"Here comes my pesky wicked stepsister now," she mumbled.

"I can't believe it's you," she drawled in her questionable Southern drawl. "I've never even been to this place before, and I decide to stop in for some dinner, and here you are!"

"Here *we* are," Julianne corrected. "I'm here, too."

Her eyes grazed over Julianne without comment before she leaned down and smacked a kiss on Will's cheek, leaving its bright red form behind.

*Like a lipstick chalk drawing around a corpse.*

"Can I join you?" she asked Will, grabbing a napkin and wiping the lipstick from his face.

"Well, we're just finishing up," he told her. "But we can sit with you while you have something."

"Delightful," she sang, and Julianne watched her slither down into the chair beside him. "You know, Julie, there's no reason for you to stay. If you want to be on your way, William and I can just—"

"Oh, no!" she interrupted. "I wouldn't dream of leaving. Besides, we haven't ordered dessert."

"Ooh, dessert." Turning toward Will, Lacey asked, "What's delicious here for a sweet tooth?"

Julianne raised one eyebrow, glanced at Will, and slid a menu across the table toward Lacey. "Here. Have a look."

*Love the unlovable,* she reminded herself. *Love the unlovable. Love the unlovable.*

"Mother says there will be no recreation
until your chores are complete," her stepsister insisted.
"And when you're finished in here, the stables need your attention."
The girl wiped the perspiration from her brow
and gazed up at her stepsister.
"What have I ever done to you to warrant your repugnance?
Why do you make it your life's work to oppress me so?"
Narrowing her flame-filled eyes,
her mother's other daughter glared at her.
"Why?" she repeated with a sniff.
"Because I can, that's why."

# 7

"**Lacey, why did** you call?" Julianne grumbled into her cell phone as she stroked Gus, Suzanne's precious blue parakeet, as he sat perched on her shoulder. "Is there something I can actually do for you?"

"I just found it ironic, that's all," she cooed. "You and I, up for the same award . . . both of us women in William's life . . ." Julianne's tongue nearly slipped right off its roller " . . . each of us attorneys in the Greater Cincinnati area."

"I'm sorry," she finally managed. "Both of us, what?"

"Attorneys."

"No. Before that."

"Oh, well," Lacey said on a bouncy little giggle. "We play very different roles, of course. I know you're territorial and all—and I do hope you're not thinking of marking him like Daddy's hunting pup, Julie—but I think we need to face facts. I mean, we *are* both women in his life, aren't we?"

So many replies came to mind that they logjammed Julianne's entrance into the conversation. She just sat there, gripping the arm of Suzanne's pretty floral chair, her eyes bulging so wide that they ached, the flow of oxygen blocked at the base of her throat by a wall of indignation.

"Fine, fine," Lacey continued. "I can see that I was wrong. I thought I'd just reach out to you, extend an olive branch."

*Oh, an olive branch! Maybe that's what I'm choking on.*

There was a salty taste at the back of her throat, after all.

"I thought we might make a day of it together. Get mani-pedis, have our hair done. No matter which one of us wins the award, Julie, there's no sense in *looking* like a loser, is there? Especially when you have a new man in your life at the moment."

"What? What did you say?"

"William told me about the new man in your life, and I thought maybe I could do my part to help you keep this one. My hairdresser can do wonders with that hair of yours if—"

"I . . ." There it was! Her voice had returned at last! ". . . don't think so."

"All right then," Lacey said with a sigh. "You'll call me if you change your mind?"

"I won't," she replied, her voice going raspy as she did. "And Lacey? My name is *not Julie*. My name is *Julianne!*"

And with that, she disconnected the call.

"What on earth was that all about?" Suzanne asked as she emerged from the closet with several hangers of clothes over her arm.

"Lacey James."

"Your arch-nemesis," she growled playfully. "Why do you let her get under your skin like that?"

"Oh, she's just so infuriating! Now, she has somehow mistaken *William* for her boyfriend, and me for her high school BFF."

"You're joking."

"I wish."

Julianne's *real BFF* dropped to the bed with the pile of clothes and grinned, her hazel eyes glimmering with amusement as she raked her auburn hair away from her pretty face.

"Okay now, focus," she said, snapping two pink-tipped fingers that Gus mistook for an invitation, and the bird flew from Julianne's shoulder and landed on Suzanne's outstretched finger. "You meet him in three hours. The Blind Lemon is very casual. You don't want to overdress. Try this. It's Stella McCartney."

Suzanne thrust a creamy white blouse at her, still on the hanger.

"Stella McCartney, Suz? What if I spill on it?"

"You won't. It works great over jeans, and it's still dressy enough to leave room for a knockout pair of shoes."

"Jeans?" she asked her friend. "Really?"

"What did I tell you?"

"I don't want to overdress."

"Right. You'll wear those distressed skinny jeans you bought at Nordstrom's. Here. Try it on while I put Gus into his cage. I don't want him lighting on silk charmeuse."

Julianne slipped into the blouse and fastened the buttons hidden behind a seamed panel. Standing in front of the mirror, she examined the long, fluid sleeves and starched cuffs as Suzanne reappeared and, reaching from behind her, adjusted the flowing tie around Julianne's collar and arranged it into a perfect knot.

"Stupendous," she said with a grin to Julianne's reflection. "And you'll wear my blue waistcoat over it."

"I'm not wearing your Stella McCartney blouse *and* your coat. Besides, it's still too warm for a coat yet."

"It's not that heavy, and you'll take it off once you're inside. You know how that navy blue brings out the color of your eyes. I'd kill for those crystal clear blue eyes of yours."

Before she knew it, Suzanne had guided her arms into the sleeves and slipped the jacket up and over her shoulders. The waistcoat fit her like a glove all the way to the waist, where tarnished silver metal clips held it shut before the silhouette flared over her hips.

"It's very military steampunk," her friend observed. "And just perfect for your figure. You should wear those navy platforms of yours—the ones with the cool straps. Do you have a bag?"

"Stop, Suz. You're wearing me out. I want him to like me . . . not just what I'm wearing."

"I just want to make sure you're ready. I have a great bag that—"

"I have a purse. Stop."

Julianne slipped out of the coat and folded it over the corner of the bed before slipping down into the floral chair again. As she unbuttoned the blouse, Suzanne dropped to the bed and grinned at her.

"What else?"

Suzanne Nichols excelled at cutting straight through to the heart of a matter. In the ten years they'd known each other, she always had.

"Will has a date tonight, too."

"Does he? Good for Willie. Who's it with?"

She slipped out of the blouse and handed it to Suzanne. "Someone from our church set him up. Alison Something. She's a teacher."

"And this bothers you, why?" she asked, folding the blouse and placing it atop the waistcoat.

"It doesn't," she replied immediately, but Suzanne's grimace reflected even Julianne's own disbelief. "Well, it shouldn't." She shrugged and sank deeply into the chair. "But for some odd reason, it does."

"Maybe you're afraid he'll move on and forget you?"

"No," she snapped. As she thought better of it, she sighed. "Will would never forget me, exactly. But I guess . . . I don't know."

"You guess," Suzanne finished for her, "he might not make you A-number-one-top-priority anymore? And that makes you feel a little bit abandoned?" Julianne's eyes locked into her friend's as Suzanne wrinkled her nose and held up her hand, showing only the slightest bit of room between her index finger and thumb. "Little bit?"

She managed a tired smile of surrender. "Maybe a little. Yeah."

Suzanne glanced over her shoulder as Gus's metal cage rattled from the other room and the bird tweeted out a stern objection to his sudden incarceration. Returning to their conversation, Suzanne dropped both hands to her lap and said, "Or else it's that other thing."

"What other thing?"

"The thing where you and Will are made for each other, and

you're both too ignorant to see it."

"Oh, that thing."

"Yeah. That one."

"No. It's the other thing. The one where I'm afraid of being left in the dust while he rides off into the sunset with Alison the schoolteacher."

Suzanne nodded.

"That's actually what they're doing, you know."

"What is?"

"They're going horseback riding at sunset."

Suzanne contorted her face slightly and moaned. "Really? That's almost a little too adorable."

"I know, right?!"

And with that, Gus suddenly winged his way into the bedroom, flew a couple of circles around Julianne's head, and tweeted out a happy little tune as he landed on her shoulder.

"What is with you and my bird?" Suzanne exclaimed.

Julianne rested her chin on her own shoulder, whistling softly at the parakeet until he ruffled his bluish feathers and pressed his beak against the corner of her lower lip.

"The true boy of my dreams, that's what you are. Aren't you, Gus?"

●  ⸺  ●  ⸺  ●

Alison Reece was a knockout, and Will watched her fly past him on Alec's favorite horse, a Morgan named Hershey because of his very dark brown, shiny coat. Alison's hair almost matched the color and sheen of Hershey's coat, in fact, aside from the horse's ebony mane.

"Come on, slacker!" Alison called out over her shoulder. "What are you waiting for?"

Will snapped Christie's reins, and the mare took off after her. Alison's melodic laughter wafted head-on into him as he trailed her up the hill, and both animals slowed as they circled the top of the ridge.

"Over there," Will called out, pointing toward the white-trunked elm tree; the one where he did most of his best thinking.

The last time he'd parked beneath its branches, Will had prayed for God to help him move past his lifelong mindset about Julianne. Minutes later, his iPhone rang and Beth Rudd suggested he call Alison for a date.

Hershey whinnied as his rider stepped down from the saddle and tickled his long snout. "Good boy," she sang, and the low-hanging sun set the red-gold strands hiding in Alison's dark hair ablaze. When she smiled at Will, a soft breeze caught her long hair and it danced over her shoulder.

"Are you dismounting?" she asked. "Or are you planning on eating up there in the saddle?"

Will laughed and shook his head. "Sorry," he said, hopping down and leading Christie closer to the tree. "Distracted. It is beautiful."

He lifted the insulated leather bag from the saddle horn and flung it over his shoulder while Alison grabbed the picnic blanket from atop Hershey. She spread it out and unpacked their meal while Will secured the horses nearby.

When he turned back toward her, she looked like a picture postcard sitting with the orange sun at her back and her long legs crossed at the ankles.

"I love this time of year," she said as Will sat down across from her. Leaning across the edge of the blanket, she threaded her fingers into a tuft of bright green grass and observed, "It's like velvet."

He brushed his open palm over the tips of the grass and nodded. "So Alison, tell me more about yourself. Did you grow up here in Ohio?"

"Kentucky," she replied, tucking a strand of dark hair behind her ear. "Just an hour or so across the river. But I was accepted to UC and came up here to go to college."

"And now you teach?"

She nodded and smiled. "Third grade at a private school in College Hill. What about you? Beth told me you're a lawyer. What kind?"

"Until recently, a corporate attorney with a conglomerate housed on two floors of the Carew Tower, Benson & Benhurst."

"Until recently?" she asked, twisting the lid on a glass bottle of lemonade. "Disbarred, were you?"

Will laughed as he took the bottle she offered him. "I went out on my own."

"Really! How exciting, Will. All on your own?"

"No, I'm the Hanes part of Hanes & Bartlett."

"And who is Bartlett? He sounds grumpy."

Will spouted again with laughter. "Good call. But he's a she."

"Ohh," she said on a giggle as she unwrapped the mile-high turkey subs he'd picked up from the deli around the corner from the house. "Sorry."

"Julianne Bartlett. We've known each other since we were kids, went to law school together. She went to work for the public defender, I accepted an offer from B&B, and then we each started to lose our separate minds over time."

"And a bouncing baby law firm was born," she summarized, handing him a plastic fork and a small cardboard bowl of pasta salad. "So how's it going?"

"Too soon to tell," he admitted. "We haven't gotten much further than hiring an admin and setting up shop. Ask me again once the paint's dry on the office walls."

Will took a bite of his sandwich and watched Alison as she did the same. Before she'd completely chewed it, she nodded. "Mmm. Good!"

"I'm glad. I was hoping you weren't going to tell me you're a vegetarian."

She chuckled and swallowed the mouthful. "Nope." Raising one hand to shield her words from the horses, she whispered, "Completely carnivorous. But don't tell them."

"I promise."

"So you go to church with Beth and Jimmy," she said.

"Yeah." He nodded, wiping his mouth with a folded napkin.

"Jimmy and I serve on the deacon board together. Are you a churchgoer?"

"I am," she replied, her dark eyes sparkling. "I attend Gracepointe Christian."

"By Northgate?"

"Yes. I don't live too far from there."

The conversation flourished in easy ebbs and flows. Alison told Will about some of her students and regaled him with tales of recent home ownership, and he explained how he'd sold his house to move in with his dad after the Parkinson's diagnosis. They moved on to talk of college days, skipped over a few childhood dreams, and landed on Alison's years of equestrian competitions.

"Your Palomino actually reminds me a little of the quarter horse I learned to ride on," she told him, and Christie whinnied, seeming to follow along. "I was only six when I mounted Nilla Wafer for the first time—"

"Nilla Wafer," he teased. "Name him yourself?"

"Her," she corrected. "And yes, I did. Nill and I fell almost instantly in love, and it was the start of a lifelong passion for me."

"I can see that," he observed. "You have horse rapport."

"Is that the technical term for it?" she asked him, and one corner of her full reddish lips quivered with amusement. "I haven't heard that one before."

"Very technical. And you, Alison Reece, have got it. Horse rapport."

It wasn't until much later, as they sat beside each other watching the sun sink into the horizon in silence, that Will realized he hadn't thought of Julianne's date with the ditch digger even once.

# 8

Clad all in black, the musician with the oiled ponytail and dazzling, deep-set eyes masterfully set an exotic Spanish mood as his hands moved in a blur over the sound hole of his acoustic guitar.

"I've heard this guy play before," Paul said as he leaned toward the center of the wobbly wooden table that separated him from Julianne. "He's rather a genius. I only wish I could do that."

"Do you play?" she asked him.

Paul's steely blue-green eyes actually twinkled as he grinned at her. "Not like that."

Julianne nestled comfortably into the padded bench seat, cupping her glass with both hands as she watched him. Not the musician, but Paul.

Threads of gold ran through his wavy light chestnut hair, and the perfectly sculpted lines of his face made her momentarily imagine him as a superhero in disguise. All he needed was a pair of Clark Kent's signature glasses. His black sweater had a silver zipper up the front, and Paul had it closed all the way to the base of the small turtleneck. It wasn't too tight, but tight enough to see that he had a few muscles on him. His broad shoulders set the frame for his athletic torso and arms and, despite all of that physical perfection, Julianne spied a soft kindness in his eyes.

"Is this one of your regular haunts?" she asked him, and he peeled his gaze away from the musician.

"I like to come here on weeknights sometimes to listen to the music when it's not too crowded. They've had some amazing performers. I'm not much of a drinker or a party guy anymore. I mean, those days are behind me now that I'm getting older, you know?"

Julianne nodded happily. "I've never been a *party girl* . . . unless you count Friday night dance parties in the basement with my girlfriends. I was raised in the church, so clubbing and the like seems kind of foreign to me."

"What do you mean, raised in the church?" he asked. "Were your parents pastors or something?"

"Oh, no. Nothing like that. I just mean we lived sort of . . . biblical lives. What about you?" she asked with hope. "Do you go to church?"

Paul chuckled and shook his head. "No." Looking around the back room, he pointed out, "It's jam-packed tonight. I don't usually come on the weekends so I can avoid all this."

"You made an exception for me," she surmised, swallowing her disappointment. "I appreciate it. Now that you've shown me a little about your world, maybe I can show you more of mine. I've been attending a really interesting Bible study on—"

"Are you good?" Paul interrupted, gulping back the last of his tea and setting the glass on the table. Tapping the rim with his finger, he nodded toward her glass of diet Coke and asked, "Or would you like another?"

"No. I'm good."

He paused for a long and somewhat frozen moment before scuffing his chair closer to the table and leaning toward her.

"So . . . why did you want to get together with me, Julianne?"

Astonished at the directness of his question, she looked into his eyes for an instant before replying. "You seemed like someone I wanted to get to know."

"Oh."

He leaned back in his chair, his focus heading toward the guitarist. Then, without any forewarning at all, his gaze darted back to Julianne.

"Why?"

She laughed. "What do you mean?"

"I mean, why do you want to get to know me?"

"Does there have to be a concrete reason?" she asked him. "I was sort of mesmerized that day when I saw you save the dog. It was such a brave and gallant thing to do, getting out in the rain to rescue him the way you did."

"Well," he said as his eyes dropped to the table for an instant, "I couldn't just leave him out there in the middle of the road like that. I'm not really much of an animal person, you know? But still."

*No church attendance, and not an animal person?* It clinked around inside her ears several times before fading away.

"A lot of people wouldn't have gone to that kind of trouble," she said finally. "You did. I think you seem like a really kind man, Paul. I enjoy getting to know kind people."

He nodded tentatively and tossed back a few half-melted ice cubes from his glass.

"I guess I asked because . . . well . . . you're a lawyer and all. Not that you look like any of the lawyers I've ever met. You're more like one of those lawyers on TV, you know?"

"What does my job have to do with anything?"

"I don't know. I guess I'm a little surprised someone like you would want to go out with a contractor from Clifton."

Julianne smiled at him. "I like Clifton."

The corner of his mouth twitched slightly before it turned upward into a full lopsided grin. "You want to get out of here?" he asked.

"Sure."

"Let's go for a walk. Maybe go get something to eat?"

Julianne sighed. "Sounds good."

She grabbed her purse and Suzanne's waistcoat, and she followed Paul Weaver through the front door.

●　—　●　—　●

Julianne stared at the screen before her. Something had changed. She tapped her pen on the desktop until it finally hit her.

"Phoebe?" she called out.

"Be right there."

A moment later, Phoebe appeared in the doorway clutching a spiral notebook and a pen. "Do you need tea? Coffee?"

"No, thanks. Can you come in for a minute?"

Phoebe folded into the chair across from Julianne's desk and adjusted the braided metallic headband holding back her dark curls. She narrowed her brown eyes and cocked her head slightly, waiting for direction.

"Did you change my sticky notes?"

"I didn't change them," Phoebe gingerly replied. "I just organized them. The personal reminders are on the left, the professional ones on the right."

"Oh." Julianne cocked her head and skimmed over the multicolored squares. "That's actually pretty brilliant. Thank you."

"If that's the form of note-taking that works best for you," she said, "you could go a step further and color-code them. Pink for personal, green for business, and maybe use the yellow for the really urgent reminders."

Julianne sighed as she folded her arms and leaned back into her chair. "Thank you, Phoebe."

*Finally, someone who understands the importance of a good system of sticky notes!*

"Hey, I was just looking over the end-of-month report from your email this morning," Julianne said, tapping on the keyboard to bring it up again. "But before I get into that, can you do me a favor, please? There's an emergency animal clinic out on Old Taylor Mill. Can you track them down and call to check on a dog that was brought in last week? It's a yellow Lab that had been hit by a car."

"Your Prince Charming's dog?"

"Yes. I'd like to find out how the dog fared."

"I'll call them right away."

"Before you do," Julianne said. "About this report . . . where did you gather these figures?"

"From the bank statement that arrived on Wednesday."

"So we only racked up sixteen billable hours last month?"

Phoebe winced. "Sorry. Yes."

"Has Will seen this?"

"I emailed it to him. But I don't know if he's opened it."

As if following a stage direction, Will appeared in the doorway right on cue. "Have you seen the end-of-month email?"

"We were just discussing it. Come on in." Julianne guessed this wasn't a conversation to have in front of their brand-new assistant. She smiled at Phoebe and said, "You can go. I'll let you know if we have any questions."

Instinctively, Phoebe closed the door behind her as she left Julianne's office.

"Were you as surprised as I was?" Will asked her.

"Yes! Even with the leftovers you brought along from B&B, only sixteen hours."

"Well. It was a short month for us. Just two and a half weeks."

"Still."

"Yeah." Will groaned and sank into the chair across from her. "I've got maybe thirty hours left on the B&B business for this coming month, but that's going to be it."

"I've got a few more hours left on the Bertinni case. And we've got Rand for however long that develops. I think that's it, Will."

"We'll have to figure out how to drum up some new clients," he told her. "We need to make that a priority."

Julianne spent their silence watching Jonah circle his fishbowl a few times.

"Do you suppose you could talk to any of your regular clients from B&B?" she asked.

"Getting a reputation as a client poacher this early in the game," he pointed out, "doesn't seem like a way to establish our new firm."

"I don't mean poaching them. Just . . . reminding them that you're out here. On your own. Hungry for their business."

Will's eyes met hers, and they both laughed right out loud.

"Okay. You're right," she said with a sniff. "If you want to go all *integrity-driven*, sure."

"What about you?" he asked. "Any coattails you can yank?"

Julianne sighed. "Want to pray?"

Will simply reached his hands across the desk and took hers. "Father, thank You. We are overwhelmed by Your goodness and love for us. You have guided us to this place and we are so very grateful. Now we lift up our business to You once again. We ask for Your favor and grace in prospering the practice by opening those doors that are meant to open. In Jesus' name we pray."

"Amen," she said with a nod.

"Amen."

Will had only just released her hand when a soft rap at the office door drew their attention.

"Sorry to interrupt," Phoebe said through a slight opening. "Judge Hillman's office is on the line for you, Julianne."

She scrunched up her face at Will before shrugging. "Thanks, Phoebe." She snatched up the receiver and tucked it into the curve of her neck. "Julianne Bartlett."

"Miss Bartlett, this is Bridget Ferguson, Judge Hillman's bailiff."

"Yes, Bridget. How are you?"

"The judge wanted me to call and ask you to come to his office as soon as possible this afternoon."

"Is this in regard to the Bertinni matter? Because that's—"

"I don't know what it's about. He just asked me to call you right away."

"All right. I'll head over there in about twenty minutes, Bridget."

"I'll tell him."

She hung up the phone, her head whirling with worst-case scenarios.

"What's that about?" Will asked her.

"I have no clue. I've been summoned to Judge Hillman's office."

"That can't be good."

"No," she said, and she pushed to her feet and headed for the door. As she slipped into her suit jacket, she turned back again. "Hey, I didn't get to ask you. How did your date go Friday night?"

"Pretty great, actually. Yours with Prince Charming?"

"The same," she replied tentatively. Unclasping the chain of her purse from the hook, she turned back toward Will. "By the way, why did you tell Lacey about Paul?"

He stared at her for a moment before replying. "Oh. Yeah. I don't know. It was just a reflex. Sorry."

"It's okay. But check us out, both of us getting back in the game."

The drive to the courthouse took all of ten minutes, but about two hours' worth of speculation filled the space. *What in the world could Judge Hillman want from me at two o'clock on a Monday afternoon? And why isn't he in court like the rest of the judges in Hamilton County?*

"Ah, Ms. Bartlett," he greeted her when she knocked on the open door and saw him seated behind the desk. "Come in."

Julianne obeyed and stood behind an empty chair, bracing herself on the back of it. The judge looked up at her and scowled.

"Well, sit down."

"Oh. Thank you, sir."

She slipped into the chair and folded her hands in her lap. She sat quietly, listening to the rhythm of her own heartbeat as the judge continued reading the brief before him. Finally, he removed his glasses and scratched the edge of his far-receding hairline as he looked up at her. She'd never noticed the deep blue hue of Judge Hillman's eyes before.

"There is a case before me, Ms. Bartlett, that's what we judges like to call a migraine with a bullet chaser."

Julianne snickered. "I'm sorry to hear that, Your Honor."

"It's a civil case. Not too complicated until this morning. It seems the plaintiff is suing the defendant for breach of contract." The judge rubbed his graying moustache and leaned back into his desk chair until it creaked. "However, the defendant's wife is also named in the suit and—*blah-blah-blah*—the two of them have now filed for divorce, the wife needs her own attorney, says she can't afford one, the public defender's office . . . as you know . . . is stacked up, so I'll bottom line it for you, Ms. Bartlett. You are going to handle her case."

Julianne blinked, and her eyes went instantly dry. "What? Me?"

"You are an attorney, are you not?"

"Well, yes."

"And I've given Mr. Bertinni a great deal of latitude, have I not?" She sighed. "Yes."

"For which you . . . what's the legal term? . . . owe me, big-time."

Julianne deflated, leaning forward slightly. "Pro bono?"

"Yes, but it won't take more than a couple of days at worst."

She inhaled sharply. "You don't understand, Your Honor. Will Hanes and I have just opened our new office, and we had only sixteen billable hours last month. We're really hurting for new clients. If I go back to the office and tell him I'm doing pro bono work right now when all we have to look forward to is a pig homicide and a few leftovers from—"

"You said a pig homicide, didn't you, Ms. Bartlett."

"Yes, sir, but—"

"Two days, tops. Just get with your co-counsel later today and she'll bring you up to speed. And I will take it as a personal favor, Ms. Bartlett. Not the kind of favor for which you can collect, just to be clear, because that would be wrong. But still, a personal favor."

Julianne held back the groan that rose from somewhere beneath her ribs. "Yes, sir."

"Now. I'm due at a little soiree at the office of some friends in an hour and my car is in the shop. Would you mind dropping me?"

She tapped her foot several times and gripped the sides of her chair, but her face betrayed no sign of her irritation. "Of course." As the thought hit her, she added, "Oh! And who is my co-counsel, by the way?"

"Lacey James," he replied.

*Of course she is.*

They chatted about the judge's daughter up in Dayton on the drive over—it seemed she was pregnant with her first child, Hillman's first grandchild—and Julianne filled in the details of Rand's run-in with Emily's pet pig. The judge never let out more than one almost-friendly chuckle. By the time they arrived at Caswell Center, Julianne snapped the button to unlock the doors as she pressed on the brake.

"Here we are," she told him. "Have a nice evening."

"My back's bothering me," Hillman stated. "Why don't you park so you can carry my briefcase upstairs for me, hmm?" She glanced at the clock, hoping for a convenient time-crunch excuse, but the judge cut her off at the pass. "I'm an old man, Ms. Bartlett. Put your youth to good use, will you?"

She pushed down the inward groan as hard as she could. "You are not old," she told him as she steered into a parking spot.

"Tell that to my aching joints."

She grabbed her purse and the judge's briefcase from the backseat and followed him toward the lobby. He gave a cursory—and unconvincing—pat to his lower back before depressing the elevator call button.

Caswell Consulting, one of the largest business consulting firms in Southwestern Ohio, occupied the entire fourth and fifth floors of the office building bearing their name. The reception area alone took up five times the space of Hanes & Bartlett and teemed with people in suits and high-ticket business attire, all of them holding glasses clinking with ice cubes and small plastic plates filled with aromatic appetizers.

Julianne's stomach growled as a smiling woman who looked very much like the cover of some corporate magazine approached.

"Bradford, I'm so happy you could make it." She air-kissed the judge's cheek and her eyes fell on Julianne. "And you brought someone. Hello. I'm Veronica Caswell."

"Julianne Bartlett."

Her handshake seemed amiable, as did her smile.

"Ms. Bartlett gave me a ride over since the Buick is in the shop."

"Again?" Veronica teased. "Bradford, I think you can afford a trade-in, don't you?"

"Do they serve coffee at this shindig?" he asked, ignoring the car comment.

"Every kind you can imagine."

"I'll get some while I mull over what kind of car I want to buy. You talk to Ms. Bartlett. She and her law partner have just opened a new firm. Didn't you mention that you're in the market for new legal counsel? Maybe Ms. Bartlett can offer you some sort of direction on that."

"A new firm, did you say?" she asked, her smile brightening as Judge Hillman walked away and she honed in on Julianne. "Do you have any experience with corporate law?"

"Actually, it's been my partner's specialty," she replied, catching the judge's unmistakable—albeit unusual—grin as he wandered away from them.

So this was why he pushed her into driving him across town. It turned out the judge had a tender side after all.

*Color me astounded,* she thought.

"Do you have a business card? Maybe I can come in and have a powwow with you next week."

# 9

"**Caswell Consulting,**" Will repeated as he straightened his apron and handed Julianne an empty platter. He shook his head. "Hold this for me."

"Can you believe that old codger? He railroads me into driving him all the way over there," she said as he loaded the platter with chicken from the large gas grill on the back deck of his father's house. "The whole way I'm thinking what a fool he is, and then he goes and does this. What a lesson."

"This could be huge for us, Jules."

"It's a sign, Will. We just prayed and asked God to help our business thrive, and He sent Judge Hillman and Veronica Caswell. It's a sign!"

"You see signs on every hill," Will told her as he set the tongs atop the chicken and took the plate from Julianne. "They're doing millions of business every quarter. If we can just get a small slice of that pie, we'll be sitting pretty."

They filed through the back door and entered the kitchen where Amanda buzzed around him, transferring serving dishes from the counter to the table in front of Davis. Mashed potatoes, steamed asparagus spears, and a bowl of wilted leaves of some kind topped with what looked—and smelled—like crumbled bleu cheese.

"What's that?" Julianne asked, her tiny nose bunched up as she leaned over the bowl.

"It's kale chiffonade," Amanda replied, and Julianne turned away immediately. "It's good for you, young lady."

"Chiffonade," Will repeated in an uppity English accent, and Julianne giggled.

"I read that kale is a superfood," Amanda explained. "It's full of antioxidants, high in fiber, and it will help Davis's eyes to ward off cataracts."

"Well, Davis, heap some of that stuff on your plate, why dontcha," Julianne teased. "You don't want to go getting cataracts."

"Sit down and be quiet, young lady," Davis snapped, and then he winked at her.

"It's flavored with turkey bacon," Amanda told them as she circled the table, placing napkins at each plate. "Try some. It might surprise you."

"If she tries some, it might surprise *you*," Davis interjected.

"I'll just have an extra piece of Will's barbecued chicken and call it a day."

The foursome passed side dishes back and forth as Amanda served up chicken for each plate: a breast for Davis, two thighs for Will, a drumstick for Julianne; another barbecued breast landed on her own plate. In that way that the mother of every family intimately knows the preferences of each of her children, Amanda had taken the maternal spot in this mismatched brood that gathered around the table once or twice each week.

"Julianne unearthed a really good possibility for some business for the firm today," Will announced, and Amanda raised a serious eyebrow that stopped him from expounding.

"You children work all the time. How about we leave business at the door for our community dinners, hmm?"

"Sorry."

"Tell us instead about something extracurricular that has no roots steeped in your law practice."

"Will's dating someone new," Julianne announced.

Davis's eyes lifted instantly and rested heavily on his son while Amanda froze, her own gray eyes wide and round. With that look on her face, Will instantly recognized the Bartlett family resemblance that had faded over the years.

"Alison Something," Julianne continued. "She teaches the fourth grade."

"Third," Will corrected just above a whisper.

"Really," Amanda remarked.

"Where did you and Alison meet, Son?" Davis chimed in.

"They were set up."

"Not by you," Amanda asked Julianne in the form of a statement.

"No. Beth Rudd. Her husband is on the deacon board at church with Will. Alison is Beth's younger sister."

The silence that followed felt thicker than the kale in that yellow bowl in front of him, and Will concentrated on his barbecued chicken thighs.

"What about you, young lady?" Davis asked, cutting through the awkward hush. "Don't I remember that you had met someone as well?"

Julianne sighed, and a grin spread out her lips like butter warmed by the sun. "Paul. He's a carpenter."

"Like *Jesus*," Will interjected.

"Not *unlike* Jesus," Julianne admonished him. "But certainly I wasn't comparing him to the Savior of the world, Will."

With one eyebrow raised and his lips drawn in a smirk, Will stared into her clear blue eyes.

"Anyway," she continued, "we had our first date Friday night, and it was . . . nice. We listened to some Spanish guitar music in Mt. Adams and went for a long walk afterward in Eden Park, and then we went and grabbed a bite to eat."

"You walked in Eden Park after dark?" Davis clarified. "Doesn't say much for your new young man's good sense."

"I was perfectly safe."

"The guy is a lumberjack," Will cut in, and Julianne chuckled.

"He's six-foot-four, and very muscular," she told them. "But he's also very kind. The first day I saw him, he was rescuing a dog that had been hit on a downtown street."

A quick flash of nausea hit Will, but it lifted as quickly as it dropped on him.

"A dog that he dumped at a clinic and never checked on again," he snapped.

"How did you know that?"

"I was there when Phoebe called the clinic and asked about him," he said. Turning to Davis, Will expounded. "The dog has a broken leg, and the vet had to absorb the bill himself. And now they're turning the dog over to a local shelter. Who's going to adopt a dog when he's just recovering from surgery?"

"You don't know that," Julianne objected. "And besides, you can't expect Paul to take on the medical bills of a dog he doesn't even own."

"No? Who would have paid for it if *you* were the one dumping an injured dog at a clinic, huh?"

"Are you going to see him again?" Amanda asked, and she shot a glance toward Will.

"I am," she answered. "We're going to the kite festival out at Winton Lake this weekend."

"A kite festival." Her mother nodded. "I didn't know you had any interest in kites."

"She doesn't," Will said.

"I don't *not* like them. We entered this same festival, you and I, once upon a time, Will. I just . . . you know . . ."

"Like them much better with a six-foot-four-inch lumberjack at your side," he surmised.

Julianne scrunched up her face and glared at him. "What is *wrong with you*?"

"Nothing's wrong with me."

The look exchanged between his dad and Amanda hadn't escaped his notice, but Will decided not to comment.

*On the grounds that it may incriminate me.*

"Amanda, I think I'll try some of that kale after all," Davis said.

"Can't be too cautious about cataracts."

When Julianne's phone sounded off, Amanda's entire face bunched. And Julianne made the same expression when she looked at the screen of her phone.

"Ahh, maaaaan," she cried before answering. Then with the push of the button, she turned monotone. "Hi, Lacey . . . Yeah, I know. I was about to call you about that."

Amusement tickled the back of Will's throat and he chuckled as Julianne got up from the table and took her conversation into the living room. Hillman had steered a substantial new client their way and polished off the good deed with a big old goose egg: A forced encounter between Julianne and the person she liked least in the whole Queen City area.

●　—　●　—　●

The pig lover, Emily Alden, sat confidently erect in her chair at the conference room table across from that porcine murderer, Rand. Her parents flanked either side of her, and Julianne thought it only mildly amusing that she and Will bookended Rand in that same parental way.

"Emily," she said softly, "I just want you to know how sorry I am about your loss. When I was your age, my dog was hit by a neighbor's car, and I remember how heartbreaking it was. I didn't get over it for a really long time and, even though I knew he hadn't meant to do it, I was just furious that the neighbor hadn't watched where he was going."

Emily didn't miss a beat. "I'll bet he didn't slam down on the gas just so he could hit your dog," she replied, and Julianne's stomach lurched slightly, realizing she'd gone up against easier opponents inside the courtroom.

"Well, no, of course not. But Mr. Winters didn't know it was your Wilbur when he fired his gun."

"No. He thought it was a *dog*," Emily replied. "Maybe like that one your neighbor killed. What was its name?"

Julianne looked into the eyes of the girl's father, who simply shrugged slightly and glanced away. The mother didn't show signs of weakness either, although she did reach over and touch her daughter's hand.

"Kellogg," Julianne replied in defeat. "I named him after my favorite cereal."

"Emily." Will took the wheel, and she stifled a sigh of relief. "Despite what you might think, Mr. Winters does regret what happened. And he understands that you're upset and angry. We all do. But what is it you're looking for here?" The girl stared Will down without reply. "I mean, you've made the flyers and you've told everyone who will listen what he's done, and you've effectively scarred his reputation in his community. What do you see happening now?"

"I thought I might sue him," she answered without flinching. "My dad says I can."

Julianne pressed her arm against Rand's in hopes of quelling his response.

"Well, that's true. You can do that. But to what end?" Will asked her directly. "You want him to pay you money? Or replace your pig? Or both? See, what I'm trying to get to here is whether you have specific restitution in mind or if you're just blindly doing and saying anything at all, anything you can in order to irreparably damage Mr. Winters's reputation. Because if it's the latter, you're actually giving him the upper hand."

Emily's eyes darted to her father's for a moment before she turned back to Will and asked, "What do you mean?"

"I mean that Mr. Winters has done everything he possibly can to resolve the situation, and any judge is sure to see that. We know how horrible you feel about the loss of your pet . . . your friend, but it's in your best interest to work with us before we go into court."

Emily blinked, and Julianne spotted the standing pool of tears in her eyes.

"So to avoid more unpleasantness, why don't you just tell us what you're looking for here. What would help you, beyond Mr. Winters's heartfelt apology?"

Rand opened his mouth, ready to speak something Julianne felt absolutely certain was going to increase the flow of hot water into his life, and she pinched the side of his knee under the table.

"Rand, why don't you tell Emily how sorry you are," Julianne suggested with an additional pinch for good measure.

He inhaled sharply, and he let it out slowly before speaking. "Look, kid, it was stupid. I thought it was the Blanchettes' ridiculous dog in my trash again. You know that dog?"

"Yeah," Emily answered him, and she looked at Julianne. "His name is Dugger. One time, he got into Mrs. Castro's garbage and spread her used . . . um . . . under-things all over the neighborhood."

"I only meant to shoot a warning shot," Rand continued, "to scare him away. But when I saw that it wasn't a dog—and I didn't quite know what it was, only that it wasn't some dog or cat from the neighborhood—I guess I panicked."

Julianne nudged his knee with hers to help him continue. *Out with it*, she thought. *Just say it.*

"Look, kid, I'm really sorry. What can I do to make it up to you?"

Emily seemed to mull it over for nearly half a minute of excruciating silence.

"You mean it?" she finally asked him.

Rand squirmed. "Yeah."

"I want you to get rid of your gun."

"Whoa, wait just a—"

"That's a possibility," Julianne interrupted. "What else?"

"The gun is nonnegotiable," the girl insisted. "Nobody in the neighborhood wants to know that, if they make a little too much noise or they skateboard into your trash can one day, you'll get out your gun and shoot at them."

"You make a very good point," Will said.

"Yeah, okay," Rand conceded. "What else?"

101

"I want a new baby pot-bellied pig. And I don't just want you to pay for it. I want you to go with us to pick one out so you can see how gentle they are."

Rand looked at Julianne helplessly.

"You know what," she said. "I'd like to see how gentle they are, too. Maybe we can all go."

"You mean it?"

"I do."

Emily seemed happy with that. "Okay."

"Okay?" Will repeated.

"And you'll stop with the flyers," Rand confirmed.

"Yeah."

"And take down any of them that I've missed."

"Okay."

"Okay!" Julianne exclaimed. "Excellent! So we've come to a constructive and mutually agreeable conclusion. Doesn't everyone feel much better now?"

Rand grunted softly, but Emily didn't seem to care. She probably came out feeling like the winner.

"And I'll bet Mr. Winters would also like to make a donation to an animal welfare charity in Wilbur's name," Will told Emily. "Would you like that?"

"In Wilbur's name?" she asked excitedly, and she waited for Rand's agreement.

"Yeah, all right," he surrendered before falling back against the chair.

In Julianne's experience, no other animal could ever truly replace a lost companion. But they'd negotiated a settlement that would give Emily a new friend, protect Rand's reputation, fund animal welfare, and rack up some billable hours for the firm.

Win-win-win-win.

As Will tied up the loose ends between them, Julianne stepped out to reception, where Phoebe had just ended a phone call and hung up the phone.

"That was the clinic," she told Julianne. "The dog had surgery to set a broken leg, and they need to keep him there for a couple more days before they turn him over to the shelter."

"Did you find out how much the bill is going to be?"

Phoebe cringed. "Just over a thousand dollars."

"A thousand!" she exclaimed. "Wow."

"I know."

●　—　●　—　●

Alison's dark auburn hair caught the sunlight through the window behind her, and Will couldn't help but notice how truly beautiful she was.

"I've wanted to try this restaurant ever since I first heard about it," she told him with a smile. "The French toast is to die for. Do you want a bite?"

She cut a small corner from the raspberry-filled confection and ran her fork through the powdered sugar before extending it toward Will. A little too sweet for breakfast fare, as far as he was concerned, but tasty enough.

"Good, right?"

He nodded. "Aside from the cavity it's digging into my teeth."

Alison giggled, and he thought how cute it sounded. "All right, that's enough out of you. So I have a sweet tooth. Now you know."

Will gulped back the last of his coffee. "You never told me," he said as the waiter filled the cup. "What were you doing out this way today? It's a little far from home for you, isn't it?"

"Oh, I'm chaperoning a group from school at the kite festival this weekend, and I wanted to stop by the boathouse and pick up some maps for some of the parents."

"The one at Winton Lake."

"Yes. We're bringing picnic lunches and sitting on the hill to-gether to watch them fly the kites. Do you want to come?"

The corner of his mouth twitched slightly before he gave up a chuckle at the irony.

"Ah, you'll be busy. Maybe we can do something another time." Then, "But I'm making my world-famous potato salad," she sang to tempt him. "And afterward . . . there are two-person pedal boats available. If you're man enough to give it a try, I mean."

"Oh, I'm man enough," he declared.

"Meet you there around noon on Saturday?"

"Sounds good."

Will replayed the conversation in his head a couple of times as they finished their breakfasts.

*Man enough.*

Yeah, he was man enough to sit with some third graders to watch a bunch of kites flying overhead, even to pedal a boat around Winton Lake with their stunning teacher.

*But am I man enough to run into Julianne and her ditch digger boyfriend?*

"Do you see him?" she asked, leaning over the branch
of the tallest tree she could find for a closer look.
"He's wearing a beautiful blue cloak."

"I see him!" her friend replied.

"If only we could get closer. You could see how the cloak
matches the blue of his eyes. He has beautiful eyes!"

"Do you love him deeply?"

"As deep as the ocean, as vast as the sky," she replied.
"He's my one-and-only."

"I wish I had a one-and-only," her childhood friend remarked.

"You do. Everyone does. You just haven't found him yet."

# 10

**Will decided to ride** his bike rather than drive the couple of miles around his circular subdivision and down to Winton Lake. He padlocked his bicycle to the rack at the edge of the parking lot before setting out to find Alison and her students, and he pulled the iPhone from his pocket to send her a text.

*I'm here. Where are you?*

*Meet you at the boathouse* came her reply.

By the time he reached the dock, he spotted Alison in a blue and white paisley maxidress that seemed to float behind her while her long auburn hair danced on the breeze. His heart fluttered slightly when she grinned at him, two large soft-serve ice cream cones in her hands.

"Bought you a present," she said, handing him one of them. He took a lick before accepting it, and she giggled. "We're over there, on the hill."

They meandered through the crowd before breaking free and hiking up the grassy hill. Scads of people dotted the lush green lawn, from families with picnic baskets seated on blankets and beach towels to teens sunning on low lawn chairs with audio buds connected to their ears. A clear summer canopy of blue, dotted with the occasional puffy white cloud, provided a perfect backdrop for the dozens of colorful kites zigzagging across the sky.

Alison led him toward a grouping of more than a dozen young children sitting on blankets pulled closely together, several adults anchoring the corners.

"Everyone," she announced, "this is my friend Will. He's going to be another chaperone for us today."

The adults nodded friendly greetings before checking him out, but most of the kids hadn't even noticed his arrival in deference to the display of color overhead. With their heads tilted back and their eyes bright and wide, the appearance of Miss Reece's friend Will held very little appeal.

One particularly large delta-wing kite drew Will's immediate attention with its colorful graphic design. "I flew one like that," he pointed out to Alison as they sank down to a large square of blue gingham fabric held in place by a bright red picnic basket.

"Have you been to the kite festival before?" she asked.

"A few times, when I was a kid. My pop helped Jules and me build pretty elaborate ones, and sometimes they even stayed in the air."

Alison chuckled. "Jules. That's your law partner? The one you said you'd known since you were a boy?"

He nodded and took a moment to tend to the stream of melted ice cream making its way over the rim of his cone. "Julianne. We grew up next door to each other."

Alison pulled her dress up to mid-calf and crossed her sun-tanned legs at the ankles. A silver chain hung loosely around one ankle, and braided white leather sandals, each of them bejeweled with one light blue stone, revealed perfect cinnamon-frosted toes.

"I've only been to this park a couple of times," she told him as she finished her ice cream cone and leaned back on both elbows, fascinated by the colorful kites flying overhead. "It's beautiful."

"You could probably blindfold me and set me loose to find my way around, and I could do it without a problem," Will replied. "These are my old stomping grounds. You can almost throw a rock and hit my dad's house up there."

He pushed the base of the cone into his mouth, and Alison passed him a paper napkin that he used to wipe his chin. "They have summer concerts out here. I remember hearing the Cincinnati Symphony do an evening of Mozart when I was nineteen."

"Mozart." She mulled it over before gazing up at him curiously. "I didn't peg you for a Mozart kind of guy."

"I'm not."

"Julianne?" she asked knowingly, and he nodded. "Were you two an item back then?"

Will chuckled. "For about twenty-six minutes."

"Oooh. Didn't make the half-hour mark. Sorry." Her mock-serious face melted away into a bright smile.

"It worked out just fine."

Somewhere out there among the hundreds of Queen City residents enjoying the day's festivities were Julianne and her perceived Prince Charming: A freakishly tall ditch digger who reminded Will of *Gaston*, the arrogant pursuer of a girl who preferred a beast over him in an animated Disney film Julianne had forced him to watch with her when she had the flu. He couldn't remember the song lyrics, but that tune about the character's brawn and good looks—if you went for the lumberjack type, anyway—hummed around in his brain every time he thought about Paul Weaver.

"Will?"

The familiar lilt of the voice that had called his name pinched him, and Will looked up expecting to see Julianne. But the golden-haired beauty who stood over him, backlit by a stream of Ohio sunshine, was not Julianne.

"Hello, Will. How are you?"

As he swallowed around the lump in his throat, he realized he hadn't seen her since the night she returned the diamond ring he'd given her.

"Holly."

●— ● —●

"You all right?"

"Yeah," Julianne puffed. "Great."

When Paul suggested a date to Winton Lake for the kite festival, Julianne had pictured the two of them sitting on a blanket somewhere, watching the colorful displays overhead, maybe sharing an ice cream cone or indulging in a couple of hot dogs. She certainly hadn't anticipated an hour of kayaking, followed by a brisk three-mile hike! Her cute pink wedge sandals were nearly ruined.

"Is it much farther?" she asked him, winded as she tried to keep up.

"About another half a mile. You think you can make it?"

"Oh yeah," she lied. "I—I can make it. But maybe you could slow down a little? Your legs are a lot longer than mine."

He stopped in his tracks and waited for her to catch up to him. "Do you want a ride?"

"I'm sorry. What?"

"Hop on my back," he said. "I'll give you a ride."

"Oh . . . no . . . I . . ."

"It'll be a good workout for me," he said, scrunching down in front of her. "What do you weigh? About one-fifty?"

"No!" she exclaimed. Dialing it back, she forced a chuckle. "No. I'm not one-fifty. I'm . . . much *less* than one-fifty."

"Okay. Well, hop on."

"No, really, Paul, that's okay . . ."

He straightened and turned around to face her. "Look, Julianne. You're really slowing me down. Hop on."

He pivoted and leaned down again, his hands braced behind him in the shape of stirrups.

Julianne glared at her ruined shoes for a moment as she considered the offer.

"I don't know, Paul. A piggyback ride? Really?"

Before she could process it, Paul lifted her from the ground.

"Wh—what're you . . . What are you doing?!"

She groaned as her fanny plunked down on the top rung of the rustic split rail fence that bordered that section of the hiking trail. Turning his back to her, Paul demanded, "Hop. On."

Julianne shrugged. After she pressed down the hem of her pink-and-white gingham top with one hand and adjusted her denim capris with the other, she tossed her hands to his shoulders for support and threw herself onto Paul's muscular back. It was the tallest piggyback ride she'd ever had.

And the most mortifying as well. Although . . .

"Wow. You're really strong, aren't you?"

Paul chuckled as he forged ahead at twice their former speed, blowing by several other hikers, most of them giggling as they passed. She guessed she really *had been* slowing him down. In no time at all, they reached the end of the trail, converging on a more dense assembly of people.

"Okay. You can put me down now," she said, but Paul forged ahead. "Okay, Paul. I can walk now."

Onlookers snickered, and Julianne buried her face in the slope of Paul's shoulder. Her words muffled by his denim shirt, she pleaded, "Would you *pleeease* put me down? People are staring."

At last, he slowed to a stop. When Julianne peeked at the world again, she saw that he stood slumped in front of a bench, and she slid down to it.

"Thank you." She resisted the sudden urge to slug him. His macho was wearing a little thin on her.

"Let me see your shoes," he said.

"My shoes?"

Instead of clarifying, Paul simply reached down and slipped off one of her sandals.

"Wait! What are you—?"

He took it with him to the water fountain. One quick splash on the shoe, and he scrubbed it with his thumb as he headed toward her again.

"That worked pretty well," he said, handing it back to her. "Let me have the other one."

She lifted her foot and allowed him to remove it. While he repeated the effort, she stepped into the clean one. When he finished, Paul knelt in front of Julianne and looked up at her as she slipped her foot into the damp canvas sandal.

"Just like Cinderella," she muttered, and a warm, broad grin spread across her entire face.

Maybe not too much macho after all. Maybe just enough.

"Except Cinderella was smart enough to wear her special shoes to a ball," he replied. "Not hiking around Winton Lake. That wasn't too bright, Julianne."

The grin melted from her face and landed in a puddle on her chin.

"To be fair, I didn't know we'd be kayaking and hiking today, Paul."

He stood up and looked down at her with a confused expression. "What did you think we'd be doing at a kite festival on a lake? Sitting on the grass eating ice cream?"

*Well, yeah. I kinda did,* she thought. But she didn't say so.

"Ice cream sounds kind of good," she suggested tentatively. "Want to get some?"

"I don't do ice cream," he replied.

"Oh. Well. Maybe . . . something . . . else then."

"We can get you some if you want it."

"No. That's okay."

"If you're hungry, we can get something."

"Maybe a hot dog would be nice."

"A hot dog!" he exclaimed. "These are the kinds of things you put into your body, Julianne? You'll be dead by the time you're forty."

"I'm pretty sure a hot dog isn't going to kill me, Paul."

She raked over him with a heated glance. With his face all scrunched up like that, and the scolding tone in his voice, she realized she might have stumbled into the wrong fairy tale entirely.

"All right, Grumpy," she teased. "Let's just go see what they have at the concession stand. Maybe you can find something that won't do us in before we make it home."

Thirty minutes later, Julianne had scarfed down two hot dogs with ketchup and relish and ordered a big soft-serve ice cream cone that she enjoyed much more under the shadow of Paul's disapproving and watchful eye.

"Just a taste?" she said, offering him her cone.

"No, thanks."

"Come on, Paul, let's relax a little, huh? We can go sit on the hill and watch the kites for a while. What do you say?"

He shrugged and thrust out his hand like it was part of his punishment. Julianne snickered as she clasped his massive hand, and the two of them headed across the green lawn, weaving around groups of suicidal people blissfully indulging in poisons like ice cream, cotton candy, and—*gasp!*—the dreaded hot dog.

*Sledability factor, through the roof,* she observed as they trudged across the lush hill. Aside from the fact that a sled ride down this particular hill might surely end in a splash into Winton Lake, of course.

When she spotted Will on a gingham blanket, Julianne felt sweet relief wash over her in a cool shower.

"Will! Hey, Will!" She let go of Paul's hand and jogged toward him, grinning. "Will! What are you doing here?"

"Hey!" he said. "Jules, this is Alison. We're here with her third grade class."

Julianne looked around at all of the children gathered nearby, and her eyes landed on Alison with a thud.

"Oh. Hi, Alison. It's good to meet you."

"Hey," Will said with a nod that made Julianne remember she had company.

"This is Paul Weaver."

"Hi, Paul. Alison Reece."

"Jules," Will said, leaning back on one elbow, "you missed the best one. They had this enormous delta-wing up in the air, just like the one my dad made. Do you remember flying that one?"

"I loved that kite!" she exclaimed. "I still have pictures of it somewhere."

Julianne glanced at Alison, and she sort of froze under Alison's dark brown stare. Her hand instinctively went to her mouth. Why was Alison gawking like that? Had she gotten ice cream all over her face or something?

"I'm sorry," Alison said in response to Julianne's obvious discomfort. "I'm staring. But it's uncanny, really."

"What is?" Julianne asked.

"The resemblance." Looking to Will, she said, "They could be sisters."

"Who could?" he asked.

"Holly and Julianne."

"What? No!" he declared. "They don't look anything alike."

"Are you kidding?" Alison grinned at Julianne and tilted her head slightly. "You look so much like her."

"Holly?" She looked from Alison to Will and back again. "I don't understand. How do you know Holly?"

"I just met her a few minutes ago."

Julianne's heart began to pound against her chest. "Will. You ran into Holly?"

He nodded, and then shrugged.

She wanted to ask him if he was okay, if the meeting had gone well, or if he needed to run screaming from the park. He hadn't seen Holly since she broke their engagement, and he'd barely spoken her name ever since.

*Poor Will! It must have been—*

Alison leaned toward Will and touched him gently on the arm as she whispered something to him softly. Whatever she'd said, it evoked a smile from him, and Julianne felt a slight flutter in the pit of her stomach.

"Well, we're going to . . . go find a spot," Julianne announced.

"Okay," Will called over his shoulder. "Have fun."

"You, too."

"Nice to meet you, Julianne."

She wanted to return the compliment, but she wasn't entirely sure it had been such a pleasure meeting Alison.

She and Paul wandered a few yards up the hill and sat down together on the grass. While feigning interest in the colors overhead, Julianne used the moments in between to get a good look at Alison.

Dark auburn hair . . . dark brown eyes . . . dark skin . . . long, suntanned legs. The woman could have been a model! She seemed like the negative version of Holly, opposite in every way.

*Opposite of me, too*, she realized. *Completely different, in fact.*

# 11

"**I like your offices.** They've got personality."

Julianne smiled as Phoebe set a cup of coffee on the conference room table in front of Veronica Caswell. "Cream and two sugars."

"Thank you."

"You're sure I can't get you something?" she asked Julianne.

"Nope. I'm good, thanks." Phoebe headed for the doorway as Julianne added, "You haven't heard from Will yet?"

"No, but I texted him and left a message on his cell."

Veronica picked up the conversation where they'd left it. "The lobby has that retro feeling that you don't find too often out where we are. I noticed even the elevator has those little details like the mosaic tiles."

"We'd seen about a dozen offices that day on our search," Julianne told her. "But the minute we pulled up outside, Will and I both knew this was the place."

"Well, it suits you."

Veronica had a polite and amiable smile, and Julianne found herself wondering if it was authentic or just practiced. After all, she'd built a mini-empire consulting people and businesses on how to build and sustain a certain image. Maybe calm and cordial was part of the appearance she'd constructed for herself, along with a subtly highlighted bob, a sensible manicure, and coiffed tailoring.

"I'm really sorry about Will," she offered. "I've never known him to miss a meeting. Something unforeseen must have come up."

Will had skipped church the day prior and gone to visit

Gracepointe Christian with Alison. It had been the first Sunday they hadn't spent together in she didn't know how long. And now he hadn't shown up for their meeting with Veronica. Julianne didn't like the way everything seemed to change so quickly.

"Well, maybe we can go ahead without him?" Veronica suggested.

"Absolutely. I'm familiar with your company's reputation, but why don't you tell me a little more about the nuts and bolts of what you do, and about your expectations for outside legal counsel."

"Good," she replied, pausing to take a sip from her coffee. "You know then that we're business consultants, but how that translates seems to be mysterious to the general public."

Julianne chuckled. "Of which I am one."

"We're fairly diversified in the services we offer, but our main division handles image for corporate business. We go into large companies and conduct seminars for their leadership called *The ABCs of Corporate Image: Attitude, Behavior, and Connection.* For the smaller businesses, we help them cut back to the bare bones to determine and establish their brand, we plug them into a good public relations regimen, and we coach the players on the front line to the customers."

"Like their customer service agents?"

"Yes. And their sales and marketing teams, even their human resources group if it's warranted. We're all about helping to shape businesses and individuals to perform at a level that will achieve the desired endgame results."

"And where does legal counsel play into that plan?"

"We need someone on retainer for consultation, to handhold the collections group when they've done everything they can to collect a fee. There's also the threat of lawsuits, which is almost a monthly occurrence in this corporate culture. Every CEO wants miracles for the price of a magic hat." Veronica ran her index finger around the rim of her cup before continuing. "We've just completed a three-month cycle at Owens Farms."

"The poultry people with the contamination outbreak earlier in the year."

She nodded. "Right. We went in and took over their front line completely. We did damage control, our in-house PR firm took the reins, and in the course of a few weeks, we were able to turn the situation around completely. The problem is, once that happened, it wasn't even thirty days before there was another instance of salmonella."

Julianne cringed. "That made your job a lot more complicated."

"Like you can't believe. And now they're threatening to sue us because we didn't do the job in repairing their image to the consuming public." Veronica sighed and dropped her hands into her lap. "You can only do so much, you know?"

"Even if they follow through with legal action," Julianne reassured her, "that's not one they can win."

"So you see why we need you."

Julianne smiled. "Who's your current counsel?"

"We've had an in-house team for the last few years that was working out very well. But the lead decided to venture out on his own, and he took his four associates with him."

Cringing, she asked, "Was he under contract?"

"It's complicated."

"How so?"

"He happened to be my ex-husband's brother." She paused for a moment before glancing up at Julianne and biting her lip. "Did I mention that my ex is also trying to take half of the company from me? Dividing up Caswell Consulting is like cutting King Solomon's baby in half—neither side can win, and the baby is dead in someone's arms."

Julianne reached over and touched Veronica's hand, and every bit of composure drained from the woman's face as she asked, "Can you help me, Julianne?"

● — ● — ●

"Mr. Hanes, follow the light as closely as you can without moving your neck."

Will stood back and watched as the doctor examined his father. He tried not to allow his thoughts to jump ahead to the possible diagnoses, but his imagination had a mind of its own.

"How long since you were diagnosed with Parkinson's?"

"About a year," Davis told him, trailing the ray of light.

"And you said the new meds have been effective."

"They have," Will chimed in. "His tremors have subsided quite a lot, and Dr. Donnelly told us that the limited movements were bradykinesia associated with the Parkinson's. But this morning was very different than it's been before. He tried to get out of the chair and fell right back down to it, two different times. His mouth looked a little misshapen, and it looked like one corner turned downward. When I tried to help him up, he became very confused. I don't think he even recognized me for a good two or three minutes."

Davis didn't seem to have anything to add. As the doctor flipped off the light and slipped the ophthalmoscope into his pocket, Davis lowered his eyes and stared at the floor.

Will touched his dad's arm until Davis looked up. "How do you feel now, Pop?"

"Like everyone's making much ado about nothing much."

Will chuckled. "That's the way he is, Doc. Not a big fan of the fuss."

"Every now and then, a little fuss is called for, Mr. Hanes," the doctor said. "Your son did the right thing bringing you in. I'd like to get a CAT scan and do some labs, just to make sure this is related to the Parkinson's and not something else hiding behind it, like a mild stroke or dehydration. Is that all right with you?"

Davis shrugged.

The doctor patted his shoulder as he nodded at Will. "They'll come and get him in a few minutes. Just sit tight."

Will helped his dad get settled before excusing himself to call Julianne.

"Where are you!" she exclaimed. "Veronica Caswell just left the office, Will. You missed the whole meeting!"

"Hang on, Jules. I'm with my dad at the ER."

She seemed to choke on whatever she nearly said next. "What happened?"

"I'll tell you all about it later. They're running some tests, and I don't know how long we'll be tied up here, or if they're even going to keep him overnight."

"What can I do?"

"I've got a couple of items on the calendar today. Will you ask Phoebe to reschedule lunch with Lloyd for me?"

"Of course."

"Will you be all right going on the pig trip without me this afternoon?" he asked seriously.

"Yes, Will. I think I can survive a pig farm on my own."

"I meant Rand. Can you survive Rand without me?"

Julianne giggled. "I'll try."

"How did the meeting go with Veronica Caswell?"

"We have a new client."

"Excellent," he said. "Details."

"Later. Give my love to your dad?"

"Of course. I'll call you later."

●  ─  ◉  ─  ●

"That one looks just like Wilbur," Emily cried, and she hurried across the barn and fell to her knees in front of the circular fenced enclosure.

The little Wilbur look-alike wobbled toward her and pushed its flat nose against her outstretched hand and squealed. In the next few seconds, several others joined him. Julianne supposed that, if she happened to be in the market for a six-week-old pot-bellied pig, she would choose the black one with the glossy gray eyes.

"But I don't think I should get one that looks like Wilbur, should I, Gramps?" Pastor Alden knelt down beside her and scratched a

121

pink piglet with his index finger. "I mean, it might feel like I was trying to replace him or something, you know?"

"I think that's very wise, Em. What about the little black one?"

Emily reached over the fence and rubbed Julianne's choice behind the ear. "I like the white spot on the tip of her tail. It looks like God dipped it in paint."

Julianne glanced at Rand, standing in the doorway to the barn, looking about as uncomfortable and out of place as his shiny leather oxfords.

"Rand," she whispered as she joined him at the door. "Maybe you could just pretend to be interested?"

"Why?" he asked. "She wants a pig. I'm buying her a pig. She didn't say I had to know which one she picks, or that I had to pretend to care."

"Tell me again why you're getting a divorce."

"Hey."

"Sorry. But still. Could you force an effort at just general human kindness, please?"

Emily rushed toward them, the black piglet squirming in her arms. "Julianne! Look at her. Isn't she adorable? I'm gonna call her Shena."

"My granddaughter loves that singer, Shena Gomez," Pastor Dean commented with a smile.

Julianne tickled the pig's fuzzy chin and giggled. How flattered the pop star would be if she knew a pot-bellied pig had been named after her.

"So that's the one, huh?" Rand asked in monotone, and Julianne suppressed a laugh.

*Well, at least he tried.*

"Uh-huh." She nodded.

"All right then. Let's go."

"Wait a minute," Emily chided. "You still have to pay."

"Right."

"And we have to talk about that other thing," she added, looking more like Rand's mother than the child who had negotiated a new pig and some gun restriction.

"What other thing?"

Julianne leaned toward him and ribbed him with her elbow. "The gun thing."

"Oh. That."

"You didn't get rid of it, did you?" Emily asked him, one arm wrapped around Shena and the other bent, her hand on her hip. "You have to get rid of it. Doesn't he, Julianne?"

"It was part of the deal," she reminded Rand, and the look on his face made her laugh right out loud.

He didn't stamp his foot, but Julianne confidently expected him to do just that from the expression on his unhappy face. Instead, he nodded for Emily to follow him through the barn door.

"How much?" he asked the farm owner.

Pastor Dean placed his arm around Julianne's shoulder and gave it a squeeze. "It's a good thing you've done here."

Julianne shrugged, and then shot him a smile. "She's a very cool little girl."

"I think so."

"And speaking of cool girls . . . thank you so much for sending us Phoebe! She's a gem."

"Phoebe?"

"Yes. Phoebe Trent. She's running the place like she invented the concept of a law office. Will and I couldn't be any happier."

"I'm sorry," he said, and he removed his arm from her shoulder and turned to face her. "I don't know what you're talking about."

"Phoebe."

"Yes, so you said. Who is Phoebe?"

"Phoebe—"

"Trent. Yes. I heard you, Julianne. But I don't know anyone by that name, and I didn't send her to you."

"That's not . . . possible. She . . ."

The brakes of Julianne's thoughts screeched to a stop as she pored over the facts, trying to make sense of things, struggling to remember how she'd come to believe Phoebe had been recommended by her pastor.

"You didn't send her."

"I did not. I referred Carmen Juarez."

"Who?"

"She's the daughter of a friend. But by the time she got to you, you'd already hired someone."

After several beats, Julianne tried to swallow around the dry lump in her throat. "Then why would she . . . How did we . . ."

"I'm ready to go home, Gramps," Emily called out to him from the doorway of the barn.

The pastor rubbed Julianne's arm. "I hope you get it sorted out. And I want to thank you for what you've done here."

Julianne absently nodded as she scratched her head. "Mm-hmm."

Pastor Dean headed toward his car with Emily, the young girl chattering away. "He won't get rid of his gun, Gramps. But he promised to lock it away in two different places, the gun in one place and the bullets in another place. We neg-ertiated it."

"That's a very good compromise," he commented.

"Bye, Mr. Winters," she called. "Thank you!"

"Yeah. Bye, kid." Rand stood in front of Julianne, glaring at her. "What's with you?"

"I . . ." No sense in sharing it with Rand. "I have to go."

"Yeah, okay. Glad this is over. Just have your girl send me the bill."

Julianne's neck snapped. "What?"

"Your girl. Tell her to send me the bill."

"Oh. Yes. I will."

"You look like you need a drink, Bartlett."

She blinked. "Rand, you know I don't drink."

"You look like you should start."

"Go," she said. "Get in your car . . . and *go*."

"Yeah. See ya."

124

# 12

**Julianne pushed through** the office door to find Phoebe on the phone. She stood in front of her desk, still unsure of what she might say, knowing full well that she had to say . . . *something*.

"Yes, the initial consultation is free, so if you'd like to set up an appointment to talk it over with one of the law partners . . ."

Julianne pointed at her office and nodded before heading in. She slipped out of her jacket and hung it on the wall hook next to the door before proceeding to her desk chair and sinking into it.

*So. You lied and I bought it.*

No. She couldn't say that.

*Who are you, really? Is Phoebe Trent even your real name?*

That either.

Phoebe appeared in the doorway with one of her big old smiles, blinding Julianne. "Did you want to see me?"

"Yes. Come in."

She sat down in the chair across from her desk, and Julianne narrowed her eyes and wondered if this was her first good honest look at the executive assistant from who-knew-where. Her dark curls framed an almost-angelic face: Turned-up little nose, full lips glossed with deep pink to highlight that bright white smile, chocolate eyes fringed by dark, full lashes. If she remembered right, she was around twenty.

"Where are you from, Phoebe?"

"All over the place," she replied.

"I think I remember your résumé saying you moved here from Florida after working for a realtor for three years? That's where you learned your office skills? Typing, filing systems, organizational things?"

"Yes."

Julianne leaned back in her chair and stared at the girl.

"Is . . . something wrong?" she asked.

"Yes."

Phoebe swallowed hard. Her pretty eyes rounded and she silently looked back at Julianne without blinking. "What is it?" she finally asked.

"Well, I'm trying to think back to the day you came into this office with your résumé in hand, Phoebe . . . and how you told me that Pastor Dean had recommended you for the position."

She looked down at the floor for an instant before lifting her head and looking Julianne directly in the eye. "I didn't say that."

"You certainly did."

"I didn't," she gently insisted. "They hadn't painted the title on the door yet, and I asked you if this was Dean & Dean. That's where my interview was supposed to be, but I couldn't find the office."

Julianne inhaled sharply before narrowing her eyes. "Dean & Dean." *Like Pastor Dean?*

"And you stood up and shook my hand," she reminded her. "You said how happy you were that I came in, and you asked for my résumé. You told me you didn't see much office experience on it, and I told you that I'd worked at the real estate office."

"Yes, I remember that. But I know I've told you at least twice how glad I am that Pastor Dean recommended you. You never thought to correct me?"

Phoebe sighed, massaging the edge of the desk with her thumb.

"Phoebe, why did you lie to me?"

"I didn't," she insisted, tipping her head to one side and looking like she might burst into tears. "I just didn't correct the assumption you made. I needed a job so badly, and you seemed so nice. I was sure I could learn what I needed to know and make you glad you hired me."

"Well, you certainly have done that," Julianne admitted.

"Really?"

"Yes, Phoebe, we're very happy with you. So happy, in fact, that I made the effort to thank Pastor Dean for sending you our way."

"Oh," she said, cringing. "I was afraid that might happen."

"Were you ever going to tell us?"

She considered the question before answering. "No."

"No?"

"Not anytime soon anyway. I love this job. I wanted to give you the time to really see what I could do." A glaze dropped over her face, and Phoebe tried to smile. "I'm sorry, Julianne. I'm so sorry. Please don't fire me."

She hadn't even noticed Will in the doorway until he spoke up.

"Fire you?" he said, and he stood behind her with his hands on both of Phoebe's shoulders. "We wouldn't fire you. Would we, Julianne?"

"We need to talk."

They used to joke about those four words. Nothing further needed. And Will got the message, loud and clear.

"Let's go then."

Julianne stood up and looked at Phoebe. "Will and I are headed out. We'll talk this over, and you and I will meet first thing in the morning. Okay?"

Phoebe nodded, and she made no move to get up from the chair. Julianne grabbed her jacket and purse. When she turned back, she noticed Will give Phoebe a reassuring pat on the shoulder.

They didn't speak again until the elevator doors closed on them.

"Your dad?"

"Home and resting."

"Shall we go check on him together? Maybe make some dinner?"

"No need," Will replied. "Your mom has that handled."

"Oh. Let's walk then. Can we go to our spot and talk? We have a lot to talk about."

"I'd say we do," he remarked. "Let's start with why you scared poor Phoebe into begging for her job."

"No, let's start with your dad, and we'll work our way around to Phoebe."

They meandered, arm-in-arm, through the crowded city streets as Will recounted the events of the morning that led up to driving his father to the emergency room.

"The CAT scan was normal, and his labs are being forwarded to Dr. Donnelly. It looks like a little advancement of the Parkinson's."

"Oh, Will. I'm so sorry."

"Things were really looking up since that last physical. But you know, you just can't predict anything with this disease."

They made their way to Yeatman's Cove and followed the winding concrete walk. Their usual spot on the third step from the top of The Serpentine Wall gave them a perfect perspective to watch one lone riverboat paddle its way up the sparkling waters of the Ohio River.

"Now tell me about Phoebe. What happened?"

"I think it's really more my fault than hers," she began, and Will poked her with his elbow.

"Are you about to beg for your job?"

"Very funny."

More than an hour later, they still sat on their step, the sun dipping low beyond the river as they went over the events of the day and sorted out the weight of their world—dispensation for Phoebe, a course of action for Veronica, continued tolerance of Lacey, concern for Davis—Julianne felt the pressure lift the way it always did when she shared her concerns with Will. When they finally landed on the details of the trip to the pig farm, he placed his arm around her shoulders and squeezed.

"Who knew, when we opened our practice, that we'd be defending a pig killer, huh?"

"Oh, I had an inkling," she teased. "I just didn't want to scare you."

She didn't want him to remove his warm embrace, but Will pulled his arm away anyhow. As they stared into each other's eyes for a moment that felt somewhat eternal, Julianne noted a slight quiver inside her stomach, and she struggled against the oddest urge. An urge she hadn't felt in many years. A flash in Will's dark eyes made her wonder if he'd felt it too.

Just about the time that the thought took full form in her head, Will peeled his gaze away from her. She turned away, too, staring at the smooth water reflecting the pinkish sky.

"So," she said to fill the suddenly uncomfortable silence. "How are things going with Alison?"

"Good," he replied in a short snap. "Paul?"

"Good."

* — * — *

"You had two reference letters with you. Those were genuine?"

"Yes, of course!" Phoebe defended.

Julianne leaned back in her desk chair and folded her hands. "Will and I talked it over, and we feel like you're a valuable asset here, Phoebe . . . part of our team. We take that very seriously."

"So do I," she said softly. "I should have told you right away that I wasn't the person your pastor had sent over."

"Yes. You should have."

"I'm so sorry."

Julianne smiled. "Phoebe, you don't have to keep apologizing. It's done. But going forward, there's no room on this team for deception of any kind." With a chuckle, she added, "At least between the three of us. I mean, we are *lawyers*, after all."

Phoebe giggled.

"So there won't be any more discussion about it. We just need you to be the best executive assistant you can be."

"I will. I'll prove myself to you, I promise."

Julianne leaned forward and reached across the desk with an open palm. Phoebe shyly set her hand into it. "You've already proven yourself. We rely on you, and we're happy to have you here."

Phoebe's dark eyes glazed with emotion. "Thank you."

Julianne gave the girl's hand a shake before she released it. When the front office door opened, Phoebe hopped to her feet and hurried into the reception area.

"Hi. How are you?"

Julianne froze. She knew that voice . . .

"Oh," Phoebe said. "You must be Miss Bartlett's . . . sister?"

"Uh, no," the woman replied. "But I get that a lot. Is Will around?"

Julianne stood up and closed the space between her desk and the open office door. Just one look confirmed her suspicion.

"Holly? What are you doing here?"

Holly brushed her blonde hair away from her peaches-and-cream face and looked up at her with wide blue eyes. "Hello, Julianne. I came to see Will."

"Does he know you're coming?" *Because I think you'd be the last person on earth—*

"No. I was in the area, and I thought I'd take a chance."

"Davis is just out of the hospital," she told her. "He's looking after him this morning."

"Oh, no. What happened?"

Julianne resented the concern she saw evident in Holly's expression. She knew how illogical the emotion was, but it burned in her just the same. Holly Corbett had given up all rights to concern over anything or anyone in Will's life the day she left the diamond ring on the table and walked out the door, leaving Will devastated in her wake.

"Davis has Parkinson's."

Holly twisted something around her finger; the long tassel hanging from her camel suede purse occupied her focus as she glared at the floor in search of her next words.

"Okay," she said when she found them. "Would you tell Will I stopped in? Ask him to call me?"

"I can ask," she said. "But I don't think he's going to call you, Holly."

She raised her eyes until they met Julianne's. "I know you're his mighty protector and all that, Jules . . ."

*Don't call me that. Will is the only one who calls me that.*

". . . but he is a big boy. He gets to choose whether he talks to me or not."

"You're right. I'm just telling you that I think I know what his choice will be."

"No disrespect, but you've always thought you knew what Will's next move was going to be. Sometimes you're wrong."

Julianne bit the corner of her lip. "All evidence to the contrary," she finally replied.

Without another word, Holly turned and left, thumping the door shut behind her. After she'd gone, Julianne stood frozen for a few seconds before she inhaled sharply and looked at Phoebe sitting quietly behind her desk.

"I'll bet there's a story there!" Phoebe said with a nervous chuckle.

"Will's former fiancée. Left him in the dust. Nothing else to tell. Would you write him a note to tell him that Holly Corbett stopped by, and put it with his messages?"

"Sure."

Julianne retreated to her office and pushed the door partway shut before sinking into the chair with a deep sigh, reconsidering whether a quick note with all of his other messages was actually the best way to go. She didn't want him blindsided. But to call him with a report, to make a big deal of Holly just stopping by the way she had, maybe that would—

"You'll never guess who I just saw in the lobby!" Lacey James suddenly exclaimed as she pushed past Phoebe and shoved Julianne's door wide open. "Holly Corbett, that's who!"

"Yes, I know."

131

"Is William here? Did he talk to her?" she drawled.

"No, thankfully," Julianne said with a sigh as she leaned back into the leather chair. "What are you doing here, Lacey?"

"We'll get to that in a minute, hon. What on God's pretty green earth was she doing here in this office after all this time?"

"Lacey—"

"He sure does have a lot of blondes in his world, doesn't he?" she remarked as she folded into the chair across from Julianne. "You, Holly, me . . ."

"Well, I think Will's days of collecting blondes are over," she said with a crooked grin.

"What do you mean?"

"The girl he's seeing now is a brunette."

All the color drained immediately from Lacey's made-up face, and she gasped. "What do you mean, *the girl he's seeing now*? William is dating someone? Is it serious?"

"Yes, he is. And I don't know. Now do you want to tell me what you're doing—"

Lacey jumped to her feet and placed both hands on her hips as she looked down at her. "How could you let this happen, Julie? How could you leave the floodgate open like that? I mean, William is a handsome, eligible guy, and—let's be honest, hon—our only real hope was that his little heart was broken over that awful Holly. Now that he's dating again, the women are going to rush in like one of those tsunamis in Asia! Is that what you want, Julie? Is it?"

"First: My name isn't Julie. It's Julianne. I don't know how many times I have to tell you that. Second: I am not a candidate to date Will. He's my best friend. Third, and most importantly," she said as she scribbled a note of reminder to call her brother Travis to wish him a happy birthday, "Will is a big boy, as was recently pointed out to me." She looked up. "He'll decide when to date and when not to, who to see and who not to."

She peeled the sticky note from the pad and stuck it to the last open inch on the frame of her computer screen.

"Oh, don't be daft, hon. What kind of woman lets a man make all of his own decisions?" Lacey sat down, crossed one leg over the other, and leaned against the back of the chair, shaking her head. "That's just crazy talk."

"And your reason for barging into my office again?"

"Oh. Well, I thought we could make some quick work of this collaboration Judge Hillman has ordered, and then move on to some talk about the gala. What are you wearing? Do you have a dress yet? Because if not, I want to put in my dibs for the color pink. I found a beautiful pink taffeta, one shoulder, and I don't want to share the color spotlight. It's just too beautiful."

"That's uncanny," Julianne replied, deadpan and straight-faced. "I just bought a pink dress with one shoulder."

"No." She took such depraved pleasure in Lacey's expression of horror as she tapped one shoulder and asked, "A big magnolia flower, right here? With pearl beads?"

"Yes!"

"Nooo!" Lacey cried.

After a moment, Julianne broke into a grin and admitted, "No."

Lacey's eyes narrowed. "No?"

"No. I was just messing with you."

An exasperated scream blew out of Lacey as she exploded to her feet and looked down at Julianne with fire blazing in her eyes.

"You are hideous!" she cried, and she spun on one heel and headed for the door.

"Oh, come on. I was joking. Come back here. I thought we were going to talk about the case," Julianne called after her, but Lacey let out another angry groan just before the outer door slammed shut behind her.

With a shrug, she picked up the phone and punched in Travis's cell number.

"Hello."

"Trav!" she exclaimed, yanking the sticky note from her screen and crumpling it in her hand. "Happy birthday, big brother."

"Listen to them," the prince remarked. "They're like clucking hens. They never quiet down."

The prince's equerry gave a hardy laugh. "They're clucking over you, Your Highness."

"Me! Whatever for?"

"You'll soon choose a wife, sir. And every one of them wants your consideration for the role."

"Well, I certainly don't want a wife who clucks like a hen," he replied. "If they can't see that, then they're daft! All of them!"

# 13

"**As you know,** *Queen City Magazine* is one of the sponsors of the Bar Association gala this year, and we're doing an in-depth feature on each of the lawyers nominated for awards. Since you're a Person of the Year nominee due to your charitable fund-raising, I thought we might spend some time talking about that. Can you spare me a few minutes this week?"

"Yes, I suppose so."

"It won't take more than a couple of hours. We'll do a sit-down, take a few pictures, and I'll get out of your hair."

Julianne's stomach lurched slightly. "Melanie, I'm going to transfer you to my assistant. Phoebe has my calendar and will be able to set something up for you."

"That's wonderful. Thank you."

Julianne placed the call on hold and hurried out to Phoebe's desk. "I don't know how to transfer! Can you just pick it up from there if she's on hold?"

Phoebe chuckled and nodded. "Yes. Who is it?"

"It's that reporter from *Queen City Magazine*. She wants to set up an appointment to come and interview me this week. Don't just give her the pick of all of the open slots dominating my calendar, okay? Give the impression I have a little something going on."

"All right."

"And try to put her off to the end of the week so I have time to shop for something to wear. She's bringing a photographer."

"You got it."

Phoebe knew just the right button to push, and she answered

in a professional voice that did Julianne proud.

"This is Phoebe Trent, Miss Bartlett's executive assistant. I've got her calendar in front of me. Why don't you tell me which day you had in mind and I'll see if we can accommodate you."

Julianne's hand flew to her chest, and she sighed. "Perfection!" she whispered, and she turned back toward her office. "Sheer perfection."

While Phoebe handled Melanie Larsen, Julianne dialed Suzanne on her cell.

"What are you doing?" she asked without greeting her friend.

"Coming out of a sales call. Why? What's up?"

"I need you."

"Outfit, shoes, or both?"

"Both. I'm being interviewed by *Queen City Magazine* this week, and they're taking pictures."

"I'm out in Kenwood, and I have one more stop to make. But I'm starving. If you bring sustenance, I can meet you in front of my closet in an hour."

"It's a date!"

After she hung up, Julianne emerged from her office to quiz Phoebe.

"We set it up for Friday morning at eleven," she said before Julianne had the chance to inquire. "Not too early so you have the morning to get ready, but early enough for you to still be fresh."

"Thank you!"

"I'll make sure everything is tidy, and set out some pastries and fruit in the conference room . . ."

"You are—"

". . . make coffee and tea, restock the fridge."

"—an angel! I could almost kiss you."

Phoebe beamed.

"I'm going to meet Suzanne for help in choosing something for the photo shoot. Something that says Person of the Year."

"You're a shoo-in."

"When Will gets in, give him the heads-up about Friday? They may want to talk to him, too."

"Of course."

"And tell him about Holly?"

"Yes."

"Oh, and can you remind him we've got a table for the gala? If his dad is feeling up to it, I thought he might like to come along as my mom's date."

"I'll tell him," Phoebe replied as she scribbled a note.

"And if you'd like to bring a date, there will be room."

Phoebe paused. "Me?"

"Of course, you! You have to be there."

"I wouldn't even know—"

"What to wear?" she interrupted, and the young woman nodded. "We'll go shopping next week."

"Well, I . . . The thing is . . ."

The light dawned while Phoebe fidgeted, and Julianne chastised herself. "Listen, I know about being on a budget. I spent five years at the public defender's office. I know some great places where we can both get something affordable. And if not, we can go shopping in Suzanne's closet for you, too. You and she are about the same size, and her closet is the square footage of a small bedroom. She has a whole section of fancy-schmancy. We'll work it out."

Phoebe chuckled, and Julianne waved at her as she headed out the door. "I'll be back in time for my three o'clock."

● — ● — ●

"I was thinking about that Burberry suit jacket with the tie-back. Do you know the one I mean?"

Suzanne nodded and took a quick bite of her salad before she hopped off the bed and disappeared inside the closet. "It has trousers with it, but they're going to be way long on you. We could do a temporary hem though."

"I don't know about pants. The last time I borrowed that jacket, I wore it with my black pencil skirt."

"Oh, right, for that lawyer lunch. And that beautiful starch-white blouse, with the rhinestone pin at the collar."

Julianne sighed. "That's right! That's what I'll wear with it for the photo shoot."

Suzanne emerged with the tailored black jacket on a wooden hanger. "What would you do if you had a normal friend who wasn't a complete clotheshorse?"

"Camp out in front of the Salvation Army store?"

Suzanne motioned toward the mirror and stood behind her as Julianne slipped into the jacket. As she buttoned it, Suzanne tied it at the back, accentuating Julianne's small waist.

"You look like a million bucks," her friend told her reflection. "I'm so proud of you, Miss *Person of the Year.*"

"Not yet. But you're coming, right? To the gala?"

"I can't, honey. I've got a sales conference in Dallas that weekend."

Julianne groaned. "You'd rather spend the weekend with a hundred pharmaceutical sales geeks than cheering me on at the gala?"

"No, I would not. But I'm already registered, and my whole team will be there."

"Traitor."

The soft lining of the jacket caused it to slide straight down her arms, and she carefully placed it back on the hanger while Suzanne retrieved a vinyl garment bag from the closet. Once they'd zipped the jacket safely inside, Julianne hung it on the bedroom door and returned to her salad.

"What are you wearing anyway?" Suzanne asked her, munching on a quesadilla wedge that came with her salad. "It's black-tie, right?"

"I found this *gorgeous* gown in that vintage shop in Clifton. It's pale ice blue with a beaded little bolero overlay with three-quarter sleeves, a rhinestone empire waist. Ah, Suz, it's stunning. It has this whole forties Balenciaga vibe . . . without the price tag, of course."

"It sounds smashing. Shoes?"

"None yet."

Suzanne's hazel eyes flashed suddenly, and she leapt to her feet and rushed into the closet. "You know, I thought of you when I bought these, Julianne. And now I feel like, I don't know, maybe it was meant to be!"

She emerged from the closet clutching a shoe box, and she plopped on the bed beside her. She opened the box as if presenting Julianne with the Holy Grail of footwear and slowly peeled back several layers of light pink tissue paper. Sounding more like the theme song to *Star Trek* than the harps-and-angels song Julianne felt sure she was aiming for, Suzanne crooned at the top of her lungs. When she got a first look at the contents of the box, Julianne gasped.

"Oh . . . Suz . . ."

"Crazy, right?"

"Completely."

Julianne moved her hand toward the shoes, gingerly touching one of them with the tip of her index finger. Four-inch spiked peep toes, three-quarter-inch platform, metallic silver underneath solid rows of sparkling crystals.

"It's like . . . a shoe made out of . . . *diamonds*."

"They're spectacular, aren't they?" Suzanne asked rhetorically, and she nudged the box closer. "Try them on."

Julianne lifted one shoe from the tissue-lined box and held it up to the light from the window long enough to watch it shimmer.

"If they don't fit, I'm going to jump off the roof."

"My condo's a single-story. There's nowhere to go. Put them on."

Julianne kicked off her own shoes and lovingly slid into one of the crystal stunners. The farther her foot went into the first one, the wider her grin became. When it was evident that the fit might work, she snatched the second shoe and happily jammed her foot into it before rushing over to the mirror.

"How do they feel?" Suzanne asked her.

"The truth?" she said with a chuckle. "They pinch."

"Ohhh."

"But I don't care. I love them!" Julianne exclaimed, turning her leg sideways to admire the reflection. "What's a little pain when your legs look like this?"

"That depends on how long you'll be in them," Suzanne remarked. "But if you're willing to endure it, I'm willing to lend them." She wagged a finger at Julianne and grinned at her. "Get that? They're on loan."

"Yes, yes, I get it. . . . I'll have them back to you before the clock strikes midnight at the end of the weekend."

With her plastic salad fork in hand, Suzanne jumped up and knighted her friend. "Then I hereby dub you . . . *Belle of the Ball.*"

Julianne beamed. "Thank you, Fairy Godmother. You kind of rock."

"Kind of?" she teased before shifting gears. "And what about your prince? Is he all set to step into the Cincinnati lawyer scene with you on his arm?"

"I haven't asked him yet."

"Well, get on it, girl."

"He's taking me to a fund-raiser tonight. I'll talk to him about it then."

"Cincinnati's Hungry Children or Cincinnatians Without Cars?" Suzanne teased.

"Legal Aid Art Exhibition," she stated. Glancing at the clock, she jumped to her feet. "I've got to go. I have a three o'clock with Lacey James."

"Oh, that sounds like your idea of a perfect afternoon," Suzanne teased.

Julianne grabbed the garment bag as she passed it, blew a quick kiss to Gus in his cage, and hurried out the front door.

She placed Suzanne's Burberry jacket in the backseat with all the loving care it deserved and slipped behind the wheel to head back to the office. At the stoplight on Galbraith and Winton Roads, she quickly punched out a text to Paul.

*Reminder re benefit 2nite. Pick me up at 7?*

By the time she merged onto Interstate 71, her phone jingled with his reply; but she couldn't read it until the light at Eighth Street.

*Sorry, meant to call. Can't make tonight.*

"Ahhh, maaan," she whimpered, and she tossed the phone into her purse.

Julianne pouted all the way upstairs to her office. She'd really been looking forward to attending this one with Paul. A lot of her peers from the legal community would be in attendance, and she thought it might be a good practice run.

She noticed Will in the conference room, and she stomped in and flopped into a chair across the table from him.

"So much for my brilliant plan."

He looked up at her and removed his wire glasses. "Another brilliant plan bites the dust?"

"Paul backed out of the legal aid benefit tonight."

"And his taking you was brilliant because . . ."

"Because if he had a good time, I might get him to agree to take me to the gala."

"Ah."

Will stretched and leaned back into the chair.

"What are you reading?"

He tilted his iPad toward her. "*Trial Lawyers Magazine.*"

She faked a yawn, and Will chuckled.

"Did Phoebe tell you Holly was here earlier?" she asked him.

"She did."

"And?"

"And I called her."

Julianne bristled. "You called her? Will!"

"Don't 'Will' me. You just didn't want me to prove you wrong since you told her that I wouldn't."

"She told you that?"

"Of course she did."

She felt a wave of embarrassment wash over her, and she pulled a face. "Of course she did."

Will smiled and shook his head. "You thought she wouldn't?"

"Never mind. What did she want?"

"To talk about the other day. It was a little awkward when we ran into each other at the kite festival."

"Yeah, it tends to get awkward when you run into the guy you—" She stopped herself just in time. "Sorry." After a long pause, she grinned at him. "You know what would make you forget all about Holly?"

"Finishing this article about Quick Response codes that . . . Never mind. What would make me forget?"

"Taking me to the legal aid benefit tonight."

Will groaned.

"Oh, come on, Will. I have the tickets already. You don't want me to go alone, do you?"

"Don't I?"

"No. You don't." When he seemed unconvinced, she added, "It's at the Radisson. I'll bet there will be shrimp. You love their shrimp."

After a long moment's thought, Will asked, "Can I have yours too?"

# 14

"**Legal Aid has** developed many programs that help people within the Southwestern Ohio region to resolve critical problems. Specifically, they make every effort to contribute to the solution of community issues, such as the health and well-being of children, secure housing, resources for low-income job seekers, and our greatest effort—providing legal services to those in need."

It wasn't that the cause was anything less than worthy, but Will had been to so many of these things over the years that the speeches had all begun to run together. He tapped Julianne's wrist with the handle of his fork, and she in turn passed him the crystal bowl of chilled shrimp sitting in front of her.

"Careful," she whispered. "Eat too many of those and you'll ruin your appetite for the rubber chicken."

"Hey. I'm here for the shrimp. You think that guy across the table is going to eat his?"

She shot him a disapproving glance before she shrugged and asked, "Can I have your roll?"

While the speaker explained the semantics of the art exhibition and silent auction, Will paused to exchange pleasantries with a couple of familiar faces and to thank the server who poured iced tea into his glass, but he'd finished off Julianne's shrimp by the time the entrees were delivered beneath shiny silver domes.

"Score!" Julianne exclaimed when the waiter removed the dome from her plate. "It's not rubber chicken after all."

Fragrant salmon fillets, garlic mashed potatoes, baby carrots, and broccoli florets.

*Score, indeed.*

Julianne looked lovely with her honey-gold hair twisted into sections and pinned at the back of her head with jewel-toned rhinestone clips. Her deep purple dress brought out the indigo of her eyes, and she'd shown off her strappy black shoes no less than three times since he'd picked her up.

"They really are pretty, aren't they?" she asked him at the door, in the car, and again in the elevator on their way to dinner.

Will could take or leave the shoes, truth be told, but Julianne . . . now she defined "pretty."

He looked on as she continued to charm the elderly gentleman seated on the other side of her, and every time she giggled at one of his remarks, Will felt the rumble of it deep within him, like the echo of a beautiful song sent down into a canyon.

"I was surprised to see you with a brunette," Holly had said to him on the phone that afternoon. "It gave me a little hope, actually. I felt like maybe you'd finally moved on."

He swallowed her comment along with a large bite of salmon.

*Finally moved on.*

He wished she'd meant moved on from her. But he knew what she meant.

*I felt like maybe you'd finally moved on . . . from Julianne.*

Will glanced over at Julianne as she ribbed her dinner companion with her elbow, and the old guy's steely eyes sparkled with delight. He saw it, too—that indescribable, indefinable *something* that she had. But then he easily moved back to conversation with his silver-haired wife on the other side of him. Will envied the ease with which he made the transition.

"Where's your mind?" Julianne asked him, and he blinked back to the current moment.

"Huh?"

"You're a hundred miles away."

"Oh. No."

"Are you thinking about your conversation with Holly?"

He twitched. "Sort of."

"Do you want to talk about it?"

"Not at all."

"Okay. Let's play the dessert game then."

Will chuckled. It was a game that had been born out of dozens of these charitable dinners, derived out of a mixture of boredom and Julianne's quirky, creative mind.

"Anyone else want to play?" she asked the other six people at their large round table. "It's called The Dessert Game. If you already know what they're serving, then you can't play. But everyone puts at least twenty dollars into the centerpiece. We go clockwise around the table, and everyone guesses what they think will be served. The trick is . . . you can't repeat what someone else has already guessed. And the winner gets to collect the money and donate it to the cause in their name, or the name of their firm. Who's in?"

Further proof of her adorability, Will noted, every person at the table tossed money at the centerpiece.

"Will goes first," she declared.

"Cheesecake," he called out. These functions almost always had cheesecake.

They went around the table. Everything from berry cobbler to Dutch apple pie to chocolate mousse found its way into the entries. Being last, all of the usual suspects had been submitted, so Julianne settled on an unlikely delicacy. "Bread pudding with warm honey-vanilla sauce."

Some of their companions pretended to swoon while the others laughed out loud.

"If we all sneak out now, we might find a place that serves it," the elder to Julianne's right suggested.

"Ooh, here come the waiters with dessert!" the woman with the flaming red hair seated directly across from him exclaimed.

They all craned their necks, and Will thought the waiter must have thought them to be the biggest collection of eager sweet-toothed philanthropists in Hamilton County.

"What is it?" someone asked.

"Key lime pie," the waiter replied.

"Key lime pie!" Julianne blurted through laughter. "No one guessed that! This is the first time we've played this game where no one has guessed the dessert!"

"Let's just donate the money anyway, in the name of Table Thirty-Six," Julianne's new friend declared, and they all agreed.

"What a fun game," the woman next to Will sang to him. "I think we want to sit with you two at every one of these shindigs."

"She's the fun one," Will told her with a grin. "I'm just along for the ride."

"How long have you two been married?" she asked, and Will froze for an instant.

"We're not married. We're partners in the same law firm."

"Oh!" she said with a chuckle. "I could have sworn you were an old married couple." Leaning around him, the woman caught Julianne's attention and told her, "I thought you two were married!"

A strange flash in her eye struck Will with a pinch as she replied, "No. Will dodged that bullet a long time ago."

"Well, if you're both single, I'd suggest you connect immediately," she teased. "You were made for each other."

They finished dessert and coffee, and a small group from the table strolled around the art exhibit together. When they had circled the room, Julianne looped her arm through Will's and smiled.

"I'm tired. And my feet hurt."

"So much for your really cute shoes," he remarked. "Can you still take them back?"

"Why would I do that when they're so pretty?"

He should have learned that lesson long ago, but he continually fell into the trap. In the same way that paper always covered rock, cute shoes trumped pain every time, he reminded himself.

"Are you ready to go?" he asked her.

"More than."

They said their goodbyes to a few of their new friends, and the

old man who'd been seated next to Julianne gave her an enthusi-
astic hug.

"You're sheer delight," he cackled. He nodded at Will as an afterthought. "Both of you."

On the drive home, Julianne rested her head against the window and closed her eyes. Will wasn't sure if she'd actually fallen
asleep until he pulled up in front of her small Greenhills building and shut off the engine. Her breathing was deep and unen-
cumbered, and her shoulders rose slightly and fell again with each
breath she took. He hadn't noticed when she'd removed her shoes,
but there they sat, overturned in her lap.

"Jules," he whispered with no response. He jiggled her arm
slightly and repeated, "Jules."

She stirred a bit, and one corner of her mouth lifted in an uncon-
scious sort of smile. Then she sighed before drifting back to sleep.

"Hey. Jules. C'mon," he said, shaking her arm until she whimpered. "Wake up, girl. You're home."

Her lashes looked longer and thicker under the shadow of
night, and her blue eyes fluttered as she struggled to open them.

"What's wrong?" she asked him.

"You're home. You have to wake up."

She glanced around, squinting. "I'm home?"

"Yes. Put your shoes on."

She lifted one of the shoes and looked at it strangely before
poking the spiked heel into her twisted hair and scratching her
head with it. "Shoes?" she repeated sleepily.

Will couldn't help himself, and he let out one unabashed laugh.
"Yes. Put them on."

When she stared straight ahead for several seconds, Will
sighed, pushed out of the car, and went around to her side. He
pulled open her door and stooped down to a squat as he removed
the shoes from her lap and placed them, one at a time, on her
smooth feet. With a gentle nudge, he led her out of the car and to
a standing position.

"Come on, Sleepyhead. Follow me."

She did as she was told, no doubt out of blind obedience rather than thoughtful choice. When they reached the front door, she leaned against the wall with her eyes closed while Will fished her keys from the outer pocket of her purse and unlocked the door.

"Don't stop or pass go," he instructed as he pressed her purse back into her hands. "Go straight to bed."

"'Kay." She stepped inside, and then she slowly turned around to face him with squinted eyes. "Nice of you . . . taking me tonight. . . ."

"Sure."

Her lips tilted into a tired little smile, and she plunked both arms around his neck. Will chuckled as he returned the embrace, but when he tried to pull away, she held him there for a moment longer, the fragrance of her vanilla hair coercing him to sigh and enjoy the moment. And when he thought she had released him, Julianne surprised him by leaning in again and pressing her mouth to his in a warm, sweet kiss.

When they parted, he couldn't do anything but just stand there, staring at her still-closed eyes, his heart pounding at double-time.

"Night," she said in a sleepy rasp, and she turned away and headed inside.

"Night," he managed as he watched her walk away, the door still wide open behind her. "Sweet dreams."

"Me, too," she muttered, and she headed directly into her bedroom without looking back.

Will staggered slightly in the doorway as his lips tingled and his thoughts ricocheted all over the place. He quietly closed the door.

● — ● — ●

Julianne leaned on her elbows and sighed. She could hardly drag out of bed that morning, and several cups of coffee later, she still struggled against weariness. Knowing that Paul was on his way, however, buoyed her alertness somewhat.

"We're all set for Friday morning?" she asked Phoebe before she even made it into the chair on the other side of the desk.

"All set. And I've got your meeting with Veronica Caswell pushed to next week like you asked."

"Good. Any word from Lacey?"

"She called earlier to say that everything is on track, and it looks like the one consult with Mrs. Blanchard ought to do it."

"Well, Judge Hillman didn't lie," she commented. "It really was quick and easy. That's a relief."

Phoebe twisted a lock of her short, dark hair around one finger, her eyes averted to the edge of the desk.

"What is it?" Julianne asked, and the girl glanced up at her as a stain of crimson washed over her cheeks and down her throat. "What's on your mind?"

"I wanted to tell you . . . about the other day . . ."

"Phoebe, I told you, we don't need to speak about it again. It's water under the bridge."

"I appreciate that, but I think you need to know—"

Interruption came in the form of male voices from the reception area, one of them Will's.

"I'll just go see . . ." Phoebe said as she gathered her things and headed for the door.

When she recognized Paul as one of the voices, Julianne glared at the clock.

*He's early.*

She quickly checked her makeup in the mirrored compact she kept tucked in her top drawer and replaced it as she scuffled to her feet.

"I'll be right out," she called to him.

Paul poked his head around the corner of the doorway and gave her half a smile. "Can I come in?" She loved the way that one lock of wavy hair fell across his forehead. "I thought maybe we could chat for a minute."

"This place is a constant stream of interruptions," she told him

149

as she grabbed her purse from the hook by the door. "Let's head out to dinner and talk there, okay?"

He lifted one shoulder into a shrug and let her pass in front of him.

Will silently leaned against his office doorway, and she gave him a smile. "I'm outta here," she told him. "See you in the morning." His silence struck her as strange, and she thought she spotted something odd and out of character in his expression. "Okay?"

"Yeah," he said with a nod, and he disappeared into the office and closed the door behind him.

*He must be preoccupied*, she thought, and she led Paul out the door and into the hallway.

Once they stepped into the elevator, Julianne turned to Paul and gave him a broad smile. "What a day it's been! It's good to see you."

"You, too," he replied, but he didn't look at her when he said it.

"I've been looking forward to this all day. You're going to love The Precinct. The restaurant is set in this old police patrol house. It's a historic landmark, and—" Paul's pained expression slammed the train of words into a collision with the back of her throat. "What's wrong?"

The elevator doors slid open, but the two of them just stood there, Paul looking through the open doors, and Julianne turned sideways and staring up at him.

"Paul?"

"Yeah. Julianne, listen . . . we have to talk."

# 15

It felt a little like cheating on Will as they sat there on the top concrete step of The Serpentine Wall, but when someone downtown gave her the "We have to talk" line, it was usually Will, and The Wall was always the first place she thought to go. As she and Paul sat side by side, each of them silent and gazing out at the Ohio River, Julianne felt a lump form in the base of her throat.

"Why don't you just tell me what's on your mind," she managed.

Without another moment of silence, Paul tossed it right out: "I don't think I want to see you anymore."

*Well, there it is. There's no mistaking that.*

"Can I ask why?" she inquired. "I thought we were getting along pretty well." The moment she said it, regret pushed a distant and bitter taste into the back of her throat. Had she really come to believe they had a future?

Paul shifted toward her and propped one ankle atop the opposite knee. "It's not that I don't think you're a sweet girl . . ." he began, and the thud of the *but* that followed hit before he even had a chance to speak it ". . . but I just don't see this going anywhere."

"You don't?"

"Do *you*?" he asked, his astonishment unmistakable.

"I guess . . . well . . ."

"How?"

A puff of a chuckle burst out. "Well, that's straightforward, isn't it?"

151

"I just mean . . . *How?* We have so little in common, Julianne. Believe me, I'm flattered that someone like you—all Reese Witherspoon-ful and a lawyer and everything—would be interested in a carpenter from Clifton. But you don't like the outdoors, and I rather live for it. You hated the acoustical show when we met at The Lemon."

"I didn't. Really. I just—"

"It's okay. You don't have to fix it. I saw that glazed-over look after about ten minutes. But it's not even just Spanish guitar. It's everything, Julianne. You like to go to these upscale restaurants and get all dressed up. I'm more of a jeans-and-a-sweater, eating a three-way at Skyline Chili sort of guy, you know? And let's just put it out there. I'm never going with you to a *Bible study*. We don't fit."

A bead of perspiration tumbled down the back of her neck, and Julianne's heart began to palpitate softly. Rubbing her temples, she thought what a ridiculous picture to get in her mind, but there was Lacey James, shaking her big platinum head and clicking her fake-Southern tongue. *"They never stick around for long, do they, Julie?"*

Paul cut into her thoughts, running a hand through waves of sandy hair. "I felt real bad canceling on you at the last minute for your fund-raiser thing last night, but I was beat. I had a long day, and the last thing I wanted to do was tighten a noose around my neck and put on a suit."

Her voice felt too thick to make it past that lump in her throat, and she felt suddenly nauseous. It wasn't usually so warm at this time of day on the river.

"You understand, though, don't you?" he asked her. "Deep down, you know we're not a fit, right?"

"Well, I understand, of course. And I guess it doesn't matter what I think if you don't think we work."

Paul looked genuinely pained. "I'm sorry," he said. "If you still want to go to dinner, I guess we can."

She summoned the courage to put full intention behind her

fake smile as she let him off the hook. "It's okay. I had some work to finish up anyway."

"Really?"

"Yes," she replied, pushing that smile up as far as the stubborn thing would go. "You go on. I'm going to sit here a few minutes and then walk back to the office."

"You're sure?"

"Of course."

He lingered for a moment before leaning toward her. "I just thought it was best to be honest, you know?"

"Yeah." She nodded. "Yes, of course. Honesty is always best." *Except when it's not.* "I appreciate it, Paul."

He pecked the top of her head with a meaningless kiss. "You take care, Julianne."

"You, too."

As Paul got up and walked away, every thud of his footsteps represented another "I told you so" in Julianne's mind.

*No date tonight, Julianne? A pretty thing like you?*

*You're not seeing him anymore? You sure do run through them fast, don't you?*

*Well, you always have Will to take you. He usually goes it alone, too.*

Julianne noted the grinding of her teeth and made a conscious effort to relax her jaw. At least when Will and Holly were together, people didn't see him as Julianne's reluctant sidekick for charity dinners and legal functions.

*Poor Julianne. But at least she has Will. Oh, wait! That's right. Will's getting married. What will Julianne do now?*

Before she knew it, she'd popped to her feet, grabbed her purse, and headed across the cove. Yes, at least she did have Will. And she needed him like crazy. He'd know just the right thing to say . . .

But by the time she reached the office again, the place was locked up tight. Will and Phoebe had both gone home for the day. Julianne couldn't manage the effort to head downstairs to her car, so she backed up to the wall across from the office door and slid down to the floor.

LAW OFFICES

OF

HANES & BARTLETT

She tried to smile at the perfect letters on the door, but her jaw ached too much to complete the effort. A mist of tears rose in her eyes and stood there, seemingly unsure of whether to back down or push forward, and her temples began to throb again.

Julianne dug out her iPhone from her purse and summoned the first number on the speed dial.

"You've reached Will Hanes of Hanes and Bartlett. I'm temporarily unavailable at the moment. Leave a message and your phone number, and I'll call you back as soon as possible."

Even his recorded voice brought her a little comfort, but it wasn't the same as the real thing.

"Hey, Will, it's me. I really need you. Call me, " 'kay?"

● — ● — ●

Will reveled in the exhilaration that came from a brisk ride across the wide-open space at the center of the Ross property. His favorite four-legged pal snorted as she flew through the high grass toward the base of the final hill, a sure sign that she enjoyed breaking loose from the stables and the boring daily regimen of simple trots. Like a premium sports car set out to the open road, Christie shifted gloriously into high gear to show Will what she had in her.

Alison rounded the curve first, and Hershey trotted up the slope of the first embankment. They were a perfect match, Alison with her dark auburn ponytail and Hershey with his deep brown sheen and gleaming black mane.

"Hah!" Will shouted, and his blond Palomino sped up, taking the hill at full charge until they galloped past Alison. "Good

154

girl," he added as they slowed to a halt at the top of the hill, and he patted the side of her neck and gently raked the coarse hair of her mane. "Good girl."

"That was fantastic!" Alison exclaimed as she dismounted, sheer joy beaming from her smiling face.

Will produced two large plastic bags from his saddlebag and tossed one of them to Alison. "Carrots, apples, and sugar cubes," he told her. "All of Christie's favorites."

"And he packed some for you, too, Hershey," she cooed, scooping out a couple of small carrots and offering them to him on the palm of her outstretched hand.

Christie pressed against the side of Will's face and nuzzled him in thanks before licking several sugar cubes from his hand. "You're welcome, girl."

The soft buzz from his iPhone drew Will's focus away, but only for a moment.

"Is that yours?" Alison asked. "You aren't going to answer?"

"Nope."

Alison grinned and shook her head. "Oooo-kay."

Christie pushed a carrot out of his hand and to the ground, and she moved in on the chunks of apple instead. "You prefer the sweet stuff, don't you?" he muttered. "I know. I feel you, girl."

Alison wrapped Hershey's reins around a low-hanging branch as they'd done the first time they visited the ridge. She inched up on Will and Christie. Patting the horse's muzzle, she remarked, "You two are good friends, aren't you?"

"We are."

She picked up the carrot and extended it toward Christie, and she happily crunched into it.

"You know, I was pleasantly surprised when you called and invited me to come riding again."

Will smiled.

"I thought maybe I'd heard the last of you after the kite festival."

"Did you?" he asked as he scooped out a few more apple

chunks from the plastic bag. "Why?"

"Well, after you ran into your ex-fiancée . . . and my remarks about the similarities between her and Julianne . . . I don't know. I just got to thinking . . ."

Her words trailed away, and Will glanced at her. "You know what I've learned about women, Alison?"

The corner of her mouth quirked as she replied, "Do tell."

"You all think too much. There's not some deep hidden motive behind everything a guy does. We're really not all that complex, if you want to know the truth. Sometimes a guy really is just busy."

She nodded and stroked Christie's nose. "Yep. You're right."

"Thank you."

"But sometimes you all use *busy* to avoid something."

He thought it over for a moment before looking up into her chocolate-caramel eyes. "You think I'm avoiding something?"

"Are you?"

"No. Not avoiding," he replied. "Just delaying."

"Oh? And what have you been delaying?"

"This," he said. Placing his hand loosely beneath the curve of her jaw before he could change his mind, he moved toward her and planted a soft kiss on her lips.

When they parted, Alison narrowed her eyes and smiled.

"Mm-hmm, yeah," she said. "That was nice, Will. But what are we *avoiding*?"

*Avoiding. Please!*

Once they said their goodbyes at the stables, Will climbed into his car to drive home. At the intersection of Winton and McKelvey Roads, he made the last-minute decision to turn right and take the scenic route instead of going straight to his dad's house.

His phone buzzed from the backseat, and he glanced over his shoulder and grimaced. Julianne calling, no doubt . . . excited to tell him what devastatingly charming thing the ditch digger had said, or that he'd agreed to escort her to the gala, or that they'd already decided to get married on a cliff overlooking the ocean or in a hot-air balloon, or maybe in a big glass carriage pulled by six white horses.

When he finally pulled into the driveway, he noticed Julianne's car parked next door at her mother's house. He didn't bother to flick the garage door open. Instead, he rolled down all of the windows and opened the sunroof before turning off the engine and leaning back against the headrest.

About ten minutes later, the garage door opened, and Davis scuffled through. He stopped at the front bumper and called out to him. "What's going on, Son? You coming in?"

"I was thinking about going for a run," he replied without lifting his head.

"Yeah, you look like it. Come on inside. Amanda's here with some of her fancy bread pudding."

Like a shot, Will found himself back at the Radisson, sitting next to Julianne and playing that silly dessert game of hers.

"Bread pudding with warm honey-vanilla sauce," she'd guessed, and everyone at the table had a sudden urge for the delectable dessert they wouldn't find anywhere in the area, aside from Amanda's active kitchen, that is.

"You coming inside, boy?"

"Yeah," Will muttered, and he flicked the handle and pushed the door open.

He grabbed the saddlebag from the backseat and, leaving all the windows down and the sunroof gaping wide open, he caught up to his dad and hung an arm loosely around his shoulder as they walked through the garage and into the house.

Fragrant spices accosted them before they even made it into the kitchen. Cinnamon, nutmeg, blended with a scent so sweet that Will began to salivate.

"There you are," Amanda greeted him with a welcoming smile. "Have you had dinner, Will? I kept a couple of plates warm for you and Julianne."

"Is she here?" he asked.

"No, I haven't seen her today."

"I saw her car outside."

"Is it?" Amanda looked to Davis curiously. "Maybe she's over at the house then."

"I'll just go clean up," he told them, and the *ps-ps-ps* of their whispers followed him all the way down the hall toward his bedroom.

As he dropped the saddlebag on the bench at the foot of the bed, the hum of his phone sounded once again. He turned away in defiance and went into the bathroom to splash warm water on his face and scrub his hands clean. When he returned, he stood in the middle of the room, straining his ears for the continued buzz to no avail. The phone had gone silent.

Will changed into gray sweatpants and a Bengals T-shirt before he finally sat down on the corner of the bed. He sighed as he emptied out the saddlebag and picked up his phone, staring at the blinking light. He sighed again as he depressed the voicemail key.

"You have five new messages," the robotic female announced. "First message."

"Hey, Will, it's me. I really need you. Call me, 'kay?"

Delete.

"Will? Where are you? I really need to talk to you, if you're up to it."

Delete.

"Will, it's Judd. Give me a ring, would you? There's been a shift in circumstances down here, and I'd like to talk to you about it, buddy."

The last thing Will could think about just then was another plug from Judd for moving to Lexington.

Delete.

"Will?" Julianne's unmistakable sniffles lassoed his full attention. "He dumped me. Are you there?"

He groaned softly, ashamed of himself, and made plans to head over to console her as he listened to the final message.

Delete.

Her stuffy nose and soft, vulnerable voice pricked something deep within Will as she stammered out her final message. "I . . . I need to get . . . out of here for a while. I think I'll take off . . . for . . . a bit. I guess I'll just . . . s-see you tomorrow."

Part of him felt almost angry. This ditch digger had appeared out of nowhere one day, just stalked down the middle of the street toward Julianne and *saved a dog*. That type of thing—rescuing an animal!—acted as her undoing every time. Had he somehow known it and manipulated her? No, of course not, Will forced himself to admit. There had been no master plan in the whole series of events beyond the cruel twist of fate that he'd answered that ridiculous ad she'd placed on the very day that Will had screwed up the resolve to tell Julianne—at long last—how he felt about her. How he'd always felt about her.

And after the ditch digger had unwittingly dragged Will along behind him that first fateful day, through the rain, bumping along on the pot-holed concrete of Seventh Street, or wherever she'd been when she saw him, now he'd gone and done the unthinkable—at least to almond-eyed hopeful romantic Julianne. Just as Will had feared, he had broken her heart.

Will dialed Julianne's number and tapped his foot as he awaited her reply.

"Hey, Will."

"Hi. I just got your message. Are you all right?"

"I guess. Disappointed. Embarrassed. But all right."

"Where are you?" he asked her.

"I'm out on The Log."

"Sit tight. I'm on my way."

Even as the maiden dangled over the cliff's edge,
she felt certain that her prince would arrive at any moment
to fight off the dragon and deliver her to safe ground.

"Here!" someone called out to her,
and she looked up and saw that it wasn't her prince at all.
"Take hold of this lifeline!"

"No!" she growled back at him.
"Get out of here. Can't you see I'm waiting for
my prince to save me?"

# 16

**Will grabbed his** wallet and keys, and he tucked them and his iPhone into the pocket of his pants as he jogged down the hallway.

"Where's the fire, Son?" Davis asked from the kitchen table.

"Sorry. I need to run out. I'll be back in an hour or two."

Before his dad or Amanda could make any further inquiries, Will rushed out the door. He ran down the driveway and along the curve of the street, waving to the Nethertons as he passed them. He picked up some real momentum on his way down the slope of Jackpine Court. Cutting across the Weylons' lawn and weaving between the two properties at the end of the cul-de-sac, he recalled the snow day of their sixth grade year when he and Julianne had discovered Jackpine's *High Ten* status on Julianne's sledability scale.

With all of the roads steeped in snow overnight, none of the city plows had been able to reach them, so they'd grabbed their sleds and started out from the top of Will's driveway. Julianne screamed bloody murder as she bumped along the curve, flew straight down Jackpine Court and through the Weylons' yard. Will's hot pursuit brought her into view just as her sled took temporary flight and zoomed across Lakeridge Drive, down the hill, and twenty yards out onto the frozen lake before coming to an eventual stop.

Will shook the memory from his head as he leapt over the ditch and thumped across Lakeridge, spotting her as he managed the challenges of the hill that led down to Winton Lake. She sat slumped over on the tree trunk that had fallen out into the lake so many years ago, her feet dangling just inches above the water.

When she peered up at him, her face looked a little like a punching bag, all red and swollen from who-knew-how-many hours of crying out there on The Log.

Will navigated the trunk like a balance beam until he reached her, and he cautiously lowered himself and sat down beside her. He reached both arms out toward her and, with a weary smile, Julianne leaned over, collapsed into his arms, and sighed.

"I'm so sorry, Jules."

As they sat there quietly, the music of Winton Lake lulled them. A flock of ducks paddled past in a straight line, the leader quacking orders like a web-footed platoon leader. Behind them, on the trail concealed by trees, horses' hooves clacked along at a slow walk. A car on Lakeridge Drive at the top of the hill gave them a short clip of a song from its radio before it faded into the distance.

*A Whole New World* by Peebo Bryson and Regina Belle.

Will recalled that it had been Julianne's favorite song the summer that it came out to coincide with one of the Disney movies. She played it so many times that he still remembered almost every lyric all these years later, in spite of his best efforts back then *not* to know them. He could still hear her off-key crooning as she reveled in the duet that represented every high school girl's fantasy of the happy ending that love would eventually bring. And while Julianne sang along with it all summer long, Will's teenaged angst inspired him to play a different song, one that never failed to tickle his soul with reminders every time he heard it, or even thought about it.

Jon Secada's *Angel.* Will's personal heart song back then—the anthem for every guy pining for something that he almost had, but lost. Two beats of those opening violins could shove him back there again, even now.

Twenty years had come between then and now, but Will knew his feelings hadn't changed much beyond the general maturity that came with time. However, he knew one thing now more certainly than he'd ever known it back then: He had to tell her how he felt.

"Jules," he said, and it sounded a little like a croak to him, so he cleared his throat. "Listen. I want to tell you something."

"I know," she said, nuzzling against his shoulder.

He wanted to laugh. Smiling, he assured her, "I don't think you do."

She lifted her head and looked at him with a sleepy smile that said she thought she knew him inside and out, that there were no surprises left between them, that he hadn't had a single feeling that she didn't understand or know about.

"Sure I do," she said as she glanced down at her dangling feet. "You're going to tell me that I got stars in my eyes when I saw Paul, that it wasn't really a sign, and that he wasn't really my Prince Charming after all."

Her mournful gaze lit a fire under Will's lips and he couldn't help but smile.

"I think I just really wanted him to be the one, you know?" She tucked a lock of honey hair behind her ear and shrugged. "I'm so sick of people pointing out that I can't hang on to a man long enough to have a real relationship, Will. I mean, I think it hurts so much because . . . it's *true*."

"It's not."

"It is, Will. And I was really excited to maybe walk into that gala with someone like Paul Weaver on my arm so everyone in the room could see that I not only managed to keep a relationship going for more than a few dates, but I snagged a twelve on the one-to-ten meter!"

"You think he's a twelve?" he murmured. "What's that make me?" After a moment, he sighed and added, "What do you care what people say anyway? Is it Lacey? When did you hand over all the power to Lacey?"

She shrugged again and fell silent, mindlessly scraping the bark of the tree trunk between them with her fingernail.

A sudden thought on how to advance the conversation tickled his funny bone. "And you know," he said with a chuckle, "I know a way to really frost Lacey's cookies . . . because you have something that she, for whatever reason, seems to really want."

She gazed up at him, and Will noticed that either the early evening sunlight or sheer emotion had glazed her blue eyes with brushstrokes of green. "What do I have that Lacey wants? . . . Besides you."

He threw his arms out to both sides in a dramatic sweep. "Duh!" When she didn't seem to understand, he puffed out a sigh. "Why don't I take you to the gala. I'll be your date."

Julianne curled her face into the most insulting form of disappointment. "What's that going to prove? Everyone sees you as my backup catcher anyway. Walking into that ballroom with you as my date just says, 'Look, she couldn't find anyone else, so here she is again with Old Faithful.'"

Will wondered if she could *actually hear* her own scorching words; or for that matter, could she hear the high-pitched sound he made as he deflated?

Old Faithful? Like a pair of stained, torn jeans that everyone thinks you should toss, but no one has the heart to tell you?

"Not that I don't really appreciate the offer," she added, rubbing his hand. "You're the best."

"I *really* am," he stated bitterly.

"Besides, I came up with the germ of an idea before you arrived. At first, I thought it was just insanity finding a voice inside my head . . . but the more I think about it, the more I think it might be kind of genius."

"Do tell."

"I know there's no chance of Paul changing his mind about us. He was pretty clear about there not being anything between us to build upon." She clicked her tongue and sighed. "But that doesn't change the fact that just one more date with him to the gala would at least make me feel better . . . you know . . . in front of my peers."

"Jules . . ."

"No, hear me out, Will. I think I might be able to convince him

164

to go out with me just one more time and be my date for that one evening. I'm going to—"

"Jules, really. I don't think . . ."

"—offer to pay him!"

". . . you should . . . I'm sorry. You want to what?"

"I'm going to offer to pay him to escort me to the gala!"

"Pay him."

"Genius, right?" And the way she sat there grinning at him made Will question his hearing. And how he felt . . .

"That's not the word I would choose."

"I'll cover the cost of his tuxedo rental, and I'll pay him for his time—"

"Like a paid *escort*."

"Sort of. But with no expectation of anything more, of course."

"Julianne."

"I think he'll do it, Will. I really do. I mean, he was willing to go to dinner with me after he'd just dumped me. Surely, he'll—"

"Ah, Jules." Will shifted his leg and turned completely toward her, gripping the side of the tree trunk for balance. Indignation flaring his nostrils, he exclaimed, "Have you lost your mind? Really. I want to know. Have you gone completely out of your gourd?"

"What do you mean?"

"What do I mean?" he repeated slowly, and he pushed himself upward until he stood on both feet. He navigated the trunk toward the shore, muttering. "What do I mean? She wants to know what I mean?"

"Will. Where are you going?"

Once he reached terra firma, he turned back and gawked at her. "Where am I going?"

"Stay here and talk to me," she said. "Tell me what you think is so wrong with paying Paul to—"

"Don't!" he interrupted. Will raised both hands, violently motioning for silence. "Stop talking, Julianne. Right now, just stop talking!" *I may need to rethink everything.*

165

And with that, he turned and stomped up the hill, across Lake-ridge Drive, and toward the Weylons' backyard.

●   —   ●   —   ●

"Have you lost your mind?"

"Why do people keep asking me that!" Julianne cried.

"Uh," Suzanne snorted, "maybe because you've obviously *lost your mind*?!"

"Come on, Suz. I thought for sure I could count on you to give me a little support."

"Julianne. Are you kidding me here? You couldn't have prayed about this. You're asking me to support you in a crazy scheme to *pay* the guy who just broke up with you to be your *date* to a formal gala when the very reason he gave for breaking up with you was that he doesn't enjoy *formality*."

Julianne deflated. "Well, when you say it like that—"

"Like . . . what? Reasonable?"

Suzanne's blue parakeet bobbed his head and chirped sweetly before he resumed his dance back and forth across the slope of Julianne's shoulder. "You understand, don't you, Gus?"

He whistled out a happy, affirmative reply.

"Julianne, you cannot do this."

"He's going to say yes, Suz."

"Even if, by some remote possibility, he actually does agree," she implored, "this just can't end any way other than badly."

"Why? It's not like I have any delusions about him dating me for real again."

"Only about making other people think he will. Aren't you the person who wouldn't go with me to a fashion show that you felt was too risqué for . . . what did you call it? . . . *the sake of appearances*?"

Julianne sighed. "When I saw him walking down the middle of the road with that dog in his arms, heading straight for me, I . . . I really thought it was a sign from God, Suz. I felt like that was my future walking toward me."

"You want a long-lasting relationship out of that one minute in time? Then go adopt the dog. Don't waste five hundred dollars on a momentary flash in the pan. It's one night, Julianne."

Julianne frowned at her friend before answering her ringing phone. "This is Julianne."

"Hi, it's Phoebe."

"Hey, Phoebe. What's up?"

"We have a bit of a situation here at the office."

"You're still there? Phoebe, it's after seven."

"I stayed after hours to clean the place and get ready for to-morrow morning's photo shoot," she rattled. "But the thing is . . . I was in the conference room dusting, and I heard something out in the reception area, and I went to check it out. That's when—"

"Is that Julianne?" a man shouted in a shrill yet vaguely famil-iar voice. "You tell her to get over here right now!"

"Phoebe, who is that?"

"It's Mr. Winters," she said, followed by a scuffle for the phone.

"Julianne? Julianne, you need to get over here to the office right now," Rand railed at her through the receiver.

"Rand, what's going on?" she asked, and Julianne popped to her feet, prompting Gus into taking immediate flight from her shoulder to Suzanne's. "You're scaring Phoebe."

"Look," he ranted between what sounded like clenched teeth, "I need you here right now, or there might not be time to talk to you before they come for me."

"Before who comes for you?" she asked him. With a gasp, she added, "Rand, what have you done? Did you shoot the new pig? Tell me you didn't—"

"It's not about pigs, Julianne! Please, just come over here right now."

Further scuffle ensued, and she had a hard time keeping up with what might be going on. The phone seemed to drop to the floor before she heard a muffled ruckus in the background. She could barely make out what came next.

"Randall Winters, you have the right to remain silent. Anything you say can and will be used against you in a court of law. You have the right to an attorney . . ."

"I have one," Rand shouted. "She's on the phone right now."

"Phoebe? Hello?" Julianne exclaimed. "Are you there?"

"Hang on," Phoebe said. "The officer's going to talk to you."

A moment later, "This is Officer Steve Lambright. Who is this?"

"Julianne Bartlett. I'm Mr. Winters's attorney. Can you tell me what's going on?" she asked.

"We're arresting him."

"Arresting him? On what charge?"

"Attempted murder, ma'am."

"Murder! Attempted murder . . . *of a person*?"

"Yes, ma'am. If you'd like to meet us at the station, we should have him processed within the hour."

A moment later, Rand's objections faded into the background and Phoebe came back to the line. "What should I do?"

"Call Will. Tell him what's happened and that I'm going to the police station to find out what I can. I'll call him afterward to fill him in."

"Okay."

She heard a slight quiver in her assistant's voice. "Phoebe? Are you all right?"

"Yes."

"Are you sure?" Julianne asked her. "Because you don't sound all right."

"No, I'm okay. I just thought . . . I didn't know why they were here, and I . . . It startled me, you know? I'm fine. I'll finish up here and have things ready for your interview and photographer tomorrow."

"You're wonderful, Phoebe."

"No. I'm really not."

"You are. And when you get Will on the phone, remind him about tomorrow, okay?"

"Sure."

# 17

**Julianne cracked** open the lid and sniffed the carton of cottage cheese.

"Ohh!" she groaned, and she sealed the lid over the mess before tossing it into the trash bag in her hands.

"Jules, what are you doing?" Will asked.

"I'm cleaning out my refrigerator," she told him. "It's like something out of a terrifying science experiment."

"Could you please just focus on this call, and tell me what happened with Rand?"

"Can you imagine if that ruckus would have happened at the office tomorrow instead of today?" she cried. "*Queen City Magazine* and their photographers there just in time to catch Rand Winters being arrested in our front office!"

Will sighed. "Jules. What led up to his arrest?"

"Hey, do you know how long you can safely keep a dozen eggs after the sell-by date? Is six months too long?" Just in case, she tossed the carton of eggs as well. "He was assigned a smash-and-grab last year," she explained while trying to pry a jar of grape jelly from the spot where it had dried to the top shelf. "The guy didn't like how it went. He served six months, and a few hours after he was released from lockup, he shows up at Rand's house."

"I told you about the dangers of working as a public defender, didn't I?"

"Well, they get into an altercation, Castillo pushes his way into the house. While Rand goes for his gun, Castillo spots his wallet and takes it. He runs from the house, Rand chases him. . . ."

"Oh, no."

"Yep. Shot the guy right outside the house on the sidewalk. I'm just glad Emily wasn't there to see it."

"What is wrong with Rand Winters, Jules? A guy like that should not be allowed to own a gun."

"If only the Emily Aldens of the world ruled our society," she remarked just as the jelly jar finally broke loose, and she let out a little squeal as it did.

"What was that?"

"Grape jelly," she replied. "So the arraignment is tomorrow morning, but I've got my photo shoot and interview at the office at eleven. Any chance you can cover it for me?"

"Yeah, sure. But don't hold it against me if I ask the court to deny bail? I'm thinking Rand is a danger to himself. Maybe some time in a cell will keep him out of trouble for a few minutes."

Julianne giggled. "You're still grumpy."

"I am not grumpy."

"Yes, you are. Are you mad at me?"

He took a moment before answering. "I'm not mad. Just a little disgusted."

"Disgusted!" she exclaimed, and she paused to inspect a plastic container filled with fuzzy white strawberries. "What a thing to say to me."

"You're paying a guy to be your date so you don't have to let me escort you. What does that make me? Lower than an *escort*?"

"Well, he hasn't agreed yet, so hold that thought," she replied, dropping the berries into the trash bag.

"Ohhh, no you don't, my friend!" he said, and she imagined him shaking his finger in her face. "If you think I'm going to be your backup last resort *ever* again, you are sadly mistaken. If this guy has the good sense to turn you down, you're all on your own, Julianne. Do you hear me?"

"Yes. I hear you," she said as she scrubbed the sticky jam off the glass shelf.

"Yes, but do you really hear me?"

Taking her head out of the fridge, Julianne replied, "I hear you, Will. I hear you. I just don't believe you. You'd never leave me twisting."

"No? Be assured, Julianne. My days as your consolation prize are over. O.V.E.R. Over." He paused and said it again. "*Over*. Got it?"

"Yeah, yeah, okay. . . . So I'll see you at the office after the arraignment? She may want you to give her a quote about how amazing I am for the article." Will's silence elicited a chuckle out of Julianne and she sang, "I love you, Will."

"Mm-hmm, I wonder," he mumbled as he hung up.

She pushed the button on the Bluetooth draped over her ear and then tossed the earpiece to the counter. The evening's refrigerator adventure had begun with her growling stomach, and she'd gone foraging for a late snack only to discover the sad state of affairs inside her pretty stainless steel Frigidaire.

Once she'd deposited the bag into the garbage can outside the back door, she returned to the kitchen and poked her head inside the open freezer.

A bin full of ice . . . a graying package of ground beef . . . three bags of frozen broccoli . . . a Lean Cuisine from 2009 . . . and a package of chocolate peanut butter cups. She removed the candy and tore open the wrapper.

*Frozen chocolate is better than no chocolate at all*, she decided, and she bit into one of the iced-over candies with a hard crunch that almost hurt her teeth.

●　—　●　—　●

"We've just taken on a big corporate client," Julianne said, "and that will keep us fairly busy. And of course we're in the midst of building our list of individual clientele."

"So for a relatively new law practice," Melanie Larsen summarized, "you're doing well already."

"They say it takes the first year to become established, so we don't have any false sense of security or anything. We're still in the growth phase, but Will and I both feel pretty confident that we made this decision at the right time."

"Well, that about does it for the interview portion," Melanie said with a rehearsed smile. "My photographer, Jasper, is all set up in your office to get some shots of you behind your desk. While he does that, I'm going to stay here and clean up my notes, and maybe have another coffee and one of these delicious biscotti."

"Help yourself to the fruit as well," Julianne offered as she unfolded from the chair and glided around the conference room table.

"Thanks so much, Julianne."

She joined Jasper in her office and settled into her desk chair while he adjusted the portable light stands.

"Let's get something nice and professional," he suggested. "Do you wear glasses?"

"No," she replied, and he clicked his tongue in a way that made her want to apologize for her 20/20 vision.

"All right then. How about you lean forward slightly, arms propped on the desk." She did as he asked, and his photographer's eye bore down on her like a butcher checking out the cow on the meat hook.

Jasper's long brown hair was tucked neatly behind his ears and pulled back into a loose ponytail. His faded denim jeans were clean but well-worn, and the tails of his black denim shirt hung loose, the sleeves rolled up to the elbows.

"Very pretty," he remarked, and he began clicking away. "Chin up slightly? . . . Nice! . . . The color of your eyes is really spectacular. You have a real sparkle."

She imagined this to be pretty typical photographer-speak in an effort to get the subject to relax and lean into their confidence a bit more; and it was working, too. For those first eight minutes, at least; before the commotion erupted in the front office.

"Jasper," Melanie said as she pushed her head through the opening in the doorway. "Bring your camera, quick! You've got to catch this." Jasper headed past her into the reception area, and Melanie turned back and looked at Julianne. One corner of her mouth quirked as she said, "You'd better come, too."

She rushed around the desk and hurried out of her office to find Phoebe standing there, her hands behind her back as a uniformed police officer snapped handcuffs into place while Jasper snapped away, capturing every movement.

". . . can and will be used against you in a court of law. You have the right to an attorney . . ." She recognized the policeman as the arresting officer who had testified in one of her final cases as public defender.

"What's going on here?" Julianne demanded. "You're handcuffing my assistant?"

"Sorry, Ms. Bartlett," Officer Peck said with a shrug. "I'm just serving the arrest warrant."

"What are the charges?" she asked with a groan as she pressed her hand in front of Jasper's camera lens. "Melanie, please!"

"Fraud," he stated, leading a tearful Phoebe toward the door. "Let's go."

"Phoebe, don't say anything to anyone. I'm right behind you."

Melanie and Jasper exchanged glances before Melanie muttered, "Oh, this is too good."

Glaring at her, Julianne nudged Jasper toward the door. "You have to go. Now!"

"My lights . . ."

"You can come back and get them later," she said, grabbing her purse from the hook inside her office door. "Go on, both of you. I've got to get to the police station."

"Just let me drag them—" Jasper shoved his camera at Melanie before he rushed into her office and wrapped his arms around the lights, yanking them through reception "—out into the hall so I can take them down properly."

The minute all three of them made it to the corridor, Julianne pulled the door shut and locked it.

"I'm sorry," she offered halfheartedly as she poked the elevator button again and again until the door slid open. "It's not usually like this. Please don't—"

"Go," Melanie said with the nod of her head.

All the way down to the lobby, Julianne paced inside her small enclosure, imagining a handcuffed Phoebe gracing the cover of the May issue of *Queen City Magazine*.

When she finally made it to her car, she simultaneously turned the key in the ignition and dialed Will on her iPhone. His voice mail kicked in as she threw the gear into reverse.

"Will, it's me. I hope your day is going better than mine," she said on a groan. "You're probably still tied up at the arraignment for Rand, but you sure have missed a truckload of action at the office. Right in the middle of my photo shoot, our assistant was arrested on fraud charges. I'm on the way to the police station now. Call me when you get this, huh?"

Julianne tried to imagine Phoebe committing fraudulent acts of any kind. What on earth could have led police to believe her sweet, twenty-year-old angel-faced assistant could be guilty of fraud? More important, how could Phoebe have brought this sort of past infraction into the law offices with her?

"Attorney Julianne Bartlett," she stated to the officer on duty. "For my client, Phoebe Trent."

"Sign here."

By the time they led Phoebe into the stark gray room and she collapsed to the metal chair across the stainless steel table from Julianne, her eyes had swollen so much that the girl was hardly recognizable. Mascara streaks formed deep scoops beneath her bloodshot eyes, and her hair looked as if patches of it stood on end.

"Julianne, I'm . . . so . . . sorry," she meted out.

Julianne handed her a fresh tissue and, as Phoebe blew her nose, Julianne leaned across the table and looked her squarely in the eye. "What is this all about? And don't tell me any half-truths or leave anything out, do you understand me? We said there would be no more deception, didn't we? I need to know the truth, Phoebe."

She nodded, dropping the crumpled tissue to the tabletop.

"The report says you stole checks from someone you worked for, wrote them to yourself, and cashed them. Did you do that?"

Phoebe's eyes welled up with tears again. "Yes."

"More than eight thousand dollars?"

She nodded. "Yes."

"Why did you do that, Phoebe?"

"I had to."

Julianne sighed. "A person has to do a lot of things, but steal someone else's money isn't one of them."

"I had to get out of Arizona."

"You're from Arizona?"

"Yes."

"Did you ever actually work in Florida like your résumé says?"

"No."

Julianne swallowed hard and considered her next question. "What were you running from?"

"My husband."

Over the next hour, a sad and frightening tale of abuse and fear unfolded. At the end of it, Phoebe had used the stolen money to escape to the last place she thought anyone might look for her, to a place she'd seen on the evening news: Cincinnati, Ohio. She'd been living a cash-only lifestyle ever since, sleeping in her car six days a week and renting a cheap motel with a shower every Sunday night.

"I'm going to see if I can get you arraigned today so you don't have to spend the night in jail," Julianne told her.

"Thank you."

"I can't promise you I can do it. But I'm going to try."

"Thank you," she repeated without lifting her eyes to meet Julianne's.

"Think about this very carefully before you answer me, Phoebe, because I need the absolute truth. Okay?"

She nodded tentatively, wringing her hands as she waited.

"Have you ever been in trouble with the law before?"

"No," Phoebe answered immediately.

"Never."

"Never. I promise."

"I don't like surprises," she warned. "So you need to tell me if there's anything else I need to know. Like . . . is Phoebe Trent your real name?"

She smiled slightly. "Yes."

"And you've never killed anyone?" Phoebe's eyes popped open wide, and Julianne chuckled. "I'm joking. Just relax, and I'll see what I can do, okay?"

She heaved a shaky sigh and nodded. "Thank you. Really."

Julianne gathered her purse and paperwork and knocked on the locked door. "You sure did liven up my interview this morning."

Phoebe's face curled into a clenched fist as she collapsed into both hands, sobbing.

Julianne hurried back to her and rubbed her shoulder. "Okay, cut it out. I'm sorry. I was just trying to cut the tension with a little humor. Stop crying, Phoebe. It's going to be okay. We're going to sort through this."

# 18

"**I have a friend** in the district attorney's office," Julianne said as she plopped tea bags into two mugs of hot water. "He called the prosecutor in Maricopa County where the charges were filed. The agreement is that you'll make full restitution and I'll oversee two hundred hours of community service here in Cincinnati."

Phoebe crumpled like a wax figure near a flame and sobbed. Julianne hurried around the kitchen counter and slipped her arms around the girl.

"What is it?"

"Now he'll know where to find me," she said, sniffling. "He'll know where I am."

"That's not going to happen."

"You don't know what kind of person he is," she interrupted. "You don't know what he's capable of, Julianne."

"But the State of Arizona does."

Phoebe looked like a child just awakened from a bad dream, convinced that the monster still lurked beneath the bed.

"The district attorney's office tells me your husband was indicted on a whole slew of charges. He's been incarcerated for a period not less than five years."

Julianne couldn't do anything except stand back and watch as Phoebe's emotions swept over her and carried her away. She crumpled, sobbing, and Julianne slipped her arms around the girl and spoke softly.

"It's going to be okay, Phoebe. I promise. You're going to be okay."

She lifted her drenched and reddened face. "I'm . . . so . . . relieved."

"I know. I know."

"And you know . . . I always intended to pay back the money, but I just have never been able to save up that much. It's not like I could start making payments without them finding out where I was, you know? I don't know how I can pay back eight thousand dollars, but I'll figure it out somehow. I can give them the two thousand I have saved up. I can't thank you enough for everything you've done for me, Julianne."

Julianne grabbed several tissues from the box on the counter and dabbed Phoebe's tear-drenched face as she smiled at her. "Two thousand is a great start. And I wired them the money this afternoon, so you'll pay me back out of your salary."

Phoebe looked as if she might choke. "You're going to let me keep my job?"

"Of course. Will and I have no hope of survival without you. Don't you know that by now?"

She shook her head and stammered, no real message emerging.

"Here's what's going to happen. You're going to move out of your car and into my guest room."

"No!" she objected, but Julianne took a firm grip on her wrist.

"Yes," she corrected softly. "You'll work at the office during the week, and on Saturdays you'll work off your community service at a few of my favorite charities. I'll deduct one hundred dollars from your paycheck every week toward the restitution and, when it's paid off, you'll start looking for somewhere to live. There will be no more sleeping in your car. Do you understand?"

Phoebe didn't look like she understood anything at all, but she nodded anyway.

"I'll cover your room and board until you can get on your feet, and tomorrow we'll go to the bank and start checking and savings accounts for you," she continued. Julianne rubbed the back of her hand. "This might all have happened exactly the way it was supposed to, Phoebe. You're getting a whole new start, so let's work together to make sure you take full advantage of it, okay?"

A fresh stream of tears plunged down Phoebe's face as she nodded.

"Why?" she asked Julianne. "Why are you doing all this?"

"Don't you know?"

Her brow furrowed, and she shook her head.

"Because I adore you," she told her. "And I think this is what you do when someone you love is in trouble. Now what do you like in your tea? Sugar or honey?"

"I have no idea," she admitted, and they both laughed at that.

When her cell phone rang, Julianne slid one of the mugs toward Phoebe as she answered it.

"This is Julianne."

"Julianne. It's Paul Weaver."

Her stomach took a dive down to her knees, and she swallowed hard around the sudden lump.

"Paul. Thank you for calling me back."

"Sure."

A man of so few words.

"Well," she finally said, "I was wondering if I could ask a favor of you."

Julianne grabbed her tea and a sweater. She gave Phoebe a quick nod before heading through the kitchen door to the glass-enclosed porch on the back of her small condo.

"What kind of favor?"

She set her cup on the small glass table next to the overstuffed chair in the corner before slipping into her sweater and sitting down.

"A sort of unorthodox one," she said. "But I hope you'll let me explain."

"Have at it," he replied.

"When we were going out, I'd been kind of hoping I could get you to be my date to a big gala at the end of the month."

"Ohh," he groaned. "I told you how I hate those things."

"I know, I know. And we're not dating anymore, so you don't have to worry about that so much, right?" He didn't answer, aside from the subtle sniff she heard on the other end of the line. "The thing is, Paul . . . this one is kind of special. I've been nominated for Person of the Year by the Bar Association. I have a pretty good shot at winning, too."

"Congratulations, Julianne."

"Thanks. The thing is . . . you're the only man I've dated for a while now, and I really hate the idea of going unescorted on my big night. I mean, you can understand that, right?"

Slow to respond, he finally inched it out. "I . . . guess."

"Paul, I would be so embarrassed to go alone. Would you consider one last date with me to save me from complete humiliation?"

The long pause told her that he needed further incentive.

"Look, I know this kind of evening is way out of your comfort zone. I get that, I really do. But I would be willing to pay for your tux rental, and even pay you for your time if—"

"What, like a paid escort!?" he exclaimed. "Are you kidding me?"

"Please don't be offended," she countered. "I just really—"

"Oh, I'm not offended, exactly," he replied.

"You're . . . not?"

"No. Just surprised. Really, really surprised."

Julianne felt pretty certain that her humiliation trumped his surprise, times ten.

"I would think someone like you could get any one of those uppity types you know to take you, for free."

Running her ringed thumb around the rim of her cup of tea, Julianne realized that the heat rising over her neck and face put the temperature of her tea to shame.

"I wouldn't ask you if I wasn't really . . ."

"Desperate?" he finished for her.

"Well. Yeah. Desperate for an escort, but also not just any escort, Paul."

His laughter caught her off guard. "You mean you're willing to pay for someone you can feel good about showing off to your hoity-toity friends."

Julianne shrugged. "Kinda."

"How much would an escort as pretty as me be worth out there on the social market?"

She cringed. "Let's say . . . five hundred dollars?"

After a long silence, Paul asked, "Can I think about it?"

"Of course. But you'll want to get measured for a tux really soon. There's only two weeks before the gala."

"The gala," he repeated. "It even sounds like something unbearable."

Biting her tongue, she forced a friendly smile to her voice. "But I'll try to make it more fun for you than the usual."

"How *much* more fun?"

She narrowed her eyes and frowned. "Not *that* much more fun . . . but it is just one night, after all."

"I'll call you at the end of the week," he conceded.

"Great." With a sigh, she added, "I really would appreciate this, Paul."

"Yeah. I sense the desperation. I'll call you in a couple of days."

She grabbed her tea and headed inside to find Phoebe curled up in the corner of the sofa clutching her cup with both hands. Julianne sank into the other corner and groaned.

"It's finally happened."

"What did?" Phoebe asked.

"I have sunk lower than I thought possible."

"I don't believe that."

"*Oh*, you can believe it," she assured her. "I just offered to pay someone to take me out."

Phoebe's eyes rounded wide. "No."

"Oh yeah. I did."

"The guy with the toolbox?"

"Yep."

"It didn't work out like you planned?"

"It did not."

"I am . . . so . . . sorry."

"Not as sorry as me. I'm as sorry as they come."

Julianne replayed that moment when she'd first seen Paul coming toward her. The events of just one random rainy morning had brought her to this; she'd gone from thinking Paul Weaver was the manifestation of that happy ending she'd been dreaming about since the dawn of time—all the while ignoring the fact, of course, that they had nothing at all in common—to actually offering to pay him to take her out and *fake it*.

Suzanne's words sang back to her: *"You want a long-lasting relationship out of that one minute in time? Then go adopt the dog."*

"Do you like dogs, Phoebe?"

"Love them. Why?"

"What would you think about a third roommate?"

●　⸺　●　⸺　●

Will set the plate of scrambled eggs in front of his father while taking a sip of coffee.

"Pop, can I get you anything else before I hit the road?"

"Go on, be on your way," Davis replied. "I can still eat some eggs on my own."

Will smiled at his dad and ruffled his full head of wavy silver hair. "I've got a meeting with a potential client this morning." He drained the last of the coffee and set the cup into the stainless steel sink. "Keep a positive thought, huh? Jules and I could really use a few monthly retainers to lean on."

"Especially if you're going to take care of all the strays that keep on turning up on your door," his father quipped.

Will chuckled as he tucked his iPhone into the breast pocket of his suit. "Oh, you heard about our administrative genius's criminal

184

arrest, did you?"

"Mandy says Julianne has taken the girl in. She's going to live with her."

"Is she?"

He knew about the deal Julianne had negotiated for Phoebe, but he had no idea she'd taken her in as well. Wondering how much they still didn't know about their assistant, he grabbed his briefcase.

"It's not really surprising, is it?" Davis said with a shrug. "She's been rescuing cats and dogs and birds and squirrels ever since she came out of the womb. Remember that little fawn she tried to drag into her bedroom with her?"

Will guffawed at the memory. The fawn had an injured leg and Julianne's father had agreed to move the car out into the snow and let her nurse it for a few days in the garage. But rather than leave it out there alone on such a cold night, twelve-year-old Julianne had put a collar and leash on the thing and tried to bring it up to her bedroom with the promise of a block of cheese and a dish of milk. The animal had broken every lamp and knickknack between the front door and the stairs before her father came to the rescue of the rest of the Bartlett home.

"She's just moved on to humans, that's all," his father added.

Will considered his dad's words as he drove to the office. Was Phoebe just an extension of that charitable heart of Julianne's? He tried to imagine what had led to opening her door to the girl. Didn't she have a home of her own?

"Good morning," he said when he walked in and found Phoebe hard at work in front of the computer. "Good to see you."

"Good morning," she returned, and then she stood up and looked at him tentatively. "I just want to tell you how thankful I am that you've let me keep my job. I promise I won't make you regret it."

"I know you won't," he told her. "I'm happy Julianne could work things out for you. Is she in?"

"Yes."

Will gave her a smile as he crossed to Julianne's office and poked his head through the door to find her sprinkling fish food into Jonah's bowl. "Got a minute?"

"Sure," she said, returning his smile with a sparkling one of her own. "Come on in."

He closed the door behind him and sat down across from her. A metallic rattling drew his attention to the wall beneath the window where a large yellow dog wearing a massive plastic cone around its head struggled to its feet atop a padded green cushion. The dog limped toward him and sniffed his leg, resting the plastic cone on his knee as it stared up at him with soulful brown eyes.

"Uh. Jules? Who's this?"

"Will, meet Charming."

"Charming?" he repeated.

"As in Prince Charming. I have decided that this is the happily ever after God intended that day that I saw Paul."

"This is the dog he saved?"

"The very one."

"What's he doing here?"

"Well, he can't stay home alone until he's much stronger," she said, as if it were some sort of explanation.

"Ooo-kay . . ."

"Charming is my dog now."

Will leaned back into the chair with a sigh. "Of course he is." After giving the dog a cursory scratch under the chin, he shook his head and regrouped. "I've got an hour before Reynolds arrives. I think I may have him in the bag to put us on retainer for his publishing firm."

"Do you want me in on the meeting?"

"We'll see how it goes."

"Okay. Just give me a shout if you want me to come in."

"Will do," he replied. "What's this about you moving Phoebe into your house, Jules?"

"My mother has a very big mouth." Shaking her head, she

186

sighed. "Will, she's been living in her car all this time."

This revelation stopped him cold for a moment. "Are you serious?"

"Yes. Six nights a week, she sleeps there. And on Sundays, she rents a cheap room down in St. Bernard so she can get a shower and iron her clothes for the week," she explained. "It just about broke my heart."

Will shook his head. "She's lucky she sees Monday mornings in that neighborhood."

"I know it. So she's going to stay in my guest room until she gets the restitution paid off and can afford a place of her own."

"Julianne—"

"Don't even say it, Will!" she interrupted. "I'm not negotiable on this. It's a done deal."

He stood up slowly and rounded the corner of her desk, and the dog followed. Standing before her, he nodded. "Come here."

She rose from her chair tentatively and stared at him with wide and questioning eyes. Before she could assume anything else, Will pulled her to him and squeezed her in a full embrace while Charming pressed against his leg and nuzzled it.

"What's that for?" she asked, chuckling.

He drew back and placed his hands on both of her shoulders. Looking squarely into her crystal blue eyes, he said, "You've done a really good thing, Julianne."

She crumpled a little and grinned. "Really?"

"Really. I'm proud of you."

"You are?"

Will felt that old familiar warmth move through him as he looked at her. He longed to keep the cork on his emotions. *I must stay guarded and remember my resolve: My days as your consolation prize are over. O.V.E.R. Over.* His heart wanted to tell her how he felt, how he had always felt. But there in the office, with a potential client due at any time? Instead of opening the confession window and flying through it, Will simply smiled.

A rather unusual electricity seemed to spark as Julianne gazed back at him.

"Every now and then," he told her, "your heart just . . . bowls me over." Pushing her hair back from her face with his index finger and thumb, he smiled down at her. "Sometimes I forget how really . . . phenomenal you are, Jules. So filled up with love, and so kindhearted."

A nervous little giggle bubbled out of her as she pushed back from him suddenly. She clumsily collided with the corner of the desk before she straightened and made it back to her chair, folded in half, and dropped down into it. Twisting a lock of hair around her finger, she fidgeted with a pen and giggled again.

"Go on," she said, her brow furrowed and her little nose slightly wrinkled as she nodded toward the door. "Go get ready for that meeting and snag us a client before Phoebe and I have to start eating tuna and Ramen noodles every night."

● — ● — ●

"No, no, no, no, no."

Julianne didn't know how many times she'd uttered the same desperate syllable, but it didn't stop the train. Her arms folded across her chest, rocking back and forth in her desk chair, she continued to berate her own treasonous imagination in hushed, jaw-clenched objections as Charming stood next to her chair and stared up at her with an expression that told her he wanted to help.

"No. No, no . . . NO!"

On more than a few occasions over the years since she'd known him, Julianne had been surprised by that same sudden spark of attraction to Will that nearly claimed her good sense and clear thinking. This day was one of those times. As he'd hovered over her, looking at her with those exquisite brown eyes, touching her face and brushing away a stray lock of hair, telling her how special she was, how "phenomenal" . . . something had happened. Something magnetic and stirring. Something . . . so . . .

Wrong!

She'd come so traitorously close to forgetting everything about who they were and what their friendship meant, so close to just stretching her neck slightly and raising her lips to his. It had snuck up on her like a thief in the cover of darkness, and it felt so natural somehow, so . . . familiar.

Julianne wondered if she'd dreamt it, but in that moment she had so clearly known the matter-of-fact touch of Will's kiss. But how could that be? She hadn't kissed him in that way since their senior year of high school!

Or had she?

"No!" she admonished herself through clenched teeth. "No, no, no, no, no."

*Not going there. Not going there. Not with Will.*

Julianne raked her fingers through the roots of her hair, and she yanked in an effort to put the scalding and lingering desire for Will's kiss out of her mind. She'd been dateless for far too long, she decided. What she needed was a real one to put the whole concept of hypothetical romance into proper perspective! After all . . . Will?

*Come on, Julianne. Get it together.*

In the fraction of a second that it took for her office door to slip slowly open, she dropped her hands from cradling her aching head, forced her stark, wide eyes to a normal level of openness, and glued an awkward smile to her seared lips.

"You okay?" Will asked her as he poked his head through the opening.

"Yeah. Great. Never better. Why? Why do you ask? What's up? I'm fine."

He chuckled and one corner of his perfect mouth quirked. "All evidence to the contrary."

"Ah," she blurted in an effort to sound casual. Waving her hand and rolling her eyes slightly, she quipped, "Too many taquitos, I guess."

"Okay. Well, Reynolds is here. Can you stop in to say hello?"

"Give me five minutes."

He nodded and pulled the door shut. At the sound of the click of the latch, Julianne melted and collapsed into her big chair with a groan.

"No, Charming, no," she managed. "God, please help me. I need some perspective. But I think no is best—no way am I going to roughen our relationship, no, no, no, no."

The pretty yellow dog seemed to shrug at her before he stuck his tail between his legs, turned around, and made his way back to the dog bed under the window.

The maiden lay in the lush green grass on the hill
and peered up at the cloudless blue sky as she wondered,
How will I ever get my prince to notice me?

"Perhaps your search for love has led you astray,"
her fairy friend suggested from the tree branch just above her.

"No, that can't be true," the maiden insisted.
"I've followed all the signs, and they've led me straight to him."

"Hmm," her friend sang. "Then I should find him lolling at your
side, should I not? If you've followed all of the signs toward him,
why are you, once again, on the hillside alone?"

# 19

**"Mr. Reynolds,"** Julianne said with her most enchanting smile, "we're so happy to have the chance to meet with you today. Will tells me your company has had quite a growth spurt over the last year."

"If all goes well, we're just a few years from making the Fortune 1000," Zach Reynolds told her, and Will couldn't help noticing that their eyes stayed locked for just a few seconds past his own comfort zone.

"That's exciting," she said, and Zach hurried to his feet in time to pull out Julianne's chair. "Thank you. Omni Publishing might just put Cincinnati on the map."

"I'm pretty sure Cincinnati has done just fine in finding its way to the map without us. But speaking of businesses on the map, I'm happy to hear that Hanes has lured you away to the dark side."

"The dark side?" she asked, glancing at Will curiously.

"Now that you've left the public defender's office, are you ready to make some *real money* for your new firm, Julianne?"

She chuckled. "Always! Are you going to help us do that, Zach?"

"Well, I was on the fence until you walked in. But it can't hurt Omni to have a fresh-faced stunner like you on our payroll."

Will considered excusing himself so that he could hurl his breakfast into the trash can. Navigating the waters of this flirting between Julianne and Zach made him a little seasick.

"Hanes, why didn't you tell me that your law partner was this charming?" he exclaimed. "How can I consider any other firm now that I've fallen helplessly in love the way I have?"

Julianne slipped one leg over the other and leaned back with a sigh. "I'm pretty sure a company like Omni doesn't make the Fortune 1000 by succumbing to the influence of anything outside of solid business sense," she told him with confidence, and Will's faith took a step toward restoration. "But I'm sure Will has drawn a clear bottom line for you about who we are and what we can do for you. If you choose us based on that, I'll be convinced that you're even smarter than you look."

Zach chortled at her reply and smacked the desktop with his hand. "I love this girl, Hanes!"

Will shook his head and forced a smile. "I can see that."

"Let's start off with copyrights and see how the honeymoon phase goes for us, shall we?"

"I think that sounds like a good start," Will replied.

"In six months or a year, if we're still standing together, we'll talk about expansion."

"Us or Omni?" Julianne inquired.

"Both."

She smiled at Will, and he read the excitement in her subtle expression.

"What about lunch, Julianne?" Zach asked. "Have some with me?"

"I'm sorry, Zach," she said as she rose from the chair. "I'm tied up for the rest of the day. But let's set something up when we sign the contracts and collect a retainer from you. I'll bet Will can get the three of us a table at Boi Na Braza."

*Good girl.*

"Did you see that, Hanes?" Zach asked playfully. "Did you see how she shut me right down?"

"Nobody does it better," he replied, swallowing the deeper truth of the observation.

Julianne shook Zach's hand, thanked him in her most charming and enigmatic way, and quickly retreated to her office.

"Is she spoken for, Will?" Zach asked softly once she'd gone.

*I wish I knew*, he thought.

"Down, boy," Will said instead. "Let's keep our business businesslike, shall we?"

Zach didn't look as if he appreciated that answer, but he endured it just the same.

"Call me when you have your contracts in order."

"Next week. I will."

Will escorted Zach to the door. As he shook his hand, he noticed that Zach's eyes had diverted to Phoebe. He stood there for a moment, watching her fingers fly across the keyboard. She was clearly unaware of his scrutiny.

"How do you do it, Hanes? You're surrounded by some of the prettiest faces in the city."

"Yeah, that's just how I roll."

Zach laughed as he left, and Will gratefully closed the door behind him.

Phoebe didn't glance up from the monitor as she dryly commented, "Very genuine guy." Will guffawed at the observation.

The phone rang, and Phoebe picked it up. "Hanes & Bartlett Law Offices." Will had nearly reached his office door when he heard her add, "Yes, Mr. Weaver. If you'll hold a moment, I'll connect you."

*Paul Weaver. Calling to deliver his decision about taking Julianne to the gala, no doubt.*

"Paul Weaver on line one."

Will dallied in the doorway until he heard Julianne exclaim, "Oh, Paul! That's so great! Thank you so much. You're saving my life!"

He pushed the door shut behind him and dropped into his chair. Leaning both elbows on the edge of the desk, he closed his eyes and massaged his throbbing temples. She was really going to *pay* Paul to take her? Worse yet, he was going to let her? What sort of dude was he?

Will heaved a massive sigh, smacking his forehead a couple of times with a soft fist before he dialed the phone.

"Hi, Alison. It's Will . . . I was wondering if you're free on the twenty-third. Would you like to attend a black-tie gala with me?"

●   —   ●   —   ●

"Why on earth have you stayed away so long?" Amanda asked as she hugged Suzanne and rocked her from side to side. "Was it something we said?"

"Of course not," she replied, grinning at Julianne over her mother's shoulder. "You know how life just gets away with you."

"Well, I used to know."

Julianne snickered as she sat down next to Davis at his kitchen table. "Don't let her fool you. She has a busier social life than either of us. If she's not movin' and groovin', she's taking a sculpting or a weaving class, or she's volunteering down at the hospital."

"Amanda," Suzanne teased. "Are you a candy striper?"

"Oh, heavens no!" she cried. "That job is reserved for the young girls with all the energy."

"You have more energy than just about anyone I know," Davis told her.

"Will's out back grilling the turkey burgers and corn on the cob," Amanda announced. "Julianne, why don't you check on his progress so we can time it just right. I've got a few side dishes to heat up."

"I'll do that," Suzanne said as she placed her hands on Julianne's shoulders. "I want to say hello anyway."

"Mom, what can I do?" Julianne asked as Suzanne headed through the back door.

"Just sit there and keep Davis company while he slices up the tomatoes and onions, that's what. We'll be eating supper in two shakes."

Julianne reached over and grabbed a tomato slice. Davis pretended to slap at her, and she giggled as she popped it into her mouth and reached for her iPhone to check email.

"Where's your foster child tonight?" Davis asked. "I thought she'd come along so we could meet her."

"Phoebe?" Julianne laughed. "She's soaking in the bathtub and ordering a pizza for dinner."

"I guess there wasn't much tub-soaking in her life lately."

"No. Not much at all. You'll meet her soon though. I'll bring her around once she's all settled in and feeling comfortable."

Isaiah, the fat old cat Julianne and Will had rescued from a stream the summer before ninth grade, waddled into the kitchen and stood near Amanda, meowing.

"I dropped a slice of cheese two hours ago, and he keeps circling back, hoping I'll do it again," she told them. "Go on, Isaiah. Get out from underneath my feet."

"Tell me what ever happened with that Prince Charming of yours," Davis said as he cautiously chopped a big yellow onion.

"Paul?" she asked with a sigh, curling her leg underneath her and staring at the screen of her iPhone as she deleted a couple of spam emails from her inbox. "Oh, he's not really all that charming, as it turns out. Or else I'm not. It seems he's not interested in going out with me anymore."

"Well, he's a nitwit then."

"Aw!" She leaned over and pecked his cheek. "Thanks, Davis."

"Gotta be a nitwit to miss what you have to offer him."

Julianne shrugged one shoulder and reached over for a dill pickle spear to munch on. "He did agree to take me to the Bar Association gala, but after that we're kaput."

"Why on earth would you want to go with him then?" Amanda asked with her back to them, facing the stove. "If he doesn't want to date you anymore, I mean."

"Well, I can't go without a date, Mom."

"He's not the only date in the world, Julianne. Why couldn't you go with Will?"

"That's like wearing an old dress to the party," Davis remarked.

"Everyone's already seen that one. She needs a new one for a special occasion like this."

"As a matter of fact, Davis, just the other day, Will told me he was done being my 'consolation prize.' So, I couldn't ask him if I wanted to."

"Ah . . . I see."

Davis's face tilted downward as he concentrated on his work as Amanda's sous-chef, but Julianne couldn't help but wonder if he wasn't serving up a little sarcasm with his chopped and sliced condiments. She nibbled on another slice of tomato as she watched him, waiting for him to lift those mischievous blue eyes of his.

"Do we want some bleu cheese crumbles for the burgers?" Amanda asked them. "I brought some along just in case."

"Sounds dandy," Davis replied without glancing up.

● — ● — ●

"Why are you asking me about him?" Will asked as he flipped the turkey burgers. "You should ask Julianne."

"I just might do that," Suzanne replied. "But right now I'm asking you."

Will tossed a glare in her general direction before returning his attention to the grill. "Yes. He called and agreed to take her to the gala for the cool price of five hundred big ones."

"Five hundred dollars, Will," she repeated, shaking her head. "And the cost of his tuxedo, too!"

"Maybe she'll get lucky and find a discount coupon in the weekend paper."

"For him?" Suzanne asked with a chuckle. "Or the tux?"

He considered biting his tongue for letting the bitterness show in his tone.

"Man, she must really be hurting."

Will jerked toward her with a laugh. "Hurting! What do you mean by that?"

Suzanne sighed. "The way that legal crowd of yours treats her.

198

All those comments people make about a cute little thing like Julianne Bartlett not being able to hold on to a guy, how you're the only one that sticks, and only because you have to. Don't you think that cuts pretty deep after a while?"

Will shook his head and fidgeted with the spatula. "Well, I'm not attached to anyone either."

"You had Holly."

"For all the good—"

"She's terrified that they're right, Will."

He turned and looked at her, taken aback by the softness in Suzanne's eyes.

"Her pride can't take any more of it. She wants the fantasy. And if she can't catch ahold of it on her own, then she'll pay for it. Even lie about it, Will. I know you realize how far out of character that is for her, but she's doing it, even though it's just for one night."

"Then on Monday," he countered, "she's unattached again and facing the same sort of comments and looks and . . . whatever."

Suzanne leaned against the wooden railing and stared at him. He tried to look away, but he felt like a fish on a hook as she reeled him back again.

"Just tell her, you dope."

Her tone blended with the look in her eye to leave a stinging sensation at the back of Will's throat.

*Tell her what?* he wanted to ask, all indignant and surprised. But he didn't have the energy in him for the deception.

"Everyone knows except Julianne," she said softly.

"They do not," he managed, and he flicked the edge of one of the burgers with the tip of the spatula. "What are you talking about?"

"Look, you've had twenty years to come clean. Don't you think it's about time that you did? Before she finds another Paul, only for real this time?"

"You said everyone knows except Julianne. Why do you suppose she hasn't figured that out, Suzanne? Huh? In all these years, why does everyone in southern Ohio know how I feel except her?"

Suzanne smacked her thighs with both hands. "I don't know, Will. Maybe because you're *both* dopes?"

"She doesn't know—" Will said, and he took a moment to swallow before saying out loud the one thing he'd been most afraid of for those twenty years since they were kids "—because she doesn't *want to know.*"

Suzanne leaned forward and looked him squarely in the eye. "Can you both really be this delusional? You're going to lose it, Will. It's going to slip right through your fingers if you don't respect the gift that's been trying to come your way. Come clean with each other."

He tossed the spatula next to the grill and spat out a laugh. "What, you're trying to tell me she feels the same way? I don't think so, Suzanne."

After a moment of silence, Suzanne pushed herself upright and headed for the back door. Pivoting toward him, she softly said, "Don't be an idiot, Will. Timing is everything, and yours is all but up."

Before she could turn the knob, the door burst open and Julianne flew out to the deck, waving her phone at him as she shouted, "Will! Will, look at this! It's on the home screen of CincyBiz.com."

He peered down at the screen and groaned at the headline: *New Local Law Firm Forgets to Check Closet for Skeletons.*

The photo beneath showed a pale and handcuffed Phoebe, Julianne behind her with her mouth wide open as she raged at the arresting officer.

"We're hosed," she exclaimed.

And Will couldn't disagree.

# 20

"It turns out that *Queen City Magazine* owns the Website," Will explained to Julianne and Phoebe. "And since the reporter and photographer were here by permission, they didn't violate any privacy laws by what they did. Moral ones are another story."

A flock of butterflies swarmed Julianne's stomach as she wondered if their fledgling firm would survive a hit like this one. Their executive assistant charged with fraud, arrested in their reception office. She imagined the Cincinnati legal community buzzing about it.

Phoebe dabbed her eyes with a tissue and pushed her chair away from the conference room table. "I'm so sorry. I've embarrassed the firm, and both of you. It seems like ever since I walked through that door and you mistook me for your pastor's friend . . ."

"Phoebe, stop it," Will told her with a sigh. "These things happen, and we will survive."

Julianne rubbed Phoebe's shoulder. "Last week, someone from the public defender's office shot someone. This week, Will and I have hired a dangerous and felonious assistant." Phoebe giggled, and Julianne nudged her arm. "Who knows what the flavor of the week will be once we wait this out."

She exchanged a quick glance with Will, and Julianne knew that neither one of them felt the lighthearted dismissal they'd donned for Phoebe's sake. But there was no use kicking her while she was down.

"If you ask me," Will offered, "I think it was a genius plan."

Phoebe looked at him with hope, tears spilling from her wide-open eyes.

"Do tell," Julianne urged, albeit suspiciously.

"Well, you were so concerned about what everyone was saying about your *love* life," he said, deadpan. "Now they won't even give it a second thought when we've got them so occupied imagining what other crimes our diabolical assistant has committed. I mean, just look at her."

Phoebe giggled again, and Julianne snickered before shooting Will a grateful smile.

"Look how scary she is! No one knows what she'll do next."

"You know what I heard about her?" Julianne teased. "On one of her cross-country sprees, she sought out a hairdresser in Abilene, just to watch him dye."

And with that, all three of them burst out laughing.

"I don't know what I did to deserve the two of you," Phoebe told them. "But I want to thank God for whatever it was."

"That's the beauty of God," Julianne told her as she smoothed one of Phoebe's wayward curls. "You don't have to earn it. He's just generous that way."

"I hate to break this up," Will interrupted. "But I've got a meeting with the assistant D.A. about your buddy, Rand. We're going to finalize the deal."

"I'm headed over to see Veronica," Julianne added. "I'm hoping the Queen of Image Repair has some preemptive advice for us. I'll head out with you."

Will squeezed Phoebe's arm as he passed. "Hang in there."

"See you in a couple of hours," Julianne told her.

She grabbed her purse and hurried out the door after Will. By the time she caught him, the elevator door had slipped open and the two of them boarded.

"She's going to be okay." Julianne wasn't sure if she meant it to reassure Will, or perhaps herself. "We all are."

After several beats, Will turned toward her and asked, "All of us? Are you sure?"

Her mind raced for his meaning, thought fragments ricocheting around her brain like some sort of intellectual pinball game. The only thing missing were the bells.

"I'm just asking," he continued, "because I haven't really been sure of that lately."

"No?" She grimaced and tilted her head awkwardly. "What am I not getting?"

Will snorted. "So much, Julianne. There's so much you don't get."

She opened her mouth to inquire further just as the elevator car shimmied and clunked to a bumpy halt, and she ended up biting her tongue.

"Ouch!" she muttered. "What's going on? Are we stuck?"

He gave her one of those crooked frowns of his, the ones that told her in no uncertain terms that she'd irritated him, that she'd come off as ridiculous somehow.

"Okay, yes. We're stuck. But what do we do?"

Without reply, Will moved to the panel and pushed a red knob until it chimed.

"The super will call someone, I guess," she deduced. "We just relax and wait, huh?"

Still no reply. Julianne blew out her frustration in a long puff of a sigh, leaning one hip against the elevator wall with a groan.

"I don't like closed-in spaces," she remarked. "It makes me feel like all of the air is sucked out of the place. I mean, I know it's not really, but it feels that way, you know? Like we might be on borrowed time, oxygen-wise; like we might . . . I don't know . . . suddenly start to feel—"

"Jules," he stated in a firm and controlled tone of voice. "Someone will be here soon. There's plenty of air for both of us. Chill out awhile."

Julianne flicked the zipper of her purse and stared at her shoes while she tried to figure out just what made Will so touchy.

"Ever since dinner at your dad's last night," she said softly, "you've been like this with me, Will. Are you going to tell me what I did to put the bee in your bonnet?"

He stared straight ahead as if he hadn't even heard her.

"What, are you in junior high again?" she prodded. "Because you look like you did that Monday after I forgot we were supposed to ride horses up at Alec's farm on Sunday afternoon."

Just when she thought he might have gone deaf, Will turned toward her and glared.

"You should have just told me you would rather go skating with Denny Witherhorn. You didn't have to keep me waiting there half the day before I found out you weren't even coming. It was two years before you finally admitted you had no intention of ever getting in a saddle anyway."

"I don't like horses," she defended. "I'm sorry. But I just don't trust them."

"How is it that you're like the pied piper of all things animal kingdom, and the one animal you don't like is the one that I connect with the most?"

She scratched her head and sighed. "I don't know, Will. I just don't."

"That was so like you, Julianne. Just taking off with Denny, and never even bothering to call next door and tell me you weren't going with me."

"I meant to. I just . . . forgot."

"You forgot," he snapped.

"Will, we were in the seventh grade! Don't you think you should have forgiven me by now? I mean, this is what you're mad at me about today, all this time later? You just woke up this morning and thought, 'Wait a minute! I can't believe Julianne didn't go horseback riding with me in the seventh grade. I think I'll treat her like dirt on my shoe.'"

He groaned and turned away from her, muttering something that she couldn't quite make out.

"What did you say?"

"I said no one would know about treating someone like dirt on their shoe better than you."

Julianne gasped, and her entire body straightened. It felt like a rod had been rammed straight up her back. "What a horrible thing to say to me!"

His expression melted slightly, and he gave a deep rub to his temple. "I know. I'm sorry."

"Will. What is wrong with you?" She waited at least twenty seconds for his answer, but it never came. "We might be stuck in this elevator all afternoon, for all we know. And I'm not letting up until you tell me what you're so mad about."

Another several beats thrummed by before he finally rolled toward her and stared her down.

"You're really going to pay that idiot five hundred dollars to take you to the gala?"

*Oh, for crying out loud.*

"*That* is what's got you all worked up?"

He sighed, shifting the weight of his entire body from one foot to the other, but he never broke eye contact even for a heartbeat.

"Will, are you kidding me? Why does this bother you so much? Okay, it's kind of humiliating that you know what I'm doing, but it's not like I'm putting him on the payroll. I just want to have *one magical night* . . . a night where all of our friends and acquaintances—for just one perfect minute—can't look at me and see Loser. Why can't I have that? And why is it so offensive to you? I don't understand. Please help me understand."

"Really?" he asked strangely. "You really want to understand why it bothers me so much?"

"Yes! Of course I do."

"Okay," he said, and without even a flicker of forewarning, Will stepped toward her, placed his hands on her shoulders, pressed her back against the elevator wall, and kissed her.

And he kept on kissing her.

Until she couldn't breathe . . . until her head began to spin . . . until she actually *saw stars*.

● — ● — ●

"Well, what did he say afterward?" Suzanne asked her, and Julianne pressed her phone hard against her cheek as she shook her head.

"Nothing. I mean, there wasn't time. The minute he pulled away, the elevator bumped, and then the doors opened, and there were uniformed guys waiting to get on and check it out."

"So, what, he just . . ."

"Walked away! Yes."

"Without a word," Suzanne recapped.

"Not a single one."

"What did you do?"

"I'm not sure. I think I just watched him leave. And then I walked to my car."

"Where are you now?"

"Still sitting here. I haven't even left the parking lot. I can't. I'm sort of just . . . stunned. Like one of those coyotes running across the road, and a car comes barreling around the corner, and the headlights hit them and they just stand there with their eyes real big and their little paws cemented to the street. That's me. I'm cemented."

"Do you want to meet me?"

"I can't. That's the worst part. I'm already half an hour late for a meeting."

"Well, call them and tell them you're on your way," Suzanne suggested. "Do some deep breathing on the drive over, and be careful. . . . And call me later."

Julianne simply nodded.

"Are you nodding?"

"Oh. Yeah. Sorry. I'll call you. Later."

"Hey, Julianne?"

"Huh?"

"How was it?"

"What?"

"The kiss," Suzanne enunciated. "How was it?"

She gulped down some air over the answer she didn't have.

"I'll call you," she finally said, and she disconnected the call.

*How was it?*

Suzanne's question reverberated. In fact, its echo was nearly deafening.

She couldn't very well tell Suzanne that it might have been the best kiss she'd ever had. Nor could she admit to the sudden memory of another kiss like it, one that took place outside the front door of her condo not so long ago, one that she'd been certain she'd dreamed until that moment in the elevator when it had come back to her at supersonic speed.

What had she been thinking? *I kissed Will.*

That night when she'd fallen asleep in the car. He'd walked her to her door, and . . . she'd wrapped her arms around his neck, pulled him toward her and . . . and . . . kissed him. And it had felt so natural—and yet simultaneously so *once-in-a-lifetime*—that she'd carefully placed it on the shelf of her memory behind some books and knickknacks and trivial souvenirs to look at more closely at a later date.

And that later date had arrived, ready or not! Julianne had become a sort of expert at not seeing what God placed before her, but that was then. And this was . . . *now*. There would be no avoidance of facing this fact anymore. She'd kissed him. And she liked it.

Had Will interpreted her kiss as a sort of sweet-tasting but unspoken pledge of some kind that had been broken with her returned attention on Paul Weaver?

But didn't he realize that it was nothing more than a date? And a paid one at that? The truth was that Paul Weaver had been a huge disappointment with his tuxedo-hating, piggyback-ride-forcing ways. He was so right when he said they had nothing in common.

And what did Will expect to accomplish by planting a retaliatory kiss of his own on her? Surely, he wasn't looking for something long-lasting and epic between them. That hadn't ever been who they were at the core of their relationship. They were best friends. Always had been. No amount of real kisses or fake romances with handsome, great-on-paper carpenters was going to change that. Their friendship was the only thing true-blue in life, in fact.

Will was just as much *family* to Julianne as Davis or Suzanne, or even her own mother! They couldn't go around messing with that. Surely Will knew that.

*Then why did he kiss me that way?*

The sudden shrill jingle of her iPhone broke her chain of thought, and Julianne quickly picked it up.

"Julianne Bartlett."

"Are you still in the parking lot?" Suzanne asked her.

"Yeah," she admitted. "I'm going. Right now."

"I knew it. Drive carefully," her friend admonished her. "Please."

# 21

"You kissed her?" Alec asked as Will tossed a saddle on Christie and buckled it beneath her belly.

"I kissed her."

"Ah, bro."

"I just laid one on her."

"And then what?" Alec asked him. "She must have been shocked."

"That's the worst part," he replied, fastening the saddlebag and tugging to test its hold. "I just walked away and left her standing there. You should have seen her face, man. She looked like she'd just been hit by a stray bullet."

"So . . . what does this mean? Do you have feelings to back up that kiss? I mean . . . what are you gonna do now?"

Will wished he had the answer.

"I'm going to take my best girl for a ride," he said, tenderly smacking Christie's flank. "She's got all the answers. I just need to ride them out of her."

"That's a lot of pressure for an old quarter horse," Alec remarked with the shake of his head. "I don't envy you, girl."

"See you later?"

"I'll be around. They're driving in with my new filly today. A Hanoverian for show."

"You're planning to compete again?"

"Yeah, it's in my blood, I guess. Stop by the east stable and check her out after your ride."

"I'll do that."

Will climbed up on Christie and gave her a loving pat. "Okay, girl. Let's roll."

The Palomino set out and walked across the open yard and past the paddock. The minute they hit the grass, Will snapped the reins, and Christie took off at a full gallop toward the trail.

Did he have feelings to back up the kiss he'd planted on Julianne? He often thought over the years that he had enough feelings for the both of them, even though he knew good and well that a whole couple couldn't exist on one person's love.

"She's not limited to having just one friend, is she?" his pop had told him that day Julianne had stood him up for a skating date with Denny Witherhorn.

And apparently Julianne just didn't see him as more than a friend. Not then, and not now.

He'd checked his cell phone a dozen times that afternoon in search of a voice mail or a text message, some indication that she'd had time to mull over that kiss and knew they'd need to discuss it. He'd even phoned the office from the car outside the stables to check with Phoebe about anything pressing . . . any inquiries . . . any sign of a conversation of substance in his future.

"Nope. We're all good here," she'd said. "See you in the morning."

"Well, just tell Julianne that I got the charges bumped down for Rand. Rand will cover the medical bills before the guy is prosecuted for robbery, and the D.A. will drop the attempted murder charge against Rand."

"That's wonderful!" Phoebe had exclaimed. "Do you want to tell her yourself?"

"Nah," he replied. "I'm in the car. You can tell her. It wasn't much of a case anyway, so we got lucky on this. If we can just get Rand to get rid of that gun like he agreed to do, he might have a shot at staying out of jail."

"That's a big *if*," Phoebe had teased. "Have a good evening."

At the top of the ridge, Will dismounted and stood next to Christie, gazing out at the horizon. He reached into the saddlebag and produced his phone, checking it one more time for any messages.

A short-and-sweet text from Alison. *Call me?*

But no voice mails.

A box full of email, but nothing from Julianne.

Flicking Christie's reins around a low branch, Will dropped to the grass and leaned back against the thick trunk of his old faithful elm. As a gentle spring breeze caressed his weary face, he closed his eyes and began to pray.

"Ah, Lord. What have I done?"

●  —  ●  —  ●

Suzanne sat on the floor, leaning into the green chenille sofa against Julianne's steely plum living room wall as Charming wrapped himself around the curve of her leg, snoring softly. She only stopped smoothing the dog's soft yellow coat long enough to draw a sip from the steaming mug of coffee and set it on the table in front of her.

"This is really yum. What flavor is it?"

"Chocolate glazed donut," Julianne replied. "With vanilla cream."

"Is that what you're having, too?"

She nodded and took a long, warm draw from her cup.

"Is it helping?"

"Chocolate always helps," she said without opening her eyes. "Even when it doesn't."

"So are you all set for this weekend?" Suzanne asked her.

"Except for my best girlfriend abandoning me? Yes. I'm all set."

"I'm sorry," she replied softly. "Especially now, I really wish I didn't have to fly out in the morning."

Julianne balanced her cup on the arm of the brown leather club chair and sighed. "Me, too."

"The dress is exquisite."

"Thank you for the shoes, Suz. They fit perfectly." On second

211

thought, she added, "Well. They don't fit *my feet* perfectly. But they fit *with the dress* perfectly. You know."

"Yes." Suzanne grinned at her. "I called Neil this morning and made you an appointment for Saturday afternoon. He's going to do your hair and nails and makeup so you look like a real glamour girl. And it's on me."

"You did?" Julianne studied her friend's soft face. "That's so sweet."

"Well, I won't be here to help you, so . . ."

"I really appreciate it, Suzanne."

"The appointment is at four o'clock. Don't be late because Neil gets pretty ugly if you mess up his schedule."

Julianne grabbed her iPhone from the table and accessed her calendar. "Putting it in right now. Five o'clock. Don't be late."

"Not five! Four!"

Charming jumped, lifting his head and looking around the room with sagging, sleepy brown eyes.

A string of giggles peeled out of Julianne as she picked up her cup again. "I know. I'm just yanking your hair."

"Don't you abuse the relationship with Mr. Neil. He's one of a kind."

"I promise," she said, grinning as she crossed her heart.

"Have you given any thought to calling it off with Paul, and just asking Will to take you instead?"

Julianne lifted one shoulder in a tentative shrug. "It would be so awkward now."

"You know what would make things less awkward, Julianne? *Talking to him about it.*"

"I know, and I will. I'm just not ready to do that yet."

"Well, you're running out of time before the gala."

"I'm aware," she replied. "That's why I'm going with Paul. I can talk to Will once I've thought it through and know just what I want to say."

Suzanne narrowed her hazel eyes and frowned. "Julianne.

You're going to put him through that? Aren't you just looking for an excuse to keep the date with Paul so that everyone can get a load of him on your arm?"

"No!" she exclaimed, and she tripped over her thoughts. "Well, yes. I mean . . . no."

"Confused much?" Suzanne remarked.

"Never more than now," Julianne muttered.

She and Suzanne finished their coffee in relative silence. Julianne spent the time staring at the gorgeous dress hanging over the door to her home office. The steel-blue color of the fabric drew her eye, complemented by a thick rhinestone-encrusted empire waist and a flared knee-length skirt supported by a stiff crinoline petticoat. Shimmering crystal beads adorned the sheer ivory bolero-type jacket, and the shoes Suzanne had purchased separately seemed like a perfectly executed match for the vintage party dress.

"Make sure to get pictures," Suzanne remarked, and the silence shattered into a million shards beneath it.

"Sorry. What?"

"Pictures. After you get dressed for the gala."

"Oh. Okay."

"I've got to get out of here," Suzanne told her as she carefully pushed up to her feet without disturbing Charming. "I'm not packed yet."

Julianne set her cup on the end table and rose from her chair to deliver a grateful hug. "Thank you so much for the shoes. And the support."

"Anytime."

As Suzanne reached the front door, she turned back and smiled at Julianne. "Ivory shimmer."

"Pardon?"

"Your stockings. You should wear ivory shimmer stockings with that dress."

"You just can't resist, can you?"

"What! They'd be fabulous!"

213

"Good-bye, Suzanne."

She stood in the doorway watching as her friend walked toward her car.

"Fashion control freak!" she teased.

"And?" Suzanne called back to her. "You say that like it's a bad thing."

Julianne chuckled, waving one more time before she closed the front door.

Settling back down into the leather club chair, she picked up her coffee mug and sipped the last of it as she gazed at the beautiful dress again.

*What a shame*, she thought. *Wasting such a spectacular dress on a phony-baloney date. That kind of dress belongs on the arm of a real-deal Prince Charming.*

And that's when it hit her like a burlap sack full of bricks and mortar.

Julianne picked up her phone and pressed #1 on the speed dial.

"Hey, Will," she greeted his voice mail as she mindlessly twisted the thin silver ring around her thumb. "It's me. Listen, I have something I want to ask you, and it's pretty important. So will you give me a call when you get this?"

The instant she disconnected, her iPhone jingled. Caller ID designated the origin as the Hamilton County Courthouse, and she shot a glance at the clock.

Nearly six o'clock. She had nothing pending; no juries out, no rulings in play. Surely she wasn't being summoned for another pro bono order this late in the day!

"Julianne Bartlett."

"Miss Bartlett, it's Bridget Ferguson. Judge Hillman's bailiff."

"Yes, Bridget. How are you?"

"I'm well. Thank you for asking. Judge Hillman has requested the pleasure of your company."

"Has he? Can you give me a clue?"

"I wish I had one for you. He just asked me to call you and

invite you to his chambers sometime before the end of business tomorrow. How does ten-thirty work for you?"

She couldn't very well turn down a judge's request, but especially not one from Judge Hillman, after what he did for her with the Veronica Caswell connection.

"Ten-thirty it is. You're sure you don't know what it's about?"

"It's a mystery."

"Well, I don't mind a good mystery every now and then," she replied. "I just hope there's a satisfying ending to this one."

"Here's hoping," Bridget answered. "I'll let him know to expect you at ten-thirty."

Still wondering about the mystery at hand, Julianne's thoughts drifted to Will. In an effort to think about something else, she decided to order a pizza and curl up with a couple reruns of *NCIS* for the night.

After a small pepperoni and mushroom arrived and she'd changed into her favorite pajamas—pink flannels with metallic hearts embroidered on the sleeve of the top and the hem of the matching capris—she grabbed a diet root beer from the refrigerator and propped a few cushions against the arm of the sofa. A couple of hours with Charming and Mark Harmon should do the trick!

Yet even Mark Harmon's piercing blue eyes and salt-and-pepper crew cut couldn't dissuade the nervous nellies from chirping out Will's name as they bounced around inside her belly.

*Just seven simple words.*

All she had to manage was seven simple words. Surely, she could utter them without somehow flubbing the line, right?

*Will you take me to the gala?*

They seemed simple enough. But for the first time, Julianne realized that simple and uncomplicated were very, very different concepts.

*"It's all about the timing, my young friend,"*
*the fairy told the maiden.*
*"You must hurry to greet the prince*
*before the time runs out.*
*Watch the hourglass, and plan your arrival with care."*

*The maiden imagined the scene in full and bright, colorful detail.*
*A beautiful dress . . . adorned in sparkling jewels . . .*
*and the magical shoes that the fairy had brought to her.*
*How could the prince resist?*
*(Especially when they were clearly God's perfect couple!)*

# 22

"**Ms. Bartlett.** I hope you haven't been waiting long."

Only half an hour!

"No, Your Honor. Not too long."

Judge Hillman rounded the corner of his massive desk and sat down behind it, adjusting his robes as he did.

"I heard that you and Miss James worked together without incident."

"Yes, sir."

"Everything is settled then?"

"Yes, sir."

"Thank you, Ms. Bartlett. It came to my attention after I asked you to co-counsel with her that the two of you are not exactly . . . girlfriends."

Julianne snickered. "No, sir. We are not."

"Making it all the more appreciated that you worked with her so efficiently to tie up loose ends."

He stared at her for a moment, almost expectantly, with his very blue eyes sparkling.

"Is that . . . all, Your Honor?"

"How is it working out with Veronica Caswell?" he asked, out of the blue.

"Oh. Really well, sir. Will and I are so grateful that you—"

"I didn't do anything," he interrupted sharply. "That might not be considered appropriate. I merely introduced you to someone I've known for a very long time. You did the rest, Ms. Bartlett."

"Well. Thank you, sir."

The block of silence that followed initiated discomfort, and Julianne squirmed a bit in her chair, repositioning as she cleared her throat.

"So. If that's all, sir—"

"Yes," Judge Hillman cut in. "There is just one additional issue I wanted to discuss."

Julianne arched her eyebrows and waited curiously. When he didn't continue, she cleared her throat again.

"Yes, sir. And that issue would be . . . ?"

"Yes. Of course. Well, Ms. Bartlett, it would appear that I am in need of legal counsel."

"Really."

"Yes. And I'm hoping you might be willing to . . ."

She waited, but the judge had stalled once again.

"Represent you?" she finished for him, and he nodded, clicking his tongue as he did.

"Yes. Well. Represent someone."

"Someone. And that someone isn't you?"

"No."

Julianne sighed. "Judge Hillman, you obviously called me here because you trust me to handle a delicate issue." She leaned forward and placed both arms on the edge of his desk as she looked at him squarely. "You can trust me."

"I have a reputation, Ms. Bartlett."

"Yes," she said, nodding. "Tough, but fair."

"Well, I hope people also know that my courtroom is dignified, and that I hold myself to a high standard of integrity."

"Of course they do, Your Honor. Can you just tell me what's happened?"

"My son was arrested."

"You have a son, sir?"

"Yes. Jason. He's twenty-three years old."

"And what are the charges?"

Judge Hillman turned away for a moment; gathering his nerve, Julianne supposed.

"Sir?"

He glanced back at her and sighed. "Indecent exposure."

"Oh. Dear."

"Precisely."

●  —  ●  —  ●

"So Jason is out on bail," Julianne said as she took another bite of her turkey sandwich that Phoebe had brought in from the deli downstairs. "But his trial date isn't until the twenty-fourth, and Judge Hillman is worried that someone like that Melanie Larsen is going to pick up the news and run with it. I'm planning to petition for a speedier court date, but beyond that I think all we can really do is pray that someone else does something far more newsworthy in the meantime."

Will nodded as he set his roast beef on rye atop his desk and wiped a dribble of Thousand Island dressing from the corner of his mouth.

"Indecent exposure," he commented. "Do I want to know the details?"

Julianne waved her hand as she told him, "He and his girl-friend were steaming up the car windows over in Eden Park."

Will cringed. "I can see where that might be an embarrass-ment for Hillman, but with that charge it could have been a whole lot worse."

"Well, that's the point. If someone reports on the charge with-out supplying the details . . ."

"Yeah, I get it." He gulped a mouthful of soda. "So when Hill-man thinks of an attorney, he thinks of you. That's saying some-thing."

"He's taken a liking to me for some reason, I guess. And you know, he's not nearly as scary as people think he is. He has a real kind side to him."

"Sure he does."

"He does! Look what he did for us with Veronica."

Will shrugged. "I guess."

Julianne swallowed around the lump in her throat. Now was the time.

*Will you take me to the gala?*

Those seven words had been bumping into one another and making her head ache for nearly twenty-four hours now.

*Just say it and get it over with!*

"Will, I wanted to mention something to you."

He took another big bite from his sandwich and spoke around it. "Yeah."

"Well, ask you something really. It's about the gala."

He grunted and pulled a face that she didn't understand. "I finally got around to asking Alison to go . . ."

"Oh. Alison?"

". . . and she turned me down . . ."

"She did?"

". . . because she has a weekend thing with a bunch of third-graders."

"Oh. That's . . . a shame. So I guess you're without a date then."

"Nah. Lacey asked me to take her awhile back, and I said I had to get back to her on it."

Julianne tossed her sandwich to the napkin spread out before her. "Lacey! Will, you wouldn't."

"Well, yeah, I would. She doesn't have a date, and like you said, a nominee for Person of the Year can't exactly go without a date."

"Yes, but—"

"Jules, I know she's not your favorite person. But Lacey's just . . . Lacey. Like you said about Hillman. She has a really warm side to her."

"Warm for *you*, maybe. But the rest of us are just your left-overs. You hear the way she talks to me, Will."

"I know, and I had a chat with her about it. If I agree to take her to the gala, she has to call a truce. No comments, no digs, no arguments."

"I don't think she has it in her," Julianne told him, her heart pounding so wildly that it took effort to draw in a sharp, deep breath. "She can't help herself."

"Well, that's the deal I struck. If she can't do it, she'll have to find herself another escort."

"About escorts . . . Maybe you could . . . you know, take me instead."

Will stared at her for a long moment, the dill pickle spear from which he'd just taken a big bite left dangling from two fingers. Finally, he dropped it to the paper sandwich wrapper that he'd constructed into a place mat, and he blurted out a hearty laugh.

"You'll do *anything* to keep me from going with Lacey!" he cried.

"No," she objected. "It's not that. I really mean it. I was thinking about it last night, and I thought I'd really like it if you took me." She swallowed hard again and screwed up those seven little words. "Will you take me to the gala? Please?"

"Oh, come on," he exclaimed. "You've got the pretty ditch digger to take you. Isn't he one-night-only, nonrefundable?"

"Nice, Will," she replied softly.

"Sorry. But I can see straight through you, Jules. If I hadn't mentioned Lacey, this subject never would have come up."

"You don't know as much about me as you think you do then."

"Right. You're going to ditch the digger so you can go with me."

"I thought I might," she said defensively.

"Pardon me if I don't believe you, huh?"

"Will."

"I'm due for a deposition out in Northgate," he said as he pushed off from the desk and rose from his chair. "See you later."

Will maneuvered over the large yellow dog with the massive plastic cone collar and left, leaving Julianne sitting on the other side of his desk for several minutes after he'd gone. Mentally kicking herself for choosing the perfectly wrong time to utter those seven treacherous—and not simple at all!—words that she'd rehearsed for hours on end, she wrapped the last of her sandwich and wiped some pickle juice from the desk with her wadded napkin. After tossing it all into the trash can, she patted her leg. Charming groaned as he got up and followed her out of Will's office, across reception, and straight into her office without a word (or a lick) for Phoebe.

● — ● — ●

"Oh, come on, George. You and I both know you're grasping at straws here. If Jason didn't have the last name of Hillman, would you even be offering this kind of deal?"

All the D.A.s in all the city, and this case had to land on the desk of George Flannigan.

"What do you mean?" He sniffed, feigning shocked offense. "That seems to indicate that I would offer an even tougher plea if he wasn't the grown son of a sitting judge? That doesn't make sense, Julianne."

Julianne couldn't avoid staring at the three locks of hair he had left, combed over his shiny bald head. They gave his skull the look of a crooked road map leading from one overgrown wooded section to another, with large, mouse-like ears holding it all in place.

"You know very well that Judge Hillman would be embarrassed by this getting out, so you're offering a plea that you think we'll be desperate enough to grab in exchange for getting this thing taken care of. But are you sure you want to play that game, George? You have a lot of cases that come before His Honor, don't you? Including that fraud scandal over at the health department? That one's yours, isn't it?"

"Yeah. So?"

"So I would think you'd be interested in a show of good faith toward Judge Hillman's only son rather than alienating him this close to trial time." She leaned back in her chair and lifted one side of her mouth in a crooked, ate-the-canary smile. "And you know, I'm obligated to tell him whether you've done your best to show good faith, or whether you've used his predicament to advance your own win rate. Which story do you want me to tell Judge Hillman, George?"

Flannigan deflated. "Okay, look, I'll knock the charge down from indecent exposure to creating a public nuisance."

"Keep talking," she said, and she scratched Charming's head as he pushed it against her knee.

"You bring your dog to work?" he said, his nose wrinkled up as if he'd just gotten a whiff of stale onions.

"Couldn't do that at the public defender's office, could I?" she commented.

"And what's wrong with him? He looks pathetic, like he's been through the war, Bartlett."

"He's recovering from surgery after an accident. All right, so the nuisance charge is a third-degree misdemeanor. Let's say no jail time."

"But a fine," he clarified, and Julianne shrugged one shoulder. "Five hundred dollars, and twenty hours community service."

"Let's say three hundred, and twenty hours."

Flannigan groaned as he tossed himself back in the chair. "Fine. It's done."

"And one more thing," she said, narrowing her eyes to convey the seriousness of what would follow. "You are going to do everything humanly possible to keep this out of the news. No sound bites, no legal comment, no reporting back to all of your colleagues. No nothing, George. That's a nonnegotiable. I don't think either one of us wants to embarrass Judge Hillman with this through a rumor mill or, worse yet, a front-page story on CincyBiz.com."

"Someone should talk to his son then," he cracked. "By the way, nice picture of you on there recently."

Julianne bit back her reaction. Instead, she simply smiled and asked, "Are we agreed?"

"Yes," he conceded with a sigh. "Fine. We're agreed."

"Paperwork by end of business tomorrow?"

"Fine."

Julianne stood up and offered him a handshake across the desk. "Always a pleasure doing business with you, George."

He sneered at her as he shook it briefly.

"So will I see you this weekend at the Bar Association gala?" she asked him.

"Naturally. The D.A.'s office has three tables." His sour face puckered up as he added, "Congratulations on your nomination, by the way."

"Thank you."

"I suppose you'll be on Hanes's arm."

Julianne disguised her own sour face as she replied, "No, actually. Will and I both have dates."

Flannigan let out a laugh that sounded like something from the horn section of the Cincinnati Symphony. "No kidding! Won't that be the talk of the town."

"I would hope our legal community has more to talk about than who I'm dating." Although she knew better.

"C'mon, Julianne. This is big local news. Even you must know it."

*Yes. Even I know it. Why do you think I'm investing five hundred dollars?*

"Have a good day, George. Thanks for coming over. I'll let Judge Hillman know how agreeable you've been, and how much you wanted to work with us to keep his name out of the gossip mill."

The moment she heard the outer door close, Julianne dialed Bridget Ferguson.

"It's Julianne Bartlett. Is Judge Hillman available?"

"He's waiting for your call. Can you hang on until he finishes up? It shouldn't be more than five minutes."

"Sure."

The hold music over at the courthouse left a lot to be desired.

Julianne pressed the speaker button on the phone base and re-placed the handset. She snapped her fingers to call Charming back over to her, and she raked through the fur at the base of his ear as an elevator version of *My Cherie Amour* vibrated through the speakerphone.

"My Char-ar-ming amour," she sang along, "pretty little dog that I adore, you're the only dog my heart be—"

"Ms. Bartlett."

She snatched up the handset. "Judge Hillman, thank you for taking my call so quickly."

"You've got news for me then?"

"Yes, sir. The charges will be bumped down to creating a public nuisance with a three-hundred-dollar fine and twenty hours com-munity service."

"You're joking."

"No, sir. You like?"

"I do indeed. Thank you, Ms. Bartlett."

"You're very welcome, Your Honor. I'm flattered that you brought your son's case to me, out of all of the lawyers you could have called. And happy I could do something to help."

"I owe you, young lady."

"Not that I could actually collect," she said, mimicking his words from the last time he'd expressed his gratitude.

"Correct."

"Because that would be wrong."

The judge laughed softly. "Also correct. And Mr. Flannigan's discretion?"

"I have his word, sir."

"Excellent. I'll see you this weekend, Ms. Bartlett."

"You're attending the gala, Judge?"

"I'm the master of ceremonies for the awards portion of the evening."

"I didn't know," she replied. "I'll see you there then."

"Uh . . . Julianne?"

*Julianne.* It was the first time he'd ever used her first name.

"Sir?"

"Thank you."

"You're welcome, Judge Hillman."

# 23

"Where did you go? ...Julianne, where did she go?"

Julianne rushed across her mother's expansive kitchen with a miniature ice cream scoop in her hand, and she adjusted the laptop so that the webcam on the desk counter faced her mother. "You have to stay in the frame, Mom," she said, pointing at the small photo box on the lower right corner of the screen. "If you move, Austin can't see you."

"Oh. I see. Sorry, honey. Can you see me now?"

"Yes. Thanks, Julianne."

She leaned over her mother's shoulder and waved the metal scoop at her brother before returning to the counter and picking up the half-empty bowl of cookie dough.

"What's she doing with a cookie scoop?" Austin cried from the computer screen. "Mom, you're not letting Julianne make my birthday cookies, are you? You know she ruins everything in the kitchen."

"Hush, Austin!" Julianne exclaimed. "I do not."

"She's not making them, honey," Amanda reassured him. "I put them together and she's just scooping them out onto the cookie sheets. I'll oversee the baking, don't you worry."

"Are they the ones I like? The peanut butter ones? Travis said you sent him oatmeal raisin for his birthday last week. You know I don't like raisins, right?"

"Yes, honey. No raisins. Peanut butter cookies, just like you like them."

"You big baby," Julianne muttered.

"What did she say?" Austin called out. "Mom, what did she say?"

"She said to wish you a happy birthday, honey. Do you have any plans to celebrate?"

"Robin and I are going to dinner at a steakhouse we discovered downtown."

Julianne knew from his wife's latest email that the steakhouse in downtown Boston would serve as the backdrop for twenty of their friends from the university and the community where they lived a few miles away to gather and yell, "Surprise!"

"Well, you have a nice time, Austin. And give my love to Robin when she gets home, huh?"

"I will, Mom."

"I love you, honey."

"Love you, too."

Julianne heard the beep indicating that the online call had disconnected, and she reached around her mother to shut down the computer.

"I'll never get used to technology," Amanda told her, reaching for the cookie scoop. "Why don't you give me that and I'll finish up."

"You're just afraid my kitchen mojo will ruin your precious boy's birthday cookies."

"Don't be silly," she said, but she got up from the chair and headed straight for the bowl on the counter. "I thought I'd wear my green chiffon to your big function Saturday night. Would that be all right?"

"I love that dress," she said, curling her legs beneath her on the chair and leaning on the table. "You look pretty in green."

"Thank you, sweetheart. It's not a full-length or anything."

"That's okay. Neither is mine."

Amanda turned around and gazed at her. "You're not wearing an evening gown?"

"No. It's more like a party dress. I found it at a vintage shop in Clifton. It has this very full skirt with crinoline underneath. It's very pretty."

"I'm sure anything you wear will be lovely," she said, returning her attention to the cookies. "You always know just the right thing." After several beats, she tried on her most offhanded tone of voice as she asked, "Are you still going on the arm of the boy who doesn't want to see you anymore?"

"Yes, Mother," Julianne droned. "And I hope you'll be nice to him in spite of his obvious lack in judgment."

"Julianna Margaret Bartlett. I am always nice."

She giggled. "Yes, you are. I'm sorry."

"I should hope so."

"And if it makes you feel any better, I did ask Will if he would take me instead." Her mother reeled around, cookie scoop in the air and hopeful anticipation in her smile. "But he turned me down."

"Oh, he did not," she said, pivoting back toward the cookies.

"No, he actually did. He's taking that horrible Lacey James instead."

"Well, why would Will do that? Unless, of course, he's finally given up on you."

Julianne's stomach turned over, leaving her wondering if she'd eaten too much raw cookie dough.

"What do you mean, given up on me? Will's never had anything but friendship in mind for me, Mom. You know that. Besides, I'm still waiting for the fairy tale."

"The shining prince on the white steed," Amanda remarked.

"Yes. But he won't ride in on a horse. In my fairy tale, he'll understand that I don't really like the idea of riding on horseback. I'll just turn the corner one day, and there he'll be. A complete and wonderful surprise."

Her mother loaded two cookie sheets into the oven and leaned across the stove to set the timer.

"You know the funny thing about fairy tales, honey? They're

just stories. Besides, no one reading them ever expects a big unexpected plot twist or has a single doubt about who the prince and princess are going to end up with at the end of the story. That's not the interesting part anyway."

"No?"

"No. The interesting part is *how they get there*. But I believe that God has an even better ending than any old fairy tale for you, honey."

●　—　●　—　●

"I'm really glad you called," Alison said as she removed a slice of LaRosa's Roma Focaccia pizza and slipped it to her plate. "I hoped I'd have a chance to talk to you before I leave with the kids."

"You didn't say," Will replied. "Where are you taking them?"

"Camping, down in Natural Bridge."

"I went hiking there with some buddies when we were in high school," he told her as the waitress filled their iced tea glasses. "It's beautiful."

"I'm really hoping for good weather. There are six chaperones, and almost thirty third and fourth graders."

Will drew a large cross in the air between them with his hand. "May you be blessed and safe, my child."

Alison chuckled. "From your lips to God's ears!"

After a short silence filled with consuming a slice of pizza, Will's iPhone buzzed.

"Go ahead and get it," Alison told him.

He checked the caller ID and saw that it was Judd. "Nah," he said, letting it go to voice mail. "It's a friend of mine from law school. I can catch up with him later."

"I love this place," she said as he tucked the phone back into his jacket pocket, and she ran her finger over the curve of the L on the front of LaRosa's menu. "I used to come here with my dad when I was a kid."

"Us, too," Will told her. "Then we'd walk next door and get a double scoop of mint chocolate chip from Grater's."

"Ohh," she growled. "I haven't had Grater's in forever! I love those giant hunks of chocolate in the chocolate chip!"

"It sounds like we have a dessert plan," he suggested.

"Well," she began, and Will caught the faint shadow of regret in Alison's remarkable eyes. "You may not want to have dessert with me, Will."

Several funny comments sprang to mind, but he felt relieved that he didn't give in to any of them when he saw the concerned expression that had washed over his date.

"What's up?" he asked instead.

Alison sniffed and tossed her dark auburn hair over her shoulder, giving Will the impression that she didn't want to get to the heart of it.

"I think you are the most wonderful man, Will."

"Uh-oh."

"You're kind and funny and sweet, and we seem to have so much in common."

He pushed his plate forward and leaned back, crossing his arms. "Okay."

"It's just that I'm not one of those people who welcomes a challenge, at least when it comes to romance. Do you know what I mean?"

He lifted his eyebrows into an arch and shook his head. "Not even a little bit."

"If it happened naturally for us, that would be one thing. I'd be all in," she explained. "But I don't really want to play the dating game."

"Ohh, Alison, look," he said as her meaning began to dawn. "If you got the wrong impression when we ran into Holly at the lake, she and I are really over. We have been for—"

"No, no," she interrupted with a raised hand. "No, I believe you. This isn't about Holly."

"What then? Not Lacey? I mean, there's nothing going on there at all. I wouldn't even have mentioned it, but—"

"Will. It's not Lacey either."

He scratched his head and narrowed his eyes curiously. Despite the fact that her meaning was becoming far more clear, he asked anyway. "Who—or what—are we talking about then?"

"Julianne, Will. We're talking about Julianne."

Will picked up the red cloth napkin from his lap, wiped his mouth, and tossed the napkin to the table as he waited for her to continue. Suddenly, the tomato sauce and oregano wasn't sitting quite right.

"You're obviously in love with her, Will. I mean, your ex-fiancée looks just like her! And until that's resolved, I just don't see anything happening for you with anyone else. Including me."

He didn't know what to say. A denial pressed on him, but he respected Alison too much to out-and-out lie to her. He actually did have feelings for Julianne. But he'd hoped those feelings wouldn't sabotage every relationship as he tried to move on without her. How was he ever going to truly press on if women kept breaking up with him over Julianne? Hadn't he and Holly broken up with virtually the same conversation about a year ago?

"I don't know what to say," he admitted, shaking his head as he stared down at the pizza between them.

"You don't really have to say anything," she reassured him with a smile. "It is what it is, Will. You love her. You've probably always loved her."

He sighed and looked away. "Please don't say that."

Alison reached across the table and touched Will's hand. "You two obviously have a whole history of complications that you don't have to talk to me about if you don't want to, Will. But you're a good guy. You deserve to find love. I hope you can see your way clear to find it with the woman who so obviously has your heart."

The waitress appeared at the table just then, and Alison pulled back her hand.

"Is everything all right?" she asked. "Was the pizza all right?"

"It was first-rate," Will told her honestly. "Just like always. We're just not as hungry as we thought. Would you mind boxing it up for us?"

"Sure."

She picked up the platter and hurried away from the table, and Alison caught Will's eye and smiled at him.

"I'm really sorry," he told her softly.

"There's no reason to be sorry. I've really enjoyed the time we've spent together. I have no regrets, and I hope you don't either."

"No," he said, shaking his head.

"I'm up for an ice cream cone before we head home though," she offered hopefully. "What about you?"

He smiled. "Sure."

After he paid the check, Will grabbed the pizza box. The two of them walked out the front door in silence. Just as he pulled Grater's door open and held it for Alison, she turned to him and wrinkled her nose.

"What?" he prompted.

"I hope you won't think I'm horrible."

"You want a double scoop?"

"Well, yes," she said with a giggle. "But that's not what I mean."

"What then?"

She looked at him seriously, so intensely that it made Will want to squirm a bit.

"Well. I was just wondering if . . . if you'd have a problem with it if I . . . umm . . ."

"Spit it out, Alison," he joked.

"The thing is," she began, and she inhaled sharply. "I really liked your friend Alec when I met him at the stables. I was wondering . . . you know . . . if it would be okay . . ."

"You want to go out with Alec."

"I really do."

Will shook his head and grinned. "It's fine."

"It is? Really? Because I get the feeling that he might like to go out with me, and I'm really attracted to him. I even thought about just picking up the phone and asking him out, but of course I had to have this talk with you first. . . . I'm sorry, Will."

"No need," he told her. "But you're buying my ice cream."

After he dropped Alison at her house, Will stopped home to check on his dad. He inched open Davis's bedroom door and found him snoozing in the recliner in the corner, soft yellow light from the floor lamp beside him illuminating the shadows of his aging face, a book open across his chest with his reading glasses propped precariously on it.

Will inspected the spine of the book. The latest John Grisham. His father certainly did love his crime mysteries. He'd thought about buying that one himself the last time he'd gone browsing for new material for his e-reader. As he moved the book and reading glasses to the nightstand, he wondered about ordering an e-reader for his dad, something simple with a backlight. He retrieved a blanket from the closet and spread it over his father. Flipping off the lamp, he crept out of the room and closed the door.

He grabbed a bottle of juice from the refrigerator and made his way outside to the deck, settling into one of the oversized chairs and propping his feet on the railing as he checked his messages.

Just one, from Judd.

"Will, it's Judd. Look, I've been trying to reach you for a while. I wanted to talk to you about a pretty great opportunity here at the firm. I remember you saying you wanted something different from corporate law after so long with B&B, and we've got a really great opportunity to expand an entertainment law division. Production contracts, publishing, things like that. I have to make a decision in the next couple of weeks, buddy, so give me a call and let me try to sway you. Or better yet, I'm going to be in Cincy for a few days, and I'll call you while I'm there. And you better pick up! You'd be a natural to head this division for us, Will. Talk to you soon."

Will set his phone down on the table and sighed. Entertainment law. His friend was right; it was something different for him, but it might still call for someone with some corporate experience in their back pocket. He wanted to think about it more, but his heart just wasn't in it.

The moon hung especially low, a full, silver orb against a clear starless sky. A sudden flash of light from the corner of his eye dragged his attention to the edge of the property where the first fireflies of the season signaled the approach of summer.

The quiet chirping of crickets lent harmony to the lyric of Alison's earlier declaration, now burning a pinhole in the blanket of his memory.

"You're obviously in love with her, Will. I mean, your ex-fiancée looks just like her! And until that's resolved, I just don't see anything happening for you with anyone else."

He took a swig of juice and let the icy liquid soothe his dry throat as he wondered why he hadn't noticed the resemblance between Holly and Julianne straightaway. Oh, people had pointed it out from time to time, sure. But now that he propped them up together against the backdrop of the dark night sky, he couldn't miss it.

*How pathetic am I?*

He wondered how long he'd been walking around Cincinnati in search of Julianne's replacement before he finally ran into Holly. He chuckled and shook his head as he tossed back another gulp of the cranberry juice.

He'd run into her in a very literal way, nearly knocking her off her feet as he flew past her in Walgreens on his way to the pharmacy to fill one of his father's prescriptions before court. They'd ended up talking for thirty minutes while they waited, and their first date had been for dinner at The Grand Finale the following night. Holly'd had spinach crepes, the same dish Julianne always ordered there; Will had chosen a steak. They'd split a bananas foster for dessert.

Regret left a sour taste to follow the tart cranberry juice. He'd been so unfair to himself, even though he didn't realize it at the time; not to mention what it had done to Holly, holding her up to the shadowy reflection of another woman in hopes that she might actually live up to it.

Will closed his eyes and tilted his face to the sky. With a sigh, he whispered out a prayer.

"Never again, Lord. Please forgive me, and don't let me do that to another woman, ever again."

He leaned forward, clasping his hands and resting his elbows on his knees as he stared out into the night. With a shake of his head, Will pressed his forehead against his hands and continued to pray.

"Maybe I should take that job with Judd in Lexington after all. Maybe I should pack up my dad and move down there, and leave Julianne behind me. Maybe my only chance of getting past her is to get off this hamster wheel and out of the cage."

A gentle breeze caressed his face as he lifted it. It felt so good on his skin.

*If Jules was here, she'd say it was a sign. A sweet tickle from the hand of God to let me know that everything is okay, that He has everything in hand.*

But Will couldn't escape the sudden notion that perhaps the soft breeze coming at just the moment that he actually considered Judd's offer, considered leaving Julianne behind at last—maybe for the first time—was confirmation that the idea was a good one.

*Go ahead*, he imagined God had said to him. *Follow this new path. It's sweet escape so you can get some perspective, so you can breathe again.*

Will chuckled, realizing he'd slipped into a Julianne frame of mind, imagining signs from God around every corner and on the wings of every waft of air.

"Or maybe," he said right out loud, "it's just a final spring breeze on a random Ohio night."

Will went into the house long enough to grab one of the dozen battery-operated hurricane lanterns his dad had purchased with possible electrical outages in mind.

"In case of a tornado or a storm," Davis had defended when Will came upon his stash under the kitchen sink. "It's always good to be prepared. Wait'll you see the light these things throw off."

He'd been right about that. Just one of the lamps easily illuminated the whole kitchen.

Will swung through the living room and grabbed the Bible he'd left on the end table next to the sofa before returning to his chair out on the deck. After downing the last drops of cranberry juice, he opened the Bible, set it on his knee, and began to read at random from the book of Isaiah.

"Do not remember the past events, pay no attention to things of old. Look, I am about to do something new; even now it is coming. Do you not see it?"

Will laughed out loud at that. He'd been looking for permission to move forward away from Julianne. Perhaps he'd just found it. The Lord certainly knew that a move to Lexington—or even just a shift of thinking where Julianne wasn't the center of his universe—would assuredly be "something new."

But then again . . .

Alison's words suddenly scraped across his memory: *"It is what it is, Will. You love her. You've probably always loved her."*

Fessing up and telling Julianne how he felt—how he'd always felt—well, that would also be a brand-new road.

A terrifying and life-altering *brand-new road*.

Suddenly, a move to Lexington didn't seem quite so crazy.

# 24

"**I've been thinkin'** about Mandy, Son."

Will glanced up at his father over their plates of scrambled eggs.

"What about her?"

"I think she spends too much time lookin' after me instead of livin' her own life."

Will couldn't resist the quiver of a smile. "Really."

"She needs to meet a good man, Will. There's still a lotta life in the old girl, and she can't see the forest for the *me*."

Will wiped the corner of his mouth and set down his fork. "You're not about to suggest that I date Mrs. Bartlett, are you?"

Davis guffawed at the thought. "No, Son. I think she might be too much woman for you. . . . I was just thinkin' I might sit it out tonight, let you young folks go to the shindig without me. Maybe you can introduce Mandy to a judge or an older lawyer acquaintance you might have."

"Pop, are you serious? Amanda's excited about going with you."

"Nah, I know. But she's in her prime. She doesn't need to think about me and if I've had enough to eat or if I'm getting overtired. She might cut loose and have some fun if I'm not there to distract her."

"Pop—"

"Just make my excuses, will you, Son?"

Will shrugged. "Sure. If you don't want to go."

"I've got a Grisham novel to finish anyway."

"I saw that. Don't donate it when you're finished, okay? I'd like to give it a read before you do."

239

"Ohh, it's a good one, too," Davis said, and he followed it with a short whistle. "Keeps you thinkin'."

"Interesting novels," Dr. Donnelly had suggested. "If he likes to read, it will help keep his mind sharp." He made a mental note to order that e-reader for his dad.

"So what's the final verdict, Son?" Davis asked, wrangling Will's wagon train of thought. "Who's goin' with whom to the big shindig? Are you taking Julianne?"

"No," he answered, shaking his head. "She's still going with the ditch digger."

"And you? Alison, is it?"

"No, Pop," he said, tilting his chair back on two legs. "Alison and I broke up last night."

"Well, that one's over before it got revved up, isn't it? Who decided? You or her?"

"She did," Will admitted. "Over pizza at LaRosa's. She sang a very familiar old tune."

"Don't tell me. Julianne?"

"Ding-ding-ding. You win the prize, Pop."

Davis shook his head and clucked, "Mm, mm, mm. Well, you aren't winnin' any of them, are you, Son?"

"Not lately."

"You think there's anything to this argument? Are you still pining for her, boy? Because if you are, it's simple enough to—"

"I have to go, Pop. I've got to pick up my dry cleaning, run a couple of errands. Do you want to come along?"

"Nah," he answered, waving a quick dismissal.

Will planted a peck on his father's cheek as he headed across the kitchen. He stopped in the doorway and looked back at him.

"Hey, Pop. I've heard they have some pretty great Parkinson's research studies going on down at the University of Kentucky in Lexington."

"Yeah?"

"You know, I was offered a pretty decent job down there recently. Do you have any interest in pulling up stakes and running away from home, just us Hanes boys?"

Davis pondered that for a moment. "You need that, Son? You need to put some miles between you and Cincinnati?"

He sighed. "I don't know."

"Well, you figure that out. If it's what you need, we'll talk about it again. Fair enough?"

Will nodded. "I'll see you later."

"Later."

"Oh," he said, stopping in his tracks. "Don't mention this to Amanda or anyone, okay?"

"Mention what?" he replied without looking up from his eggs.

"All right," Will said over a chuckle. "I'll be back in an hour or two."

● — ● — ●

"Suzi Q didn't tell me a thing about how gorgeous you are," Neil told Julianne's reflection as he tossed a cape around her neck. "She just said you're about to win a big award, and you have to be the belle of the ball."

"That sounds just like her," Julianne said on a giggle as she admired her subtle—but flawless—makeup. She almost recognized the bright-eyed girl in the mirror as an airbrushed version of herself.

"Now that I'm looking at you," he observed, "I'm thinking curls. Lots and lots of curls."

She shrugged one shoulder and nibbled the corner of her lip. "I always wear my hair straight. It might be nice to switch things up tonight."

"And switch them up, we shall!" he exclaimed with flair. "You just put yourself into Neil's hands, and let me do the magic."

Julianne needed a little magic in her life that night. No reason not to start early.

Neil produced a cone-shaped ceramic iron, and he plugged it

in to warm up while he combed out Julianne's hair. When he tossed the comb to the blue enamel counter of his station, he tugged a black knit glove out of the drawer and put it on.

"What's that for?" Julianne questioned him.

Neil chuckled as he snapped the wrist of the glove. "So I don't burn the skin right off my fingers in the name of glamour."

He wrapped a section of golden hair around the cone of the iron and held it into place with his gloved fingers. A few seconds later, a beautiful spiral curl bounced into place, and he did the same with the next section.

"Your hair is like spun silk," he told her. "Not like our Suzi's. It takes monthly gloss treatments to tame that mop of hers."

"You're kidding!"

"Oh, no, *giiirl*," he sang, an animated smirk on his handsome African-American face. "But she's a stunner when I'm through with her. Can I get an amen on that?"

Julianne giggled, shrugged one shoulder and said, "Amen."

She smiled at Neil in the reflection of the mirror as he continued to turn her sleek tresses into spirited, exuberant curls.

"You wouldn't believe what I can take and turn into something," he told her as he worked. "Not for you, though. You were a head-turner when you walked in here. But some of my clients, child. A lesser artist would turn them away with a screech!"

Julianne tumbled into a fit of muffled laughter. "Mister Neil," as her friend called him, had turned out to be everything Suzanne had depicted over the years. "A drama queen with an attitude," she'd once told Julianne over lunch. "But a DaVinci with a blow-dryer."

"Girl, I've got a client coming in here in thirty minutes that any other artist would have turned away on the second visit. Every time she comes back to me, she's turned my work into a helmet of hair spray."

"So why do you keep doing her hair then?" Julianne asked him. "I would think that would be frustrating."

"Ooooh, girl, you have no idea." A moment later, he leaned over her shoulder and whispered, "Rumpelstiltskin! You get to see for yourself. Look what she's done to my body wave!"

Julianne glanced into the mirror to catch the reflection of the front door.

"Hi-dee hi-dee, *Mistah* Neil!"

Her heart thudded downward as she caught a glimpse of Lacey James standing at the front desk.

"Julie?!"

"Ooh-ooh," Neil hummed. "How could I ever have known you would be friends with her?"

"You couldn't. And I'm not. There's a hundred bucks in it for you if you give her a bad perm."

Neil cackled like a hen. Julianne could see that he loved a good catfight, and she sensed that he wasn't above starting one himself, a suspicion set in stone when he seated her elbow-to-elbow with Lacey for their pedicures a short while later.

"I can just hardly believe you're a client of Mister Neil's!" Lacey exclaimed after several minutes of ignoring each other. "I mean, I can usually tell, you know? With that plain-Jane hair of yours, it just wasn't even in the realm, Julie."

"Well, your record stands. I am not a client. In fact, this is my first visit."

"Oh, well, that explains it, doesn't it then?"

"Yeah," Julianne said with a sigh as she closed her eyes and leaned back to enjoy a relaxing foot massage—to pretend at least. "Normally, I just cut it myself with the chicken scissors from the kitchen, rub a little Crisco through it for shine, and call it a day."

Lacey's total silence indicated that Julianne's mother had, as suspected, been one hundred percent wrong all those years when she declared that "sarcasm accomplishes no good purpose."

"Color choice?" the manicurist asked her, and she opened her eyes with regret.

"Very pale pink," she replied. "Or clear."

"Nothing so provincial for me," Lacey told the woman at her feet. "I'd like Pink Hottie for my toes, and Tickle Me Pink for my fingernails. They'll go perfectly with my evening gown. Tonight's going to be my night."

Lacey looked over at Julianne and sighed when she didn't get a reaction.

"You're going somewhere special?" the woman asked her, and Lacey fell into her most Southern explanation of the Person of the Year nomination process, the award's ties to the Bar Association, and her supposed ambivalence about winning.

"It's such an honor to be nominated," she declared, and she took in a sharp breath before adding, "Isn't that so, Julie?"

"Mm-hmm," she said with a smile and a nod before turning away again and closing her eyes.

After several minutes, Lacey spoke so quietly that she almost missed it. "Why do you hate me so much?" Julianne's eyes fluttered open, and she looked at Lacey curiously. With an unexpected amount of emotion, she repeated the inquiry. "Please just tell me, Julie. I really want to know."

Julianne sighed, and she locked eyes for a quick flash of a moment with the woman painting Lacey's toenails a shocking shade of neon pink.

"I don't hate you."

Lacey clicked her tongue and puffed out a sigh of exasperation. "We both know that isn't true, so can't you just do me the courtesy of telling me what it is about me that screeches on you like unmanicured fingernails on a classroom blackboard?"

The sudden prick to her conscience surprised Julianne. She hadn't counted a single cell in her entire body or spirit that cared one iota what Lacey thought. And yet in that moment, sitting next to the woman who rubbed her the *wrongest* way of anyone she'd ever met, she felt an unexpected apology bubbling up inside her.

"If we're going to have this conversation," Julianne said, "you're going to have to tell me something, too."

"What is it?"

"Why are you so mean to me all the time?"

The wheels turned behind Lacey's dewy eyes, and then she groaned. "When am I mean to you?" she asked. She sniffed before adding, "When it's not provoked, I mean."

"Every chance you get, you make side jabs about my hair, my clothes, my love life."

Lacey's lips parted for only an instant before she clamped them shut.

"See!" Julianne exclaimed. "You were just about to say something, weren't you? You were going to say, 'What love life?'"

Lacey's eyes lowered and she smiled. "You're right. I was."

"See what I mean?"

"That's why you hate me so much?"

"I don't hate you," Julianne repeated. "You just . . . *bother me*. It's like something out of my control. I try to tolerate you, Lacey, I really do. But it's like a chemical reaction. I just can't help myself."

Lacey looked up at Julianne with a serious expression and asked, "Could you try?"

"Can you try to stop insulting me all the time?"

"I can try."

"And stop taking every possible opportunity to embarrass me in front of other people? Especially Will?"

"I can do that."

Julianne didn't know what to say to that. She hadn't expected Lacey to make any concessions whatsoever.

"And you'll try to stop insulting me?" Lacey asked her. "Stop taking every opportunity to embarrass me in front of others? *Especially Will?*"

Julianne laughed. "I don't think I've ever heard you call him Will. It almost sounded strange."

"Tonight means a lot to me. I know you think it's the most ridiculous idea since colored nail polish, but the fact is . . . I really like him, and I'd like to see if there's any chance of a future with him, Julie." She glared at Lacey until she recanted. "*Julianne.*"

She smiled. "Was that so hard? It's my name."

"Truce?"

Lacey extended her hand, and Julianne stared at it for a moment before she took it. "Fine. Truce."

Grinning from one ear to the other, Lacey shook her hand with vigor.

"But don't make me regret it." *And Lord, please help me!*

Thirty minutes later, Julianne drove home wondering if she'd fallen asleep under the lull of a gentle foot massage and dreamed the most outrageous dream where lions lay down with lambs, dogs and cats played together, where she and Lacey James had come to an understanding.

"Hi, Paul," she stated after dialing his number at the stoplight on Winton and Sharon Roads. "Just wanted to leave a little reminder about tonight. Arrive at my place by seven?" She swallowed and inhaled sharply before adding, "Please, please don't cancel, Paul. Okay. I'll see you then."

The moment she walked through the front door, Phoebe gasped and hopped up from the sofa wearing the formal black dress she'd found at the vintage shop Julianne had pointed her toward. Her hair didn't match the sight at all, pushed into several directions with clips, her face devoid of even a speck of makeup.

"Julianne?"

Laughing, she replied, "Yes, Phoebe. It's me."

"Your makeup! You look . . . Can you do that on me?"

"Probably not. It took a village."

Phoebe giggled. "Well, you look so beautiful. I love the hair."

"You don't think it's a little too . . . electric shock?"

She belted out another laugh. "No. It's lovely, really." Then she added, "I made some snacks. Want to join me? It's a big night for you. The protein will do you good."

Julianne lifted her shoulder and one hand. "Duh. Whatcha got?"

"Ham and cheese roll-ups," she said as she stepped out of the dress to reveal a tank top and jeans underneath. "Some strawberries, a little hummus."

"Did you raid someone else's refrigerator?" she asked as she followed Phoebe into the kitchen and climbed up on one of the stools. "The neighbors don't like that."

"I went shopping," she replied as she slid several plates to the counter. "It's really a miracle you're not malnourished the way you eat."

"I think that's why my mom and Davis insist on us coming to dinner over there once or twice a week. Just to make sure I'm not eating moldy cheese and outdated peanut butter from the jar."

"Now that I've gotten to know you better, I understand."

Julianne's phone jingled, and she dug it out of her purse as she stuffed a small strawberry into her mouth and quickly swallowed it.

She looked at the caller ID and told Phoebe, "It's Veronica Caswell." Wondering about a phone call from a client so late on a Saturday afternoon, she answered quickly. "Veronica. How are you?"

"I'm terrible, Julianne. I'm sorry to call you on a Saturday, but I need your help."

She wondered if she might be asleep and dreaming
as a beautiful glass carriage appeared,
drawn by four magnificent white horses.
"How can this be?" she exclaimed.

"You can't very well go to the ball on foot,"
her fairy friend said with a twinkle.

# 25

**Julianne stood in** the open doorway, willing her mouth to close. She couldn't seem to help it. Paul looked so exquisite in his tuxedo that her jaw had dropped open when she saw him, and it took a few seconds before she could manage to crank it shut.

"You came!" she exclaimed.

"I said I would."

"Do you want to come in, or just . . . be on our way?"

"You didn't tell me there would be wheels," he stated, nodding toward the street where a long white limousine hugged the curb. "I don't think we should keep the driver waiting."

"Oh," she said, craning her neck to get a better look. "Sorry to disappoint, but I don't think that's for us."

"Yeah, it is. The driver told me so. Your friend Suzanne arranged it."

"What! Phoebe, there's a limo out front," she called. "Do you want to ride with us?"

"A limo?" she said, poking her head around the corner. "Really?"

"Suzanne sent it."

"She really is your fairy godmother, isn't she?"

Julianne chuckled. "I guess she is."

"Your mom called and asked me to be her date," Phoebe said. "I'm picking her up in half an hour. Hey, do you have the paperwork?"

Julianne grabbed it from the table by the door. "Got it. Did you arrange for the messenger to meet me at the hotel?"

"They'll be there at eight o'clock."

"Excellent."

Paul grimaced as Julianne tucked the paperwork under her arm, grabbed her purse, and headed out the door.

"You're doing business at this thing?" he inquired.

"I have a client in some trouble. I'm just trying to help without missing the gala."

The driver appeared out of nowhere and opened the limousine door, standing next to it like a uniformed sentry.

"You look enchanting," he told Julianne, and she thanked him, wondering why Paul hadn't been the one to compliment her.

Once they settled on the long bench seat, Paul turned to her and smiled. "Speaking of doing business at the gala," he said, and he raised his eyebrows. When she didn't grasp the meaning, he finished the thought. "Are you going to pay me up front, or afterward?"

Julianne's heart thudded at the question.

"I thought I could write you a check when we get back home. Is that all right?"

"I guess so," he conceded. "Okay."

She started to ask if he wanted her to get cash from the ATM instead, but she lassoed the sarcasm before it popped out. A good thing, too, because she feared he might have taken her up on it.

⬤ ⸺ ⬤ ⸺ ⬤

Despite the fact that she made him think of a plantation owner's daughter heading for the cotillion, Will had to admit that Lacey looked rather beautiful.

"Pretty in pink," he told her when she opened the front door and grinned at him.

"Really?" she asked, and he realized it might have been the first time he sensed real insecurity in her.

"You're stunning, Lacey."

She sighed. "You too, William."

"Ready to go?"

"Let me just get my wrap."

*Who talks like that?* he remembered Julianne asking him once when she'd used a similar word; he couldn't remember which one.

He took the silky shawl from her and placed it around her shoulders as they stepped off the columned porch and followed the stone walk toward his car. He imagined every day was a little like coming home to Tara for Lacey, and he smiled at the thought. His buddy Wyatt Benson, the son of one of the partners of his old firm Benson & Benhurst, hailed from Atlanta, and his home had that southerly mark upon it as well. In fact, Lacey and Wyatt might make a pretty good pair, now that he thought about it.

As Lacey slipped her arm through his and grinned up at him, Will realized she might not be as open to the pairing as he would hope.

Once they'd settled into his car and gotten under way, Lacey turned to him and said, "I want to thank you for escorting me tonight, William."

"Back atcha," he replied. "I'm happy to have a date."

"You decided not to invite your Alison?"

Where in the world had she heard about Alison?

"Alison and I split up."

He didn't have to glance over to feel the flood of light emitted from her smile.

"It's just as well. I'm not interested in a relationship at the moment." Surely that would get his point across.

"No?"

"Lucky for me I have such pretty female friends willing to fill in the gap for me on nights like this one."

Oh yeah. That one took root. The glow of her smile dimmed considerably.

To lessen the burden of his proclamation, he eased to a stop at the light before he smiled at Lacey and touched her hand. "Thank you, Lace. Your friendship means a lot to me."

"And you don't think you could ever see your way clear, somewhere down the line, for it to be more than friendship between us, William?"

*Straightforward.* And he knew he owed it to her to reciprocate.

"I'm sorry," he told her gently. "I really don't."

"I see."

Her disappointment choked him a little, but he knew from his experience with Holly that honesty now rather than heartbreak later was the way to go.

He offered Lacey his arm, and they walked into the ballroom, already teeming with people. One of them caught his attention in such a way that Will found it difficult to breathe.

Julianne looked like a contemporary princess in an ice-blue dress with a sheer cropped jacket over it. Her short dress revealed shimmering legs and a pair of spiked crystal heels that made her pretty legs look longer. Surprised, he realized he hadn't noticed that the man talking to her was none other than Judge Hillman, and it appeared that the two were conducting some sort of business.

"Excuse me for a minute, Lacey?"

"Of course. I'll just find our table."

● — ● — ●

"Ms. Bartlett, I am not here tonight in the capacity of an officer of the court," Judge Hillman told her directly.

Julianne touched his arm and looked into his very blue eyes. "I know that, Your Honor. I really do. But we're facing a real time crunch at the moment. My client's estranged husband is trying to sell half of her business before the divorce settlement has been finalized. We're not asking you to make any judgments about anything that can wait until then, sir. I'm just asking that you place your *Judgeship* behind us so that the sale can be delayed until we find out if he even has a right to the business at all."

Hillman lifted one gray eyebrow and stared at her for a moment. "What would your course of action have been had I not told you I would be here tonight, Ms. Bartlett?"

"Oh, I don't know. I might have shown up on your front lawn," she replied with a chuckle, silenced almost immediately by his reaction. "Of course, I'm only joking. I would never. Well, almost never. I mean, obviously . . . in some instances . . . there are extenuating circumstances . . ."

He turned the page and inspected the paperwork more carefully. "This is Veronica Caswell we're talking about?"

"Yes, sir."

He shot her a piercing *"Why didn't you say so?"* glare before he turned to the last page of the document. "Do you have a pen, Ms. Bartlett?"

She rummaged through her very small purse and suddenly grabbed the arm of a passing waiter. "A pen? Can you get us a pen?"

"Certainly," he answered. "Just one minute."

"My kingdom for a pen!" she joked as Hillman skimmed over the injunction document.

"I'm surprised at him," the judge muttered. "He's been sticking it to Veronica all along, as if she's the one at fault here, as if he's played no part in it."

"That's what I'm trying to stop," she said, snatching the pen from the approaching waiter and placing it into Hillman's hand. "And you can help me, Your Honor."

He scribbled his name on the paper and handed it back to Julianne. "You realize this is only a temporary fix, Ms. Bartlett. My *Judgeship* doesn't carry much weight when all is said and done. You need more than my signature for a binding—"

"Yes, sir. We just needed something for opposing counsel, something to get us through the weekend; a sort of spirit-of-the-law kind of thing until I can request a hearing first thing Monday."

Will suddenly joined them, and Julianne smiled. "Oh, hey, Will. I was going to find you in a minute."

"Evening, Hanes," the judge said with a nod.

"Judge." He returned the nod before his eyes landed on the paperwork passing between them. "What's this?"

"It's for Veronica. I'll tell you all about it over dinner." She turned toward Judge Hillman and said, "I can't thank you enough, sir."

"Good luck," he said as a woman hurried toward him and asked him to come along with her. "And keep me posted on this, Ms. Bartlett," he said before he followed.

"I'll do that."

Julianne bottom-lined the story for Will, from Veronica's panic to her conference call with the other attorney and her revelation that Judge Hillman was scheduled to attend the gala, as they slowly headed across the ballroom. She spotted Paul at a large round table next to Lacey, and the two of them chatted amiably.

"Your date looks very nice," Julianne teased. "Did she tell you we had a little mani-pedi session together today?"

"She did not," Will replied, a strange and crooked smile spreading over his face like warm butter. "That must be quite a tale."

"You have no idea."

Will touched Julianne's wrist, and she looked up at him curiously.

"Jules. You look . . ." He waved his hand from head to toe and shrugged.

"Magnificent?" she finished for him.

"Beyond."

"Ah, thanks, Will." She planted a kiss on his cheek and squeezed his hand. "My own date hasn't even said that."

"You're joking."

"Nope. I guess I forgot to add that clause to the dating contract. Oh! But guess what. Suzanne sent her company limousine to pick us up! We actually rode here in a white stretch limo. Can you believe that?"

By the time they reached the table, Phoebe and Julianne's mother had joined them.

"Don't you two look beautiful," Will said as he sat down next to Lacey. "Weaver and I are the luckiest guys in the place tonight."

"Paul, you've met Phoebe, and it looks like you've met Lacey James already," Julianne told him. "But this is my mother, Amanda Bartlett."

It looked a little like an afterthought that followed a few tugs to his bow tie, but Paul at least got to his feet as he shook her hand. "Pleased to meet you, ma'am."

Amanda's smile didn't betray to anyone except the two people who knew her best that she didn't really mean it when she replied, "Glad you could join us, Paul."

"And Mom, this is Lacey. She and I are up for the same award tonight."

"Well, you're both People of the Year as far as this table is concerned," Amanda told them. "Nice to meet you, Lacey."

One of Lacey's coworkers and his wife rounded out the table of eight, and they all settled in just about the time that the salads were served. Phoebe took the paperwork from Julianne and slipped it into a cardboard envelope. Julianne slid it into the groove between the back of her chair and the upholstered seat before she sat down between Paul and her mother and unfolded her napkin.

She wished the awards ceremony could precede the meal because of the butterflies swarming around her stomach, and her mother seemed to sense it because she reached over and smoothed the stiff skirt of Julianne's dress and whispered, "You look really lovely, honey."

"Thanks, Mom. You do, too."

Amanda leaned close to Julianne. "I can see why your head was turned," she whispered. "Paul *is* sort of a hottie."

Julianne giggled. "Mother!"

"I'm not dead yet, you know."

"I am aware."

Lacey caught her eye for no more than an instant, but something seemed odd and unmistakable. On such a festive evening,

Julianne thought it uncharacteristic to find Lacey's enthusiasm so diluted. She waited, hoping she might stumble into Lacey's line of sight one more time, but her focus had been wholly captured by the salad that apparently needed to be cut into five thousand minuscule bites. When Will looked at her instead, Julianne scrunched up her nose and gave her head a quick nod toward his date.

"What's going on?" she mouthed.

Although his expression confirmed that there was indeed something to tell, he hadn't betrayed another speck of information.

"Don't let me lose track of the time," Julianne announced. "I have to run down to the lobby at eight to meet the messenger."

She wondered if Paul had really groaned under his breath, or had she imagined it? The thought of going anywhere in those tight shoes made her want to groan a little, too. Maybe his bow tie had choked it out of him.

Somehow, the idea entertained her.

# 26

Will pushed away the plate of rubbery chicken as Julianne greeted a passing colleague from her days with the public defender.

"Janice, I'd like you to meet my mother, Amanda Bartlett. And this is my date," she said and beamed, "Paul Weaver."

*Determined to get her money's worth*, Will decided. She had introduced the ditch digger to every person in the room except the uniformed waitstaff. Just about every third step she'd taken that night had elicited a wince, and when she rose from her chair to greet Janice Buckholt, the corner of her mouth curled up tight in an instant replay. Will recognized it as the too-tight-shoe dance she did so often. Although the crystal-encrusted ones she wore for this special occasion were indeed dazzlers, he couldn't understand why she didn't simply invest in a couple pairs of more sensible everyday shoes.

"I'm going down to meet the messenger," she told him when she returned to the table and grabbed the envelope. Waving it, she called, "Be right back."

When she reached the ballroom door, he caught sight of her as she kicked off her shoes and carried them into the hallway.

"I probably should have gone instead," Phoebe speculated. "She can't be late for the awards."

"She'll be back in two shakes of a lamb's tail," Amanda replied, patting Phoebe's hand. "Don't you worry."

With Lacey immersed in conversation with the group at the

257

next table, Will went over and took Julianne's chair between Paul and Amanda.

"Have I told you how spectacular you look tonight?" he asked Julianne's mom.

"You have, but feel free to tell me again."

"You're breathtaking," he said, and her cheeks blushed as she placed her hand over his and squeezed. "Pop doesn't know what he's missing."

Amanda's expression dimmed, and she leaned toward him. "Why do you suppose he didn't want to come tonight? Is he feeling worse than he's telling?"

"Oh, you know . . . aside from seeing you looking so pretty, Pop wouldn't have enjoyed this kind of thing. He's not comfortable in big groups these days."

Weaver squirmed next to him, tugging at his collar.

"This thing is a torture device," he said when he caught Will looking at him. "I don't know how you do it so often."

"I only break out the tux a few times a year," he replied.

"Yeah, but you wear a suit and tie every day, don't you? Man wasn't meant to be all packaged up like this all the time."

Will suppressed the reply that ached inside him. Instead, he simply said, "I guess you're right."

Will raked his fingers through his wavy hair, pumping up the volume on the Disney song about the muscular oaf who wanted to marry Belle. He had to push it out of his mind when the ditch digger turned to him and asked, "How much longer do you think this thing will last?"

"They still have to get the awards ceremony under way."

He groaned, squirming in his chair, looking like a ten-year-old who'd had his ice cream and wanted to go home now.

"Look, Weaver—"

The overhead lights slowly dimmed, and a representative of the Bar Association tapped on the microphone at the podium.

"Thank you all for coming tonight," she said.

"Finally," the ditch digger puffed.

"Should I go find Julianne?" Phoebe asked Will.

"I'll go."

Just as he pushed up from the chair, Lacey grabbed his wrist. "William, you can't go. They're just about to start."

"I have to. Julianne will miss it."

Will put several paces between himself and Lacey's sour, disappointed face, and he hurried from the ballroom just as Judge Hillman took his place at the podium as master of ceremonies.

The elevator whisked him down one floor to the lobby, and he jogged across it until he spotted Julianne and the messenger.

"Jules!" he called. "They're starting."

"Ohh," she squealed, and she shoved the clipboard back at the messenger. "I have to go. You know what to do with this, right?"

"Yes, ma'am."

"It has to be delivered tonight."

Will took hold of Julianne's arm as she snatched her shoes from the seat of the upholstered chair, and they ran across the polished marble-floored lobby toward the elevator.

"Every attorney in Cincinnati is in that ballroom upstairs," she exclaimed as they boarded, "except the one I need to serve with paperwork! How far into the ceremony have they gotten?"

"Judge Hillman was up when I left."

"Oh!"

The instant the elevator doors slid open, Julianne bolted across the threshold, hopping along as she attempted to slip into her shoes and run at the same time. Will reached her when she paused in the doorway.

". . . all such worthy nominees, but our sixteenth annual Cincinnati Person of the Year is . . ." Hillman tore the seal on the scroll and opened it ". . . Lacey James."

The room erupted into applause, and a white spotlight roamed the ballroom until it landed on Lacey, already weaving her way through chairs on her way to the stage. Julianne joined them, clapping as she craned her neck to watch Lacey accept the engraved plaque that she'd been coveting for herself.

"Oh, well," she said, shooting Will a conciliatory smile. "There's always next year, right?"

He slipped his arm around her shoulders and squeezed. "That's the spirit."

The subtle deflation under his embrace could not be missed, but Will decided to pretend that it was.

"There's going to be cake," he bolstered. "So all is not lost. Let's go back to the table and indulge, shall we?"

"I'm just so honored and humbled," Lacey said over the loudspeaker. "Certainly we don't invest our time and energy into these worthy causes for the accolades, but the fact that the legal community has taken note of my efforts . . . well, that's gratifying. Thank you so much."

●  —  ●  —  ●

Paul had excused himself to find the men's room, and Will stood a few tables over chatting with some friends from his old firm. Julianne kicked off her shoes underneath the table with a sigh as Lacey slipped into Paul's chair and leaned over toward her.

"You just couldn't let me have my moment, could you?"

"I'm sorry," she said, shaking her head slightly. "What are you talking about? You won the award, Lacey. I'd say the moment was all yours."

"You know what I'm talking about. You disappeared on purpose so William would come looking for you and leave me sitting all alone when they called my name."

Julianne inhaled sharply and grazed Lacey with a controlled glance.

"Yes," she said between clenched teeth. "You're right. I broke up Will and Alison, manipulated him into bringing you instead so that I could arrange for my client to have this last-minute crisis. I called the messenger service to make absolutely sure that they arrived late, and I bribed the Bar Association to give you the award that I'd been nominated for, all to the endgame of Will leaving your side just before they called your name, shined a spotlight on you, and gave you an engraved plaque with your name on it. I guess I showed you, didn't I, Lacey?"

Her shocking pink lips parted, but just as she began to speak her retaliation, Paul appeared behind them, his bow tie undone and hanging loosely around his open collar.

"Can we go now?" he grumbled.

"I just have to speak to Judge Hillman before we—"

"Oh, come on," he said. "Is there one person left in this en-tire room that you haven't paraded me past yet, Julianne? I think I've more than done my part here. There isn't enough money in the world . . ." Julianne's heart stopped with a thud ". . . to make me want to stay in this place with these hoity-toits another minute. Let's go."

A serpent-like grin slithered across Lacey's face, igniting it with sheer glee as she asked, "What did you say, darlin'? Julianne Bartlett has . . . *paid you . . . to be her date?*"

Paul leaned down toward Julianne. "Can we go?"

"Oh, wait just a minute," Lacey continued. "Indulge me for one golden moment, would you, please? Are you Julie's *hired escort?*" Before he answered, Lacey burst into laughter, looked back at her companions and asked, "Did you hear this?"

"Julianne? What's going on?" her mother inquired.

"Oh, this is priceless," Lacey clucked.

Julianne's heart had started to beat again, but in tinny, pound-ing rhythms that echoed in her eardrums. Without another breath, she plucked her shoes from beneath the table, grabbed her purse, and ran for the door.

"Julianne! What's going on? Lacey, what did you do?" she thought she heard Will ask as she escaped the ballroom and raced toward the elevators and pounded on the call button.

"Jules!" Will called out, but the elevator opened and she jumped onboard. "Jules, wait!"

He reached her as she pushed the button for the lobby.

"You just had to bring *her*, didn't you?" she shouted at him. "You couldn't let it be just me and you."

"Jules, come on. Wait."

"No, Will. I'm through waiting. I'm just . . . *through!*"

"Hanes!" The sudden shout caught the attention of them both, and she squinted at the familiar face grinning at her as he jogged down the corridor toward them.

"Judd," Will said. "I didn't know you'd be here."

"Yeah, I told you I'd be in town this weekend, remember? I came in for this, and for a few rounds of golf for the charity event tomorrow."

"Can I catch up to you in a few minutes? I've just got to settle something here with Julianne."

"Hey, Julianne. Good to see you again."

"Hi, Judd," she managed.

"Listen," he said, turning back toward Will. "Let's make sure we talk. I want to discuss the offer I made you about coming to work for us in Lexington."

Julianne felt all the oxygen deflate from her lungs. "Offer?" she somehow managed.

"No, I—"

"He didn't tell you?" Judd cut in. "Yeah, I've got a job tailor-made for him. And with all of the Parkinson's research going on down there, I think it's the perfect time. With Davis's situation and all."

And with that, Julianne wielded one of the crystal shoes directly at Will. He moaned as the spiked heel hit him dead-center in the chest and the elevator doors slid shut.

● — ● — ● 

Will could hardly think straight. He stood in stunned silence in front of the closed elevator, clutching the shoe she'd sent barreling toward him like a spiked cannonball. Before he'd fully gathered his wits again, Judd smacked his shoulder.

"Angry cat out of the bag, huh? I'm sorry, buddy."

"Can we talk later?" Will asked him. *After I've started breathing again and find the presence of mind not to wring your neck?*

"Sure. Why don't I call you after the fund-raiser tomorrow. We'll get a bite and talk."

He nodded Judd off and focused on drawing some air back into his lungs. Before he could fill them, however, Paul Weaver appeared beside him and pressed the call button on the elevator.

"Did she leave without me?" he asked, incredulous. "She actually left me here? And she didn't even pay me. Nice, huh?"

Will turned to him, slowly and with deliberation. "You want your payment, Weaver? I'll give you your payment."

He whipped his checkbook out of the breast pocket of his jacket and frantically wrote a check for five hundred dollars, tearing it off with such force that he left a ribbon of it behind. He chucked it at the ditch digger with a sneer, and it fluttered to the floor in front of him.

"Never mind that you humiliated her in there, huh? As long as you got your money."

Will turned and stomped away from him, but Weaver just didn't have the good sense to leave it at that.

"Hey, I'm not the one who made the big announcement to the rest of the people in the room, buddy. Your date did that. That part's on you."

It took every ounce of resolve not to turn around and pound the guy's pretty face with everything he had. But somehow, Will managed to keep walking; back through the doors, across the ballroom, and straight to their table.

Standing over Lacey, he glared down at her. "We're going."

"Will, did you catch Julianne?" Amanda asked him. When she noticed her shoe in his hand, she grimaced. "Is she all right?"

Will placed a hand on Amanda's shoulder, as tenderly as he could manage at that very un-tender moment. "She's gone home."

He looked back at Lacey and repeated, "We're going."

"You go ahead," she snapped. "It's what you want to do anyway. I'll get home on my own."

"We can take her," Phoebe volunteered. Will glanced at Phoebe to confirm, and she nodded. "It's fine. Go."

Without another word to Lacey, he sprinted across the ballroom.

"Tell her to call me tonight," Amanda said after him, and he nodded over his shoulder without slowing down.

# 27

# "Thanks, Archie."

"It was my pleasure, Julianne."

She'd sat up front with him, but Archie did his job and went around to the other side of the limousine and opened her door. She slipped out and gave him a peck on the cheek.

"Thanks for the ice cream. And for the shoulder."

"Anytime. I'm here for all your limousine and bad-date needs."

Bad date.

"The understatement of *my* lifetime," she muttered as she hobbled up the sidewalk on one bare foot and one four-inch heel. "Night, Arch," she called back to him.

"G'night, Miss Julianne."

She stopped just inside the door and caught a glimpse of her reflection: Wild hair in every direction, mascara-stained cheeks, one missing earring, and a dribble of Rocky Road down the front of her light blue vintage dress. She suddenly remembered Suzanne's request that she remember to snap a picture, which of course she hadn't, and the memory ignited uncontrollable laughter. Maybe she should take a picture now? Something to remember the moment; a reminder about what pride gets you.

Just about the time she pulled herself together, her mother's voice pierced the solitude of her laughing jag.

"I made tea."

Just three simple words, and they set her face on fire with embarrassment and emotion. Her expression crumpled like wax paper over a lit match.

"Come here."

Her mother extended her open arms, and Julianne headed straight for them.

Clomp. Clomp. Clomp.

"Oh, honey, take that shoe off."

She kicked it off in the middle of the room and kept going, directly into Amanda's embrace. After she hugged Julianne, and smoothed her crazy wild hair with the palm of her hand, Amanda gave her a little nod. With her arm around Julianne's shoulder, she led her to the kitchen counter.

Julianne climbed up on the nearest stool while her mother set a cup of steaming tea before her. After she'd taken a sip, Amanda approached with a damp paper towel and began to wipe off the mascara mess under her eyes and down her cheeks.

"Oh, Mom, I'm such an idiot."

"You'd better narrow that down for me, honey."

"I paid a guy to take me out." Julianne bit her lip, realizing she hadn't actually *paid* him.

"Yes," she said, focusing on the line of her jaw with the towel. "That was not your finest moment, I'll admit."

"It was so important to me, caring so much about what they all thought. I wanted to show them that they were wrong about me, and all I showed them was that they were right. Pride took ahold of me, and I couldn't think straight."

"And now?" her mom asked as she tossed the paper towel in the trash.

"Now? I'm just mortified." The tears began to fall again, and she caved in to her folded arms on the counter. "And that awful Lacey!" she exclaimed. "I told you about her, didn't I? She's just horrible!"

"Well, it wasn't very nice of her to ridicule you like that. But I got the feeling she just couldn't help herself. That tends to happen when we're focused on our own pain. We lash out and splash it all over the nearest person. And you happened to be closest, honey."

"I hate her!"

"You *do not* hate her. But you surely hate what *she did.*"

Julianne looked around the kitchen and asked, "Where's Phoebe?"

"She's in the shower. She said she'd drive me home whenever I'm ready to go, but I wanted you to have some hot tea to come home to."

Julianne chuckled and reached across the counter to take her mother's hand. "That's the answer to all the world's problems for you, isn't it, Mom? Hot tea!"

"It doesn't hurt any, but no. It's not the answer."

Her face fell and crumpled again. "Then what is?" she whimpered.

Her mother didn't reply with words. She simply pointed one finger heavenward.

An hour later, they had moved the somber party to the living room, and Phoebe had joined them. Julianne sat perched on the floor in front of the coffee table, the skirt of her chocolate-stained dress hiked up and her bare legs folded beneath her. Charming sat at attention, pressed against her, sniffing at the dried ice cream. Every now and then, he gave her dress an affectionate lick.

The lamp next to the sofa spilled a yellowish glow over the silent group, and music played so softly from the radio in Phoebe's room that Julianne couldn't make out the song.

Phoebe was first to shatter the silence. "Do you want to talk, Julianne?"

"Not really."

"Okay."

"Then I think I'll have Phoebe drive me home now," her mother piped up. "Unless you want me to stay."

"No, Mom. You can take off. But thank you for being here."

"Sometimes a girl just needs her mother," Amanda said, and she pushed up from the sofa. "Do you want to come spend the night with me?"

"Next door to Will? I don't think so."

"All right. But you're going to have to talk to him sometime, young lady."

Julianne looked up as Amanda stood over her.

"That sometime isn't tonight," she said softly as Judd's words roiled around inside her like a shot of acid.

*He didn't tell you? Yeah, I've got a job tailor-made for him. And with all of the Parkinson's research going on down there, I think it's the perfect time. With Davis's situation and all.*

"I love you, honey."

"I love you, too, Mom."

She leaned down and kissed the top of Julianne's head. "Promise me one thing?"

"Hmm?"

"No more Paul Weavers."

Julianne raised three fingers, even though she'd never been a Girl Scout. "No more!"

"Good. A pretty face and good hair does not a husband make, you know."

"I am aware; I was so foolish."

"All right. Sleep tight."

She watched them walk out the front door, and she tucked her arm around Charming and pulled him in for a nuzzle. They'd hardly been gone a full minute when the front door opened again. She looked up, expecting to find that her mom had forgotten something, but Will stood there looking at her instead.

Even without his jacket and his bow tie hanging loose around his neck, he still looked every bit as handsome as he had at the gala. He combed his dark hair from his face with both hands and tilted his head slightly.

"Can I come in?"

"No."

"Come on, Jules."

"*No*," she said, and she popped up to her feet and rushed toward him.

She put her hands on his shoulders, turned him around, and pushed as hard as she could until he stood on the porch looking back at her. It wasn't until then that she noticed her shoe in his hand.

"Julianne, this can't wait anymore. I have to tell you—"

"There's nothing you can tell me tonight, Will. Go home."

One corner of his mouth quivered and turned upward before he dropped to one knee like some ridiculous, disheveled prince at the end of one of those obnoxious fairy tales that had caused so much trouble for her.

Will extended the shoe toward her. "Fair Julianne!" he exclaimed in his most noble voice. "I've traveled a great distance to reach you, and to tell you that *I love you*. I've always loved you. And I want you to know—"

"Oh, hush," she muttered, and she turned around and slammed the door between them.

●　—　●　—　●

The echo of the thrown dead bolt stayed with Will all through the night. Julianne had slammed the front door, locked it, and shut off the porch light, all with him still on one knee declaring his undying love. He didn't know how long he'd stayed there, but when he finally got up, he left her shoe on the mat outside the door and skulked away.

Suzanne had been right; they *really were* morons, both of them.

She hadn't shown up for church that morning, and Beth Rudd told him she'd called early to ask her to cover the David and Goliath lesson in Sunday school. Will had been so preoccupied with her absence that he couldn't even faintly remember the topic of the pastor's message.

As he pulled his car up to the stables, he noticed Alec standing there with a young woman. When she turned around and smiled at him, Will recognized Alison waving the horse brush at him.

"I thought you were camping at Natural Bridge this weekend," he said as he climbed out from behind the wheel and grabbed his saddlebag.

"I was. I got home this morning, and Alec invited me over to meet his new filly."

He hadn't seen that sort of light in Alison's eye when they dated. Come to think of it, he'd never seen it in Alec's. They were actually a pretty fair match-up.

"How was the gala?" she asked him, and his expression wilted. "That bad?"

"It was the Murphy's Law of evenings."

"Everything that can go wrong," Alec said, nodding, "will go wrong."

"You got it."

"Did Julianne win the award?"

"No. She did not."

Alison and Alec exchanged glances before Alec smacked Will's arm. "Sorry."

"Was she terribly disappointed?" Alison asked.

"With everything else that went wrong last night," he answered, "I think losing out on the award was the last thing on her mind. Although I wouldn't know, really, because she's no longer speaking to me."

"Oh." Alison cringed. "Well, maybe a good ride will cheer you up?"

"Let's hope."

He headed toward the stable, and then he stopped in his tracks. "Hey," he said to them. "I'm glad you two are giving it a go."

Alison sauntered over and pecked his cheek. "Thanks, Will."

●　—　●　—　●

Julianne noted that Will's car wasn't in the driveway, so when she didn't find her mother at home, she felt safe wandering across the lawn to check with Davis. Sure enough, the two of them sat at the kitchen table with a pitcher of iced tea and a plate of butter cookies.

"There she is!" Davis exclaimed when he peered through the back door.

"I knew I'd find my mom here," she said with a smile as she slipped in and sat down next to Amanda. "I just wanted to drop by and thank you for last night. I really appreciated you sticking around and making me feel better."

"That's what mothers do."

Julianne winced as her eyes met Davis's. "I guess you heard about last night."

"I heard plenty," he replied.

"Well, I hope you won't think less of me, Davis. I lost my mind."

"Which part has you losing your mind?" he asked directly. "The part where you offered to pay the louse, or the part where Will wrote the check?"

Julianne's pulse began to pound. "Will paid him?"

"He did."

She fished into her purse and produced her checkbook. "I'll leave him a check then. That was . . . really . . . unexpected of him!"

"I guess that's not all that was unexpected last night."

The minute their eyes met again, tears plummeted down Julianne's face. "Are you two really moving to Lexington, Davis?" she asked. "When was Will going to tell me?"

"What!" her mom exclaimed with a gasp. "No one's moving *anywhere*, Davis Hanes! I suwanee! What, you're going to just up and leave me? What would I do without you?"

"You might find a dancing partner who could give you the life you deserve," he replied.

Julianne looked on as her mother's eyes misted with emotion. "You old coot. I don't need a dancing partner. I just—" She lowered her head and whispered, "I just need you."

"You're crazy, woman," Davis said. "More crazy'n your daughter."

"Hey!" Julianne interjected. "How did this get turned around on me? Let's hit rewind because I thought I'd never see the day when you two *finally* admitted you have feelings for one another,

271

and you were getting very close there for a second."

"Julianna Margaret!" her mother exclaimed.

"Well, for crying out loud, Mom. You and Davis have been like an old married couple for years now, except for that patch of grass between the two houses."

"Look who's talking about this!" Davis cackled. "Julianne, you don't know a confession of feelings when it's right there on its knee in front of you."

"What?"

"Will had other things to tell you before we decided about Lexington," he said, leaning forward and locking Julianne's eyes with his. "And I hear you didn't have much to say when he finally did."

She scratched her temple as she said, "I don't know what you mean."

"That boy's been screwing up his courage for twenty years, Julianne. And he finally manages to tell you his feelings, and you shut the door in his face."

"He . . . What? . . . What are you talking about?" Amanda asked.

Davis tapped his fist lightly on the tabletop before turning to Amanda and shaking his head. "Will got on one knee and declared his love for your daughter last night."

"He what?!" Her mother smacked Julianne's arm. "You didn't tell me that."

"There's nothing to tell. He wasn't declaring his forever love, Davis. He was mocking me."

"Will wouldn't do that," Amanda said. "Tsk, Julianne."

"Well, he did."

"Are you really that daft, girl?" Davis asked.

She frowned at Davis. "I am not daft."

"Well, honey," her mother cut in. "You aren't exactly the sharpest knife in the drawer when it comes to love."

"The girl is thick as two short planks!" Davis exclaimed.

"Davis!" Julianne said as she hopped to her feet. "You're hurting my feelings."

"Everyone in southern Ohio has known what you can't seem to figure out, dumplin'. My boy is silly with love for you. He wasn't mockin'. He was confessin'."

Julianne looked from Davis to her mother and back again. "Confessing . . . *What?*"

"Oh, honey. God put him in your life long ago. Will has loved you since before you shaved your legs for the first time," Amanda said with a smile.

"What?"

"You gonna stand there askin' *What?* Or are you going to get in your car and go find him?"

"I . . . I don't know where . . . Are you sure about this?"

Davis thumped his fist on the table again and leaned back into his chair with a groan. "He went ridin'," he told her. "Over at the Ross place." When Julianne just stood there, frozen to the linoleum kitchen floor, her thoughts all logjammed together, Davis clapped his hands in front of her. "Get on the stick!"

Julianne turned to Amanda, her brain twisted like a question mark. "Mom?"

"Do you love him, honey?"

"I . . . I . . . don't know. He's . . . *Will!*"

"That's close enough," Davis snapped. "Go on."

One more smile from her mother, and Julianne reeled into action and ran for the door. Before it closed behind her, she heard Davis pipe up. "Now, why don't you tell me more about how you can't live without me."

Julianne hadn't heard her mother actually giggle in . . . maybe ever. But giggle she did before adding, "You old coot."

## 28

**Julianne hadn't** been to Alec's place in years. She made a wrong turn off McKelvey Road twice before she finally got it right, and a cloud of dirt rose in her wake as she made it to the property and headed toward the stables.

She saw Alec as she climbed out of her car, and the long-ago scent of horses and stables tackled her before she reached him.

"Julianne?" he called out with a laugh, and he jogged toward her. "I haven't seen you in ages! You look great."

"Good to see you, Alec," she said, and they exchanged a hug. "You looking for Will?"

"Is he still here?"

"Yeah," he said with a sideways nod. "Riding up on the ridge."

"Ohh. Any idea how long he's—" Julianne tripped all over her words when she noticed the woman heading toward them. "Is th— that . . . *Alison*?"

"Hi, Julianne," she said. "Great to see you again. You must be looking for Will."

"O-oh, so I guess you're here . . . with . . . him."

"Oh!" The light dawned quickly and Alison grinned at her. "No! I'm not here with Will. I'm here . . . with Alec."

Julianne's thoughts muddled again, and her legs felt like mush.

"Alison and I are . . . friends," Alec explained.

"You are? Does Will know?"

"Of course. Here, let me saddle a horse for you," Alec offered. "You can ride up to the ridge and talk to him."

"Oh! Oh, no! No!" Julianne began wringing her hands, and

her feet unexpectedly transported her two steps backward. "I don't ride horses. I don't . . . No!"

Alison moved next to her and placed an arm around her shoulder. "Will told me you're like the Animal Whisperer. You can certainly master a horse."

"No!" And she flew back another couple of steps.

"Why don't you put a saddle on Eeyore," she suggested to Alec. Turning back to Julianne, she explained, "Eeyore is a very slow-moving, older horse. You'll do fine."

"No! No. Please."

Alec jogged off toward the stable, and Alison faced Julianne with a serious expression.

"Will told us that the two of you had a falling-out, and I think he's pretty torn up about it. You came over here to go after him, didn't you?"

"Yes."

"Then climb up on that horse and follow the trail to the top of the ridge. That's where you'll find him." When Julianne just stood there, shell-shocked, Alison shook her gently. "You can do this."

Alec led a saddled gray horse toward her and plopped a step stool to the ground. "Come on," he said. "I'll help you up."

Julianne gazed into the distance, searching, searching for some sign of Will. "It's okay. I'll just wait here. I'm sure he'll be back soon."

"Julianne!" Alison reassured her. "You can do this. Come on. Take my hand."

She absently allowed Alison to lead her by the wrist toward the horse while Alec steadied the step stool with his foot.

"Left foot in the stirrup," Alison told her evenly. "Then lift your right leg over the saddle."

She started to follow the directions, and then she paused and smiled at Alison. "I see why you're so good with children."

Alison chuckled. "Here. Hold the reins like this."

It took three tries before Julianne plopped into the saddle and squealed, and she held the reins so tightly that her hands ached.

"Hi, horse. How are you? I'm Julianne. Please don't hurt me."

Eeyore whinnied, and Julianne screamed like a swimmer in the sights of a twelve-foot gator.

●　—　●　—　●

Will's eyes had been closed for a long time up there on the ridge. On his knees under his favorite elm tree, he asked the Lord to give him wisdom and guidance, and most of all grace. He didn't know how the situation with Julianne could possibly be resolved, but God knew. And he wanted more than anything to trust Him with it, so he laid it all at the foot of the throne and worshiped the God who turns very crooked roads like this one into straight and smooth boulevards. He gave his love for Julianne over to the Lord of the universe. Then he shifted to sit on the grass, his back pressed against the tree, and his head tilted up toward the very blue Ohio sky.

Yeah, his eyes had been clamped shut for a very long time. So when he saw . . . what he thought he saw . . . out there in the distance, he had to blink several times. Very hard. And he blinked again, shaking his head like a wet dog.

When the sound of Julianne's screech reached him, it acted like a pinprick that catapulted Will to his feet. What on earth was she doing . . . *on a horse*?

"Will, help me!" she cried when she saw him, her face contorted and her mouth wide open. She held Eeyore's reins in the air with both hands, her arms stiff as rigor mortis. "He's not listening to me. I think he's trying to throw me off! Help me!"

Will clicked his tongue a couple of times, and Eeyore headed straight for him. He tried to take the reins, but Julianne had them in a death grip and couldn't seem to let go.

"Jules, what are you doing?"

"I'm . . . riding a horse, Will."

"I can see that. Why?"

"Because," she said, prying her fingers from the reins, "I needed to talk to you, and Alison didn't think it would be romantic if I drove up the trail in my PT Cruiser. Personally, I think it would have been fine."

Will's heart leapt inside his chest, leaving a hollow sort of ache where it had been.

"This is you being romantic?"

"Well. It's me trying. How do I get down?"

"Oh, you don't," he teased. "I just need to take this in."

"Will!"

With a laugh, he opened his arms to her and she slid straight into them and allowed him to pull her out of the saddle. It didn't go as smoothly as he'd imagined, and she kicked Eeyore in the belly on her way. The horse whinnied, Julianne screeched, and the two of them tumbled to the ground as Eeyore galloped away.

"He's getting away!" she whimpered as they lay there on the ground.

"He knows his way back," he reassured her, and Julianne began to giggle.

"Can you imagine Alison and Alec's faces when my horse returns without me?"

Will smoothed her honey-blonde hair and gazed into her glistening sky-blue eyes.

"What are you doing here, Julianne?"

"Oh," she said, pushing herself upright. "Well, I thought you were making fun of me last night, and then I talked to your dad this morning—"

"Oh . . . no."

"—and he told me that you were serious, that you were just telling me what you'd wanted to tell me since before I shaved my legs for the first time."

"He said that?"

"No. Maybe it was my mom who said that."

"Your mom was there?"

"Yeah. And remind me later to tell you about how your dad and my mom have finally admitted out loud that they have *feelings for each other!*"

His thoughts twisted into a slight spin. "What?"

"Anyway, for right now, let's get back to the other feelings on the table, please." She shifted to face him, and Will bent his knees and leaned slightly into them. "Is that true? About your feelings? For me?"

Too late to turn back now.

"Yeah, it's true."

"You weren't mocking me?"

"No, not mocking."

"So you've always felt like this?"

"I can't remember a time when I didn't love you, Jules."

His pulse began to pound, and the scenery began to gyrate a little. Too many years of suppression, he supposed. Now that the words had finally escaped and the sentiment had tumbled out to the grass between them, instead of the relief he'd always imagined, Will felt nothing but terror.

"So . . . when I was dating that drummer . . ."

"Then." He nodded.

"And Billy Rampart?"

"The whole summer. Torture."

"And in law school—"

"Are we going to relive every horrible moment?" he cut in.

"No," she replied with a smile. "I'm sorry."

And then it happened. The thing Will had imagined and dreaded for more than twenty years. Julianne fell silent.

"Please say something," he finally urged.

She sighed, and a couple of eternities passed before she finally spoke. "Remember when we had that first date in high school?"

*Remember? It's been my constant companion ever since.* He shrugged one shoulder and nodded. "Of course."

"I doodled your name in my diary that night."

279

"You keep a diary?"

"Well, I did then. Anyway, I wrote that you were the Prince Charming I'd always dreamt about. I wrote something like, 'Mark this date! It's the date I'll look back on and know that my whole life changed.'"

"So what happened?"

"You were different. You started acting all ooey-gooey, and you wrote me that love poem."

Will tossed back his head and laughed. "You're the silver light of the moon, the fireflies in June; you're the one and only—"

"Song that I croon," she finished for him on a string of giggles. "Very bad poetry, Will. And I didn't want us to boil down to ooey-gooey and bad poetry. So I tucked those feelings away, and I moved you from the Prince Charming shelf to the Forever Friend shelf."

He swallowed around the lump in his throat and asked, "Can't I be on both shelves?"

"I didn't think so then."

"And now?"

"The princess never ends up with her best friend, Will. She doesn't find him on a ten-speed bicycle right there in the cul-de-sac."

"Jules," he said, leaning forward and looking squarely into her eyes. "I know this has always been a tough concept for you to grasp, but you're not a princess."

She smacked his arm with a gasp. "What a horrible thing to say," she said with a chuckle.

"And I'm no Prince Charming, I can promise you that."

Julianne narrowed her eyes, and her full red lips shifted into a pout. "You're pretty close though. You know, when you met Holly and asked her to marry you, I felt like I might die."

"You did?"

"Yes. I didn't really understand why. I just knew I could die at any moment. Just the thought of losing you to someone else . . ."

As her words trailed off into silence, Will stared into her eyes, and he thought that they looked like the ocean on a stormy day. Blue falling into blue. He wanted to dive in and swim around for a while. Instead, he stroked her cheek with his thumb.

"The thing is, Jules . . . I love you."

"I love you, too."

"No," he corrected, and he pushed upward and knelt over her. "I mean, I really *love you.*"

"I really love—"

"Jules," he said, placing his hands on her shoulders and holding her firm. "I . . . love . . . you."

"I get it, Will. You love me." After a long and silent moment, she tilted her head slightly. "Are you going to kiss me now? Because this is where Prince Charming would kiss her."

"Do you want me to kiss you?"

Melting under his touch, she proclaimed, "So much."

And Will Hanes took Julianne Bartlett into his arms and kissed her. Twenty years' worth.

And as her Father had always promised,
True Love's kiss caused the stars to swirl
and the breeze to sing a beautiful song
between the leaves of the elm tree.

"At last," her fairy friend declared.
"She's found her Happily Ever After."

# About the Author

**For more than a decade**, Sandra D. Bricker lived in Los Angeles. While honing her chosen craft of screenwriting in every spare moment, she worked as a personal assistant and publicist to some of daytime television's hottest stars. When her mother became ill in Florida, she put California in her rearview mirror and moved across the country to take on a new role: Caregiver.

"I guess most people would see my career as a publicist as a sort of dream job. But giving it up turned out to be the best thing that could have happened to me!" she declares. "Not only was I given the gift of getting to know my mother as an adult woman before she passed away, but I was also afforded the blessing of being able to focus completely on my dream of a writing career."

The author says that it was her 8th novel that opened the door to finding her way as a writer. "I'm a Christian woman, first and foremost," she says. "So it was a bit of a dream-come-true when Summerside Press chose me as one of two authors to launch the Love Finds You line."

Sandie's real-life role as cancer survivor has parlayed into her steadfast commitment to raising awareness and funds for ovarian cancer research. Spearheading a series of devotionals for Summerside Press (such as the popular *His Grace is Sufficient . . . Decaf is Not*), the author has stipulated that a portion of each contributor's proceeds will go to the Ovarian Cancer Research Fund.

*Always the Baker, Never the Bride*, released by Abingdon Press in September 2010, garnered phenomenal reviews and spawned a series of three more novels based on the popular cast of characters at The Tanglewood Inn, a wedding destination hotel in historic Roswell, Georgia. The Another Emma Rae Creation series of novels has cemented Sandie's spot in publishing as a flagship author of Laugh-Out-Loud Romantic Comedy for the Inspirational Market.

"Being allowed to combine my faith and my humor with raising funds for my pet projects . . . and still pursue my writing dream," says Bricker, "well, that's the best of all worlds, as far as I'm concerned!"

And one of the author's pet projects is animal rescue, evidenced by the special bond she has created with one particular formerly abandoned puppy—a red-haired collie with "killer brown eyes and the heart of the class clown."

Connect with Sandie at SandraDBricker.com or LIKE the Facebook page exclusively for her readers titled Fans of Author Sandra D. Bricker.

## FICTION FROM MOODY PUBLISHERS

River North Fiction is here to provide quality fiction that will refresh and encourage you in your daily walk with God. We want to help readers know, love, and serve JESUS through the power of story.

**Connect with us at www.rivernorthfiction.com**

- ✔ Blog
- ✔ Newsletter
- ✔ Free Giveaways

- ✔ Behind the scenes look at writing fiction and publishing
- ✔ Book Club

MOODY
PUBLISHERS
www.MoodyPublishers.com